BESTIAL

by

Arielle K Harris

Copyright © 2016 by Arielle K Harris

Published in the United States of America

ISBN 978-1537060101

Title page images and in-text clipart courtesy of http://cliparts.co

Cover design by Amelia Royce Leonards
For full color prints of the cover artwork please contact Amelia Royce Leonards: amelialeonardsart@gmail.com

For Jen and Alex who brought me home; for my parents for everything else.

PART I: Bestial

Chapter 1

Once upon a time there were twin brothers, Beau and Désiré. Their mother had named them for those qualities which had drawn her to their father: his beauty, her desire for him.

Beau and Désiré's parents, Guillaume and Fleur Saint-Christophe Desjardins, were both mainly decorative by function and design, the product of their upbringing. They lived in a city of modern decadence, in a country of romance and refinement, in a world where magic was rare, but not unheard of.

For those who had the exceptional gift, casting enchantments was a certain path towards wealth and autonomy, for what king would cross a wielder of magic? They were sought out by both well-intentioned nobility and those with less than sparkling consciences, by stepmothers with too many inconvenient stepchildren, and by simple peasant girls hoping to change their fates into something more extraordinary, even if they had to put the very mice in their pantries at work.

But using magic did come at a price, for the mind cannot easily reconcile the impossible. Few knew what this cost entailed, and even fewer lived to speak of it, for the gifted ones were cautious and guarded about their reputation. Most ordinary people merely thought of these enchanters as individuals to be at once both feared and sought-after, hopeful that their magic may change their fortunes, for everyone knew of at least one friend or relative who had benefitted from their help.

Fleur Desjardins, for example, had been brought up as the daughter of a wealthy family whose fortune had been founded on the happy circumstances of a blessed kiss from an enchanted sparrow, in the gardens of a country manor house. Her grandparents lived there still, and it is said that her grandfather had always had an unusual liking for seeded tea cakes.

Her education, however, mostly comprised those lessons in frivolity and fashion which made one young lady stand out preferentially amongst a crowd of her peers, and so better to attract a suitable husband. Never forgetting, of course, to keep one's eyes open for a likely creature whose courtship would bring about good fortune, or an individual who might grant much-desired wishes.

Guillaume Saint-Christophe had been raised as the son of a gentleman of who never disclosed the precise history of the making of their own family fortune, which was significant, to his son. Guillaume's education had mostly centred on the notion that a man of fortune was only as good as he appeared to be to others. He was actively discouraged from the idea of gaining a profession, as that was a poor and common goal, and his parents could not imagine what need he would have for one with the more than substantial accounts he had at his disposal.

Guillaume was therefore a young man with a sizeable enough entailment to make him suitably attractive even if there were no other favourable attributes to be had. However, Guillaume was also the sort of rare male beauty seldom seen outside of classical sculptures or paintings by the Masters. His hair was softly waving shadows, his eyes lit from within by some arcane fire. His unmarked skin was smooth, his arching eyebrows and lips were in the shape of Cupid's bow. Yet, he was no girlish figure for all his beauty, being wide of shoulder and firmly muscled.

Guillame Saint-Christophe was simply beautiful.

Fleur had placed Guillaume in her sights from the moment she saw him, and desire had flooded her with a flush she had not yet experienced in her young life. But she was not alone in this pursuit. Fleur despaired at the thought of letting Guillaume's beauty pass her by, and she prayed for divine assistance, hoping for an enchantment to help pave the way for her success.

But none were forthcoming, as the enchanters of this world were capricious and much in demand by people who were far more worthy of an enchantment, or at least with deeper purses. So eventually it was clear that Fleur had to rely on herself alone.

She knew the key in love, as in haute couture (her one area of expertise), lay in clever details and flawless execution. Therefore she laid a plan in which the principal players were a dropped glove and a rainy afternoon, a flash of dampened ankle and a rueful smile. It is a universal truth that many a romance has begun under the confines of a shared umbrella, and this was no exception.

Guillaume and Fleur Saint-Christophe Desjardins were married in the spring, to the collective tears of mourning from all the eligible, and most of the ineligible, women in the city, and to the sighs of jealous relief from all the eligible men. The newlywed couple combined their fortunes as well as their names, and were happy.

Guillaume soon found that he enjoyed a new popularity in their social circles, as his company was still so pleasing to look at, but now without anyone worrying about bringing unattached young ladies into his sphere. They might still flutter their eyelashes and sigh at him, but there would be no more than that.

Fleur blossomed under the attention of her peers, who loved her simply because they could not love her husband themselves, and she soon became known for throwing the most magnificent parties that all the fine people in society attended. With Guillaume's wealth, and Fleur's eye for fashion, together they took the city by storm. All the people of means attended their soirees, and on one notable occasion they even hosted royalty, the crowning jewel of their social accomplishments.

Even Fleur's advancing pregnancy was an item of fashionable perfection, toasted by their guests and the entire city. And the perfect twin boys who were the product of it were proclaimed as darlings of the fashionable elite.

Beau and Désiré grew up in a glittering world of laughter, decadence and indulgence. They were the double mirrored image of their father with their shining dark hair and golden brown eyes. Sometimes they were dressed in matching outfits, the perfect miniature of haute couture, and paraded in front of applauding guests before bedtime, supervised by a smiling nanny. Grown women sighed over the beauty of them. It was an age of profligacy, when all around them were shows of excess and overabundance, and the two young boys were the physical embodiment of their time. They played with toys cast in precious metals, dandled on the knees of nobility.

But it had to come to an end eventually. For the Saint-Christophe Desjardins this end came more suddenly than anyone had planned.

The family fortune had been well maintained by their bankers, and it should have lasted for several generations of Saint-Christophes. However, the exorbitant cost of hosting the city's crème de la crème for nearly two decades had steadily drained their accounts, and they were now piling debt upon debt.

Guillaume had to begin curtailing the delights they could provide for their guests, which led to such whispers as 'miser' and 'penny thrift' to hiss through his halls. It was bad enough that such easily living had widened his girth, had greyed his hair and dulled his eyes. It was bad enough that he was plagued by gout and dyspepsia. Fleur and Guillaume Saint-Christophe Desjardins were now falling from social favour, which was by far the more discomforting of conditions.

Guillaume began to fear for his family, especially his beautiful sons. He feared that they would need to take professions, if he could not find a way to change their fate. And he feared that he could not.

Beau and Désiré, however, were completely unaware of their father's anxieties. They loved their life, their freedom and licence. They did not notice the preoccupation of their father at the dinner table of late, when he was usually so vivacious and charming and full of good humour.

Or, at least, if Beau noticed it, as he noticed everything in his usual quiet way, Désiré certainly did not.

Désiré was the younger of the two by minutes, and by far the more impetuous, the more wild and passionate. He laughed and cried, and fought and flirted, easily and by equal measures. He had a gift of speaking so that the listener was drawn into his words and carried away by the sound and meaning of them, so that any suggestion Désiré made was seen as instantly agreeable and obvious. This silver tongue got him into, and out of, more scrapes than could be counted.

Meanwhile, Beau was the restraining hand, the voice of reason, who did everything that was right and expected of him. Every word he spoke was the truth, straightforward and unchallengeable, though sometimes that truth was unwanted and awkwardly forthright. He was also so unfailingly honest that he was blinded by how dishonest others could be, and Désiré took advantage of this, though without true malice, by making Beau an unintentional player in his wild schemes. Beau was shy by nature, and uncomfortable with strangers, unfamiliar places and new situations. But through the influence of his brother's schemes and japes he was included amongst his peers in a way he would have never been otherwise.

Beau also came to the realisation that he was unaffected by those things intended to evoke an emotional response, such as music, poetry, and art, all of which could have Désiré weeping openly and without shame. He sometimes wondered if his brother was given all the emotional sensation of the two of them, while he himself had all the common sense. If they could have been combined into one whole they would have made one balanced person, but they were two unequal halves instead.

The only thing they had in common was their identical beauty, which outstripped even that of their father's in his heyday.

The brothers were now young men already, well versed in leisure. They had numerous friends who they joined in hunting, hawking, dancing and fencing to wile away their days of ennui. Afterwards, their evenings were spent gambling and drinking with the sort of abandon found in those who know they will not be required to wake at any particular hour in the morning, nor be expected formulate any coherent thoughts once that time eventually came.

When their father sat them down with a solemn, grey face, to discuss the shadowy future, and their possible need to gain employment, they were both entirely at a loss. Their easy life and upbringing had spoiled them for the demands of a profession, if indeed any employer would have them if he were aware, as the entire city was, of their uncircumspect and rakish habits.

The same could have been said of Guillaume himself, spoiled by his own lifestyle. He tried to do right by his family and sacrificed his pride in search of a new living, to the scorn of his peers, but he could not find one. As a last resort, he took the remainder of the family assets and trusted in an old acquaintance to make an investment on his behalf – which lost them everything in one dire turn.

The banks began to refuse him any new lines of credit, and his debts were now being called upon to be repaid. They were forced to sell everything they owned of great value, and terminate the employment of all their household staff. Their well-placed townhouse would be reclaimed by the bank, having been mortgaged heavily.

The only asset left to their name was the old manor house, Maison Desjardins, owned by Fleur's grandparents who had recently, and somewhat conveniently, departed from this mortal soil. But they had no funds for wages, so would have no servants, no grooms, and even the very landsmen who worked the fields would be relieved of their services. They would have to work the land entailed on the estate themselves.

'It will have to be our living,' Guillaume said to his family. 'We can feed ourselves, and clothe ourselves, on the products of our own land and toil.'

'But, *Guillaume*!' Fleur was aghast, 'Are we farmers? We have never done such work in our lives, and your health is too poor to let you labour as hard as it would require. Surely we would be better off selling it, even if it is not much?'

He shook his head, 'I am afraid it is simply not worth enough to give us any benefit. It is too far from the city, and too small in acreage to be much of a boon to anyone looking for large profits. We would starve within a year or two from the proceeds of its sale if no other avenues open to us. That is, if my failing body does not fall beneath the plough of our very toils.'

Pale, Fleur turned her face to the wall and the fine wallpaper of their emptied parlour mocked her with its bright and fashionable pattern. She had only just picked it out with her decorator three months prior but was now regretting its outrageous cost, though it had seemed so necessary at the time. She could not keep her hands from shaking. She had already sold her evening dresses, her furs, her hats, her wigs and her jewels. She had not thought to ever be contemplating something so demeaning as debts and commerce, and *work*.

'You cannot work hard labour, Father,' Beau said, his bald statement spoken mildly. 'You would seriously harm yourself to attempt it. We will do it for you.' He did not need to clarify who 'we' were; although the twins differed so much in personality and taste, they always came as a set.

Désiré cast a flashing glare at his brother for that unasked-for volunteering of his services, but knew that he could not argue. Though he could not help but mutter an aside, 'Yes, until one, or both, of us dies out of pure incompetence in a profession so ill-suited to us.'

Fleur began to weep at the poorly chosen words of her youngest. She could not bear contemplating the fine figures of her sons who were now reduced to this poverty, and being forced to endure such base drudgery that they were, indeed, so ill-suited for. No, she could not bear it at all and fled to her chamber, though its bare walls and empty wardrobes held little comfort now. They had nothing but their meanest clothing and those few possessions which held little value above sentiment and therefore useless to sell. There was only one allowance Guillaume made to their old life.

'We might each keep one thing from our past life,' Guillaume said. 'Only one memento, which we will promise one another never to sell even in times of need. We will not forget who we are, even despite what we are forced to endure.'

And so Désiré kept his horse, a prancing and useless hunter but he looked so fine upon its back. Beau kept his sword, its name was Honneur and given to him by his fencing master in honest pride. Guillaume kept his finest suit of clothes in which he used to strike such a fine figure, though the buttons would no longer fasten. Lastly, Fleur kept her wedding ring which she had once thought of as the symbol of her life's triumph.

Thus poorly equipped, they began their life in exile.

Chapter 2

The Maison Desjardins was once a beautiful stately home. It was small, by the contemporary scale of these things, without many of the modern additions which typically featured. There was one central fireplace, shared between the kitchen on one side of the wall and the sitting room on the other. Up the flue, the two bedrooms above each had a conservative hearth to combat the draughty window panes which did not quite meet their frames. There was one outhouse beside the wood shed with damp, moulding brick and a warped roof. There was, at least, an established kitchen garden, a good deep well, and those extensive, labyrinthine flower beds which gave the house, and the family, their name.

It had a smallish but well-drained acreage of arable farming, in addition to a steeper and rockier pasture for the keeping of hardy sheep whose wool and milk or cheese would be an asset for the family's income if they could sell those goods, or to their own larders if they could not.

To reach the Maison Desjardins they hired a carriage, the last nod to their old life and insisted upon by Fleur who would not travel by commoner transportation – or worse, be *seen* to. They left the city and headed west by south west, and it was the longest journey any of them had ever taken, and for the cruellest of destinations. Their life was behind them, their damnation was ahead.

Many lived poorer than the Saint-Christophe Desjardins would live now, but to them it was as if they were cast into the desert naked. It was incomprehensible how they, or indeed anyone, could live this way.

Fleur spent their first week locked in the master bedroom. Guillaume became a hollow-cheeked, paunch-bellied shadow, distant and spectral in his absence from himself. Désiré wept at night, when he thought Beau was asleep in their too-small, shared bed, and was snappish and ill-tempered in the daytime hours. Sometimes he prayed, at times aloud in desperation, for the pity of an enchantress in the hopes that his beauty would sway her, despite his poverty. All he needed were three wishes, and he knew exactly what they would be. But he was never granted them, as no enchantress ever appeared before him to hear his pitiful tale.

Only Beau remained untouched, as he had always been. He realised that, due to the deficiency of his emotionlessness, he was the only one of them currently capable of setting himself to the herculean task ahead. As such, he rose before dawn every morning, to first clean and cook in lieu of the servants they could not afford. Then after serving breakfast to his family, at which point at least one of the party would begin sobbing anew, he began to shoulder the weight of working the farm entailed onto their living.

How does a courtier begin to bear the burdens of landsman and servant combined? It was a sudden and sobering education. Beau had no pricking of pride to contend with, so was unashamed to accost their nearest neighbour and gain instruction, given with some bemusement and pity. They had dismissed the lands' usual tenants just before the harvest season, the sort of amateur mistake which showed their unsuitability to this life. Beau had to bring in the summer wheat before the weather turned, which seemed nearly impossible, but its sale to the miller might assure their survival through the winter months, so it had to be done.

Every hour of daylight saw Beau with his scythe in the fields, and Désiré beside him with a sideways look and an upturned lip, roused from his bed against his will. Between them they worked steadily through the crop and gathered the wheat into bales to dry in the late summer sun.

'I cannot live like this!' Désiré protested, and not for the first time. 'I was made for better things!'

'I see you have two legs, and two arms,' Beau said. 'A head as well, for all that it seems to be absent at times. You were made as every man was made, before us or will be after.'

'I will go back to the city,' his daily threat began, 'I will seek our fortunes in a far more suitable way than this.'

'And do what?' his brother asked. 'Beg? Dance in the streets for pennies? I fail to see how your desertion and prostitution would profit this family.'

Désiré snorted a sardonic laugh at this. 'Well I have friends, still.'

'What, those ones who never replied to our letters, when we were reduced to begging friends for favours?'

'Our missives may have been waylaid,' Beau's raised eyebrow told his brother how likely he thought that was, 'It could have happened! They have always proclaimed their everlasting love and fidelity.'

'And much good that proved, when we were selling our very possessions like gypsies.'

'Then I will go to a beautiful enchantress and she will cast a spell to return our lost fortunes,' Désiré said, finally admitting those hopes which saw him standing awake at their window every moonlit night, his lips moving in silent study.

Beau shook his head. 'With barely two pennies to rub together? How would you pay for such a miracle?'

'I have convinced those of the fairer sex to do plenty of things, and for far less. Enchantresses are still women, after all, under all their magics and potions.' And Désiré preened for a moment, attempting a seductive look and forgetting that he was covered in dirt, sweat and bits of straw.

Beau gave his brother a well-practiced look of exasperation and heaved his scythe once more. He was the only person he knew who was immune to his brother's silver tongue. Or maybe it was simply that Beau was his brother's mirror and it was impossible for Désiré to truly delude himself, or to make a successful argument when he was so acutely aware of its inherent flaws.

Their father was not so resistant to Désiré's solution, however. Perhaps his hope for a successful outcome blinded him to the true state of their situation, and the unlikelihood of these schemes of a hot-headed young man. Perhaps he was too much like his son, or was once, and had hopes that the talents which had first gained him popularity might do so again for his offspring. Whatever the reason, he eventually capitulated and gave his blessing after the harvest, when the leaves began to be touched with gold. He agreed to let Désiré return to the city and try his luck at gaining them back a sizeable enough living to win back their old life.

'One year,' Guillaume repeated. 'Just the one, then you return regardless of what fortunes, for good or ill, you have gained.'

Désiré agreed, full of confidence, 'Of course, father. I am sure to gain some kind of riches through adventuring and daring acts. No one can refuse me.'

'Apparently not,' Beau said with a frown, but he spoke quietly so that his father would not be troubled by his censure. He knew this decision weighed terribly on his father, and that it was a permission not given lightly.

So it came to pass that Guillaume gave his son his cherished remaining fine suit of clothes so that he would not appear penniless in the streets of the city. Fleur gave him her wedding ring, so that he would have something of worth to use as a wager, though her hands shook while she pressed it into her son's palm.

The brothers then bade each other their farewells, the first they had ever had to make since their paired birth. Beau gave Désiré his sword, Honneur. 'You are far more likely to need this than I am, unless the blade of the plough breaks.'

'That would be a poor use for something so noble. Thank you.' Désiré embraced his brother tightly, and could not help but weep at their parting. It was like leaving himself behind, even if that self was largely insufferable and superior.

'We will always be brothers, no matter the distance,' Beau said, shrugging, unmoved as always. 'I will see you in a year.'

Désiré mounted his horse, who pranced and shied in daft excitement. 'In a year,' he promised.

And so it was that Beau and Désiré spent a year apart from the other halves of their whole, neither aware that this separation would continue for far longer than either had anticipated. Magic was at work, but not in the way they had hoped for.

Chapter 3

Once upon a different time, the Beaumont Castle in the heart of the mountains of Le Morvan was the home of the Marquis de Beaumont and his wife Lunestra.

It was a prosperous time, and the castle bustled with industrious servants and important visitors. Every room was warmly furnished and every hearth lit with a welcoming fire, and while the castle was in an ancient style the furnishings and décor were at the height of fashion. No townhouse in the city would have put these rooms to shame in their opulence, size and comfort.

The Marquis was from an old, respected family, and he had married well. Lunestra was a pretty, doll-like woman with a ready smile and an effusive temperament. However, she suffered from miscarriage after miscarriage, and then stillbirth after stillbirth for many horrible years after the wedding's first consummation. It seemed like there may never be a live heir, but the Marquis refused to annul the marriage and find another woman to bear his unborn children. He had made a promise to his wife, to honour and cherish her, and he would not put her aside.

When at last the marriage was finally blessed with a child, a healthy and round-cheeked girl, the whole household rejoiced and celebrated for an entire week. The Marquis and his wife loved their daughter Yvaine, perhaps too well, and gave her all that she could have asked for as she grew into a young lady. She had every toy she wished for, every delicacy and sweet thing she wanted to eat, and lovely little dresses enough to not have to wear the same one twice in a month, should she wish. Her father only insisted that she have a tutor to educate her, and even that was exactly as Yvaine desired, as she became a curious child who enjoyed reading and learning, when it suited her. However, the fact remained that Yvaine was dreadfully spoilt. She never had to put her own desires aside to please anyone apart from herself, and did not see why she should ever have to.

As she grew older, Yvaine became more and more demanding. Her servants bore the brunt of her tempers if a certain dress had not been mended or cleaned in time, or if a certain culinary delight was unable to be made quickly enough. She would shout and cry and threaten and stamp her small but well-heeled feet. At the same time, she was bright and outstripped her tutor's expectations at her lessons, but she grew presumptuous and bold in her address towards the old scholar who was scandalised and outraged by her behaviour daily.

Yvaine's parents could not see where they had gone wrong, and so continued to placate her simply by giving in to her demands and wiles. 'She will grow out of it,' they thought, with naïve optimism.

In time, they decided that it was marriage that would change her for the better. 'She will have to bend to her husband's wishes,' her mother thought, in her sweet idealism, 'and by loving him she will learn to put another's needs before her own. All the better if there is a child quickly! For no mother can put herself first before her child!'

So they looked to find Yvaine a suitable husband, from a good family of the same standing as their own. One likely young man was a Duke's son several provinces away, whose father the Marquis had had dealings with in the past. It was a fair distance to travel, however, so arrangements had been made for the Marquis, his wife and Yvaine to all visit with the Duke, under some vague but reasonable premise, so that the young people could meet and their parents could discuss the match in person.

'I will not go!' Yvaine said, to the consternation of her mother, who had thought that she had explained the benefits of marriage rather succinctly. 'And you cannot make me!'

'But dearest darling,' her mother tried to reason with her, 'this young man would make you an excellent match. And by marrying someone you may finally understand the need that others have to please each other, and put themselves aside for another's gain and benefit.'

'That does not at all appeal to me,' she said, with crossed arms and a frown. 'I cannot imagine any worse state than that of matrimony. To be beholden to another? Rubbish. To put his needs before my own? Nonsense. To hope to have a child who, besides ruining me in body and probably in mind as well, would then further require me to prioritise it as well? Am I to cater to its every mewling whim, then that of my husband, and only lastly undertake my own wants and desires? I simply cannot fathom why this is the done thing, and why so many women decide of their own will to undertake it.'

'Oh, but my sweetest dearheart, it must be so! If you do not marry then the family line will end, and your father's very name will die with us! And what of the people who depend on us, the servants we employ, the landsmen to whom we provide the means for a livelihood with their tenancies on our land? Without a Beaumont in the castle there will be ruin for all who rely upon its employment! It is something which simply must be done!'

'I have already said that it is not to be borne, and I will not change my mind!' Yvaine stamped her foot, used to that being the end of any such argument.

'My beloved lovely, it is going to happen,' her mother spoke with unaccustomed firmness beneath her dulcet tone. 'We are going to see the Duke, whether you come or not, and the matter will be settled between us.'

'Well I certainly am not going,' she scoffed. 'And any marriage agreement you make will be very hard to honour if the bride refuses to take part.'

Her mother sighed, and later spoke to the Marquis, 'In time, perhaps we can beseech her enough for her to see the right in this action, how necessary it is, and that it is the only choice we have. If only we had had more children,' she wept.

'Now, now,' the Marquis tried to comfort his wife, holding her close. 'Yvaine will see the right of it, just as you say. Only let us give her time and go on this journey without her, as you cleverly suggested. With time to think on her own, without us telling her how important this marriage will be, maybe she will come to that same conclusion independently.'

And so with many kisses and farewells, the carriage drew away with the Marquis and his wife, leaving Yvaine in the keeping of her servants and tutor, and none of them were happy about the situation at all.

For her part, Yvaine did not allow her parents' absence to alter her usual behaviour, and she terrorised her servants and scandalised her tutor just as she always had. Only without the Marquis and his wife to exert their small influence on her, if indeed there had ever been any at all, and to provide support for their decisions and disagreements, the household staff grew quickly weary of this state of affairs.

Bad weather soon turned on the castle, and driving winds and rain pelted the castle walls for days, turning the courtyard into a muddy pond. One day Yvaine was having one of her quieter, more agreeable moments reading a book at the window of her room when a thudding noise startled her terribly, making her cry out. Her maidservant, sitting outside the door, heaved a sigh before attending to her.

'What is it, my lady?'

'Something just hit the window, Eugénie! What on earth could that have been? Come! Let us find out!' And she ran down the hall and down the stairway into the garden, without even a backwards glance.

She did not heed the rain and mud, or how it might stain and spoil her dress and petticoats and delicate indoor slippers. Yvaine skipped out into the garden to find the place below her window with zealousness inflamed by forced time indoors.

'Eugh!' she cried out. 'Eugénie!'

'Coming, my lady,' the maid hesitated at the door, seeing no option but to ruin her own clothes as well. 'What is it?'

'Look!' and Yvaine pointed into the soggy grass, where a black shape lay heaped and spotted with droplets of rain. It was a dead crow, its head bent at an improbable angle. 'How ugly and horrible it is! Get rid of it, Eugénie, I cannot bear to touch it!'

'Can we not leave it for the foxes and stoats, my lady? Even if it is moved and buried, they will only find it and dig it up.'

'I cannot sit at my window, knowing this is right below me! Get rid of it now,' she repeated, stamping her foot – which squelched rather than stamped, and spattered mud across them both.

'Very well, my lady,' Eugénie sighed.

That night, in a fresh dress and petticoat, and new shoes and hose, while the servants of the laundry gritted their teeth and muttered in low voices, Yvaine sat in comfort in front of her hearth and did not even think about the incident at all, or its repercussions for her household staff. It did not bother her what others must do at her request.

A knock came at the door.

'My lady,' Eugénie entered, her own dress still stained with the dried marks of mud, hastily brushed as well as she had been able during a spare moment. Unlike Yvaine, she did not own so many dresses as to be able to change in the middle of the day, nor the luxury to attend to her appearance. 'There is someone at the door.'

'Someone at the door?' Yvaine repeated, frowning. 'Whoever is it?'

'A traveller, my lady. Who begs us grant her shelter for the night.'

Yvaine shook her head before Eugénie had even finished speaking. 'No, no, I cannot see how that would not inconvenience me terribly. A stranger in my house, I do not think so.'

'Very well, my lady.'

But after several minutes, she knocked again.

'The traveller insists she must speak to you, my lady. She wishes to make her case in person.'

Yvaine heaved a huge sigh, 'But I am so comfortable here, Eugénie. I do not wish to move.'

'It will be comfortable in the hall as well, my lady,' Eugénie hesitantly pressed, fearing it might rouse her temper. 'She says she really must speak to you, and that she cannot make another mile in the foul weather, or it will be her demise.'

'I simply do not care for what she has to say.' Yvaine frowned. 'If she really must speak to me, she must come here and do so.'

'My lady?'

'Yes, that will do,' she nodded. 'I can stay here and she can still make her vain request. Only, if she drags mud and water through the castle you all must give the floors a thorough washing!'

Eugénie tried to hide her sigh under pursed lips. 'Very well, my lady. I will bring her here.'

After several minutes Eugénie knocked again, and opened the door to make a quick curtesy before stepping aside to let the traveller make her way across the threshold, hanging back to await any further direction from her young mistress.

The old woman limped forward, her back hunched and her legs twisted. She grasped a walking stick in one gnarled, wind-reddened hand, which shook and quivered with cold and ague.

'Speak what you will quickly,' Yvaine said, pitiless and demanding. 'I was in the middle of reading a very good book.'

'You are a very rude girl,' the old woman said. 'Have you no manners? Were you raised in a barn instead of a castle?'

'Excuse me?' Yvaine did not quite believe what she had heard. Eugénie was forced to stifle a surprised giggle from the doorway, but could not entirely stop her lips from twitching.

'Bad enough to force a beleaguered traveller to beg twice for admittance, but then, when finally granted an audience, you make her traipse through your castle's inner rooms, and come to the chamber you are too idle to stir from? What noblewoman's grace is this? What responsibility to the people under your own position?'

Yvaine finally collected her dropped jaw from the vicinity of her knees, and regained her scattered wits, as well as her temper. 'Who are you to speak so to me, old woman? I am the daughter of the Marquis de Beaumont, and I will not be spoken to in such a fashion in my own home, and by a penniless beggar woman, no less!'

'Who am I?' the traveller asked, her voice raising in volume. 'Who am I to ask you such things? Why, girl, I am the miasma in the air that turns the colour of the leaves in autumn; I am the first pink of sunrise; I am the space between the stars. Do not ask me who I am, when you have such a rank notion of your own importance in the world, when you are not the barest insect ever to be stepped on by a careless boot!' She cast off her dirty cloak, and stood before Yvaine tall and proud and beautiful.

Yvaine was not sure how she could have ever thought this was an old beggar woman, seeing her now. She was obviously a powerful enchantress, and Yvaine felt fear for the first time in her life.

'I should think-,' she tried to speak, feeling the colour draining from her face, leaving behind a cold chill and a premonition of terror.

'You should be silent, is what you should be,' the enchantress interrupted. 'I can see through you, girl. I can see exactly who you are, and what you have done to those around you. Never once considering the comfort of others before your own, acting like a primitive beast to those who love you dearly. For the insults you have given them, and myself, I shall make you understand the truth of the matter. I shall show you what your true form is, and make your outer shape finally match your nature within!'

Yvaine tried to speak again, but found that she could not. She was caught in a spell, a spell which changed her as it worked its dreadful magic. Her dress ripped clear of her body and fell in shreds to the floor, as her shape and size was no longer that of a girl. Her face elongated, her legs and arms lengthened and warped into a new form. Then wings unfurled like the snapping open of a new starched bed sheet.

Eugénie had remained in the doorway, wide-eyed and mostly amused by the tone of things happening to her mistress, but now she screamed and fled the scene. A fonder maid, in the employ of a family whose daughter was the centre of her world, would have stayed and fought her fear of her mistress's new appearance. She might have helped her mistress to accept her new nature, and assist in whatever way possible to ease the horror of the situation. But a fonder maid would have been in the service of a kinder young lady, a young lady who would not have found herself in such a situation. As things stood, Eugénie felt no qualms about abandoning her young charge whose beastly personality had now taken physical form.

At last the change was complete, and Yvaine stood, cramped now in her apartments, trying to see what she had become by twisting and craning her neck.

'What have you done to me?' she spoke with difficulty through her beak, and it was only through the enchantress' power that she was understood at all. 'What am I?'

'A beast,' the enchantress said, satisfied with her work. 'Your family's heraldry is the griffin, and so you have taken on this mythic animal as your poisoned soul's new housing. May it serve you well,' and she made as if to leave.

'Wait!' Yvaine cried out. 'You cannot leave me this way! I am not a beast, I am a girl!'

'Not from what I have seen of you,' the enchantress spoke wryly. 'And as long as that beastly nature of yours continues to sit at the core of your person, you shall stay this way. However, I am not an unforgiving sort of person. If you should learn to become someone who is good and kind to others, who could even inspire love in another person, love which is pure and selfless, and in turn love that other person enough to place their own comfort and needs before your own, then the spell will be broken. It will be as if it had never happened, upon the very moment that other person speaks the true state of their heart's emotions and admits their love aloud, and then you admit yours in truth and sincerity in return.'

'Then you are indeed unforgiving, and cruel,' Yvaine clacked her beak with avian scorn, 'to say that there is a chance for me to change back, but then for that chance to be so slim as to be impossible. Who indeed could love a beast? What person would have feelings of aught but horror to be confronted by such a terror as I am now?'

'Who indeed,' the enchantress let a small smile play on her lips, 'could love the beast you were, even before your body changed to match? Who catered to your every whim, and listened to your every demand with patience and affection?'

With that, the enchantress swept from the room, leaving Yvaine alone. The only sounds echoing through the castle were the screams of servants and their fleeing footsteps.

Yvaine sat down in an untidy sprawl of feathers and limbs as an unfamiliar sense of panic set in. *I must be calm*, she thought. *Mama and Papa will be back soon, and when they come back they will break this spell by showing they still love me. And of course I love them, what daughter could not love her parents? I will have to prove it, and make some gesture to show my sincerity. I will have to bend to their wishes and agree to something I would not have agreed to before.*

Yvaine lifted herself with effort and began to pace on unfamiliar limbs, sending furniture tumbling over, casting paintings and wall-hangings askew on their fixings, some tearing off the wall completely to lie in shards and heaps on the floor.

There is nothing for it, she decided. *I will have to agree to marry that Duke's son. I have no choice in the matter now.* And she sighed, for still she really wished she did not have to marry, and hoped that the gesture alone would be enough, even if perhaps she did not actually intend to carry out the plan.

So Yvaine waited for her parent's return. She stayed in her chamber and tried to reclaim the sense of comfort she always found within its walls. Her favourite chair no longer fit her, however, and by attempting to sit in it she broke it into pieces.

Soon hunger gripped her insides, and she found that she could not ignore its call. 'I will have my supper while I wait,' she decided, 'though I will have to find it myself, I wager,' and with much difficulty managed to push her new body through the doorway, knocking the door itself off its hinges as she passed.

As she walked down the hallway towards the kitchen, Yvaine struggled to find her bearings. Her sight was too sharp, everything was too bright and too much in focus. Every small movement, like the wind stirring a wall hanging from where an open door let in a draught, made her jump and turn her gaze towards it. Her hearing was similarly too keen, and to her it seemed that her every footfall was as loud as a thunderclap, the scraping of her talons on the stone as harrowing a sound as branches across glass windowpanes.

Screams echoed through the corridors as the nervous servants, standing around in clusters to discuss the rumour Eugénie's terrified flight had caused, caught sight of her. They fled in haste, overturning objects and discarding them at random. Here, a cup rolled against a wall, its contents spilled in a wet spiral. There, a basket of soiled linens dropped in a heap by a doorway.

Yvaine did not pay them much attention, too fixed on her goal and her roiling stomach which demanded sustenance. As it happened, she was no more or less troubled by the reactions of her servants than she normally was. They never used to scream when she approached, but they might as well have for all they dreaded her usual demands and tirades.

Once inside the kitchen she went to the pantry where her usual favourite morsels and sweets were stored. But they did not entice her any longer. She pawed through the contents of every cabinet, but nothing seemed appetising to her. Until eventually she found the doors to the cool cellar larder, and the hanging carcasses of deer and wild boar within made her growl in hunger and desire.

With a leap, she tore the nearest off of its iron hooks, and gorged herself on its raw flesh. Then another, and another. Her hunger was overwhelming, all-encompassing, and unavoidable. It consumed her as she fed, though she still felt unsatisfied. She cracked the bones for marrow, and tore each carcass limb from limb. She gorged herself, then rested, then ate again. The castle grew quiet and empty, which suited Yvaine just fine.

She rested again for a time, heedless of the passage of day into night and into day again, exhausted from her transformation. Then she awoke to a familiar voice calling her name.

'Yvaine!' called her mother in the distance. 'Yvaine!' Her voice was panicked and on the edge of hysteria.

'Mother,' Yvaine said, or tried to say, with a mouth that was no longer her own. She bounded up the cellar steps and out of the kitchen towards her mother's voice, and could hear her father's lower register rumbling through the walls, trying to comfort his wife's sobs.

Yvaine scrabbled through the hallway, and soon saw them. They were holding each other, looking mournfully into Yvaine's devastated rooms, the scene of so much wreckage and destruction.

'I am here!' she tried to call to them, but struggled with the sounds coming out of her beak. They turned towards the noises, and screamed.

'No, it is me! It is Yvaine!' she tried and tried to speak the words properly, but could not quite manage. All her parents saw was the gore-spattered maw of a terrible beast, the beast that must have entered the castle and killed their only child. They saw her, and ran in terror.

'No, no, wait!' She tried to catch up, but her body was too clumsy in its unfamiliarity. Yvaine slid and skidded across the stone while the Marquis and his wife deftly turned and twisted through the hallway and its intersecting corridors.

'Philippe!' her mother shrieked, grasping at her husband's arm as she slipped on her trailing hemlines.

'To the carriage, Lunestra, we can perhaps still get away!' The Marquis pulled his wife along behind him. They fled out into the court-yard, running for the carriage which was still being held by their head groom. 'Hector,' the Marquis shouted to him. 'We must flee! Get up and be ready to run for it!'

Perplexed, but spurred by their obvious anxiety, the man did as he was told, and drew himself up into his seat, gripping the reins at the ready. Then Yvaine burst into sight, and the man and his pair of heavy horses all screamed together. The horses bolted, and the empty carriage flew forward, bouncing across the gravel and out of the castle gates into the road beyond.

'We are doomed,' the Marquis panted, his energy spent from even that short sprint, as they watched their means of salvation vanish without them. 'We cannot escape.'

'I am scared, Philippe! I do not want to be eaten alive, I do not want to die that way!'

'Then come, Lunestra,' he took her hand. 'Let us meet our end on our own terms.' He gathered his strength and they began to run once more, heading into the forest.

'Will you not wait and just look at me properly?' Yvaine called out in garbled tones. 'It is I, your dearest daughter! It is Yvaine!' She had no choice but to follow them through the trees, willing her strange body to work at her command.

The forest was thick and difficult to traverse even if you were a slender human being, but for a huge creature with a wingspan more than twice the height of a man it was impossible. She could not keep up with her parents, only seeing, now and again, a flash of their garments through the branches.

Still, somehow she managed to keep pace with them, helped by their own unsuitability to the terrain and their inconvenient garb, fashionable travelling clothes never having been designed for this purpose, and Lunestra kept catching her slippered feet on her long skirts until finally she lifted the heavy fabric well above her ankles in desperation.

'Wait, wait!' Yvaine kept calling, but her grunts and hisses only served to spur her parents on further.

At last they came to a part of the forest which fell into a steep ravine. There was no direction her parents could now flee that could allow them further progress.

'Please,' Yvaine panted, her beak agape with exertion. 'Just look at me, and see. I am your daughter!'

'This is it, my darling wife,' the Marquis gathered her to him. 'Are you prepared?'

'I am, my beloved. Let us join our murdered daughter, and be happy in the afterlife.'

'I am not going to eat you!' Yvaine stamped her foot, exasperated.

'And ever it draws near, its talons at the ready, reaching for us,' the Marquis intoned. 'It is now, or be at the mercy of this pitiless beast.'

'Then now it must be,' his wife said and she let out a fearful gasp as she clutched to her husband's chest.

They took a step back in unison, and fell.

'No!' Yvaine shouted, trying to make her body work, trying to grab them as they fell from sight. 'NO!'

But it was done.

And now Yvaine was truly alone, and she keened to the sky above in heartbreak and fury.

Chapter 4

With the death of her parents, Yvaine felt her last chance to reclaim her humanity die alongside them. In desperation, guilt and loneliness, she buried herself in her base and brutish inhumanity, trying not to think or feel anything that might remind her of the horror of that day. She did not want to believe that she had been the cause of her own parents' death, it was too much to bear. They who were the only ones who had ever loved her, even if they had loved her too well.

She ate when she was hungry, and slept when she was tired, and in that way she was the same as she had always been, as a girl or as a beast. She found that the kitchen's larder was soon depleted of flesh, and spent two days in hungry misery uncertain how to supply herself with what she needed. None of the servants had returned, but she had not expected them to. Her anxiety of other people, and their inevitable horror, kept her from the towns and villages, so there would be no one to help her for the first time in all her sixteen years.

In the end she had no choice in the matter. Her hunger consumed her every thought, and it helped her drown out all the other insidious voices in her head who cast blame and guilt upon her conscience. But one early morning as she watched a deer pick its way across the lawns she did not even have the presence of mind to stop and think before launching herself inexpertly at it. Only her sheer bulk and the desperate frenzy which ensued allowed her to catch it, and once she did there was one baffled moment of uncertainty before she simply allowed her animal instincts to take over for her.

Afterwards she felt mentally sick, horrified and disgusted with herself. Her paws were stained with new blood, a vibrant and alluring shade of red, and the remains of the deer lay spread across the grass. If she had been able to vomit in revulsion, she would have. Only this body did not work that way.

From that moment, a small part of her retreated into the back of her mind and did not come out again. It walled itself away like a hermit monk in a monastery of its own self-refusal, unwilling to ever reveal itself again. Or perhaps it was banished like an evil spirit, she once thought in dull misery. No, she quickly corrected, this part of her had been a benign part, even if useless; it was the part of her which could not bear to touch a dead thing, or a fat spider in the corner of a room, and cried shrilly for Eugénie to help her. It was an entirely human reluctance, a fear of something dreadful and unknown, but that was gone now. She did not know whether to feel exultant in her new freedom, or mournful at the death of her humanity.

Yvaine soon gained better mastery over her body, learned to walk and run with something resembling a natural leonine grace. She relearned the power of speech, though she would often remain in silence for whole seasons at a time, preferring not to remind herself of her lost humanity and those powers of elocution and self-awareness which separated man from beast.

The next step was learning what to do with her enormous wings.

Flying looked easy, from an outsider's perspective. You start flapping, and that gains you altitude, and then you just need to steer. How wrong that was, as Yvaine soon learned. Firstly her body was so large and cumbersome that she feared she would never leave the solid earth, and that her wings must be purely an irritating decoration. But with practice she found that leaping upwards with her muscled back legs, and then snapping open her wings to begin her heavy oar-like flaps, actually got her several feet above ground. With further attempts she got higher and higher, and soon was able to ascend to the parapets of the castle's turrets, where she could then jump from those heights to allow her wings to act as sails and carry her soaring across the sky.

Steering was still difficult, as she had no natural rudder as a bird does with its long feathered tail. She had to make due with slight movements of her muscled body, and attempt to aim for particular landmarks as exercise. More often than not she fell shy of, or over, the mark, but over time improved dramatically.

And Yvaine had nothing but time. Seasons came and went, then years, until it seemed like she was always as she was, and had been no other way, time being the great acclimatiser of one's current and present state. How could she have been a girl, when she was so used to her life now as a beast? Keeping her edge of hunger always at the forefront improved her chances of thinking very few human thoughts. Mostly she considered the hunt, the weather and its impact upon her flying, the migratory patterns of certain prey, and the improvements she was making on her nest in the South Tower.

No, Yvaine was not a girl, surely never had been, not when she had never acted that way before. She was now, and always, a beast – a terrible, inhuman creature – and deserved to live her dismal, solitary existence.

Twenty-one years passed, and then everything changed.

Chapter 5

Absence can be a strange thing. If you are the one left behind you first cannot imagine how your life could continue free of the person who has left you, but over time you start to forget it was any other way. Your risings and wakings begin to have a whole new pattern, and new thoughts and distractions take over from old worries.

And if you are the one leaving, at first you cannot imagine how your life can carry on outside of the people and places that were once so familiar, but over time you start to forget those familiar faces and sights, and new ones take their place.

So it went for Beau and Désiré:

Beau was left behind but he did not have the overabundance of emotion required to pine over his brother's lack. He missed his twin like he would have missed an amputated limb, but with the steady temper of a man who sighed once over the loss, the agony of parting, but then quickly learned how to exist with three limbs instead of four. A casual rebalancing, and nothing more.

Beau tried to learn how to be a single human being instead of one half of a whole but while he carried on as if he were complete, he was always aware of the missing parts of himself.

His parents struggled with the loss of their son, as the newest blow to their abject situation, far more than his twin did, as they lacked Beau's nature and resolve. Fleur still kept to her bedchamber most of the day, the sounds of newly intensified weeping carrying through the walls. Guillaume wandered the gardens as a shadow, sometimes speaking softly to himself in self-castigation. Beau once heard him utter, 'Where is that damned sparrow?' in tones of pure desperation.

Beau himself was something of a spectacle among their new, widely-scattered community. Word of their former position, Beau's beauty and his determined self-education spread across the fields and estates. These country people were generally dismissive of their city counterparts and their decadent lives, so it would have been easy for them to hate the newcomers forced into their intimacy. But no one, watching Beau in the fields, could think him a work-shy dandy.

His beauty was undiminished by work, if anything it was enhanced by his labours in the sun, and he could never quite get out of the habit of shaving and dressing himself with care, even in the very meanest of his clothes. That beauty and care could have been another point of disdain against him, and if Désiré had been there to preen and show away with himself, it would have likely been a cause for their alienation. But Beau made no show of himself, his concerns lay in providing for his parents, and that filial duty moved them.

And so Maison Desjardins was a scene of pity for the family's few neighbours, a sad tale of unhappy circumstances befalling people who, while not entirely untarnished, were not wholly deserving of their fate.

This brought the Saint-Christophe Desjardins to the attention of the local gentry, who send over his card one morning.

'Father,' Beau tried to catch Guillaume's attention over the breakfast table, 'have you heard of Captain Merreux?'

'Hm?' his father lifted his bleary eyes from their contemplation of the tablecloth. Beau repeated his query. 'Captain Merreux, no, I never have. Why do you ask?'

'He has asked if it would be convenient to call round this afternoon, "for a matter of mutual interest",' Beau read the small, neat hand aloud. 'And his man is waiting outside for our answer.'

'Well I suppose we cannot refuse. I will tell your mother, maybe the news of some company will cheer her.'

It was a kind thought but instead of being a source of comfort, the prospect of hosting someone of obvious wealth and social standing, even among this provincial community, made Fleur panic and fret. First that there was no respectable tea service, and then that there would be no discreet maid or footman to do the serving.

'It does not matter, Mother,' Beau said. 'This man has made his address to us knowing full well our circumstances. He will not expect more than a sturdy chair and a cup of tea.'

'And serve what with the tea? We have nothing but the commonest bread and cheese!'

'Then he will be happy with cheese sandwiches, and think nothing of it,' Guillaume said, trying to calm her by patting her hand. His wife merely frowned at how easily he dismissed those social niceties which had previously been her life's work to navigate, and was not calmed in the least.

Fleur fussed and fussed until the hour of their guest's designated arrival, and even then she could not help but wring her hands and pace, then smooth the front of her dress, now her best but once considered one of her least, and then pace again.

'He arrives,' she gasped out, breathless, by the window. Beau stood at her side, fearful that she might faint from nerves. 'And we have no maid to even see our guest in!' They stood in stupid silence for a long moment.

'I will go,' Beau said into that silence, and he went.

Captain Merreux was a tall man in his late middle age, grey-haired and dressed in country fashion a year or two out of date but without any self-consciousness of that fact. He stepped from his carriage smartly and addressed Beau with a quick smile.

'Ah, you must be the industrious young man from the city I have heard about!'

'Captain,' Beau gave his bow and addressed him formally by the habits of all but the last few months of his nineteen years spent in society. The words rang genuinely, if woodenly, 'You do honour us with your visit.'

'Such manners! I am delighted!'

'May I show you inside?'

'Please, please,' he nodded, and Beau led him to the sitting room cum dining room, as it was indeed their one and only reception room.

'Captain, may I present my parents, Fleur and Guillaume Saint-Christophe Desjardins.'

'Charmed, I am simply charmed,' the Captain grinned, evidently more than pleased by the humble nature of their arrangements when sat in their best chair and given a cup of tea by Fleur's shaking hand. 'I do apologise for not making myself known to you sooner, I have had business in Marseilles that has kept me away the last month. But I arrived home to such news! New neighbours, and such a sad tale of life's cruel twists of fate! I felt I had to come at once, as I may have some knowledge which may help your current position.' And here he paused and sipped appreciatively at his tea.

'What knowledge would that be, Captain?' Fleur asked, when the pause had gone on too long to bear.

'Maison Desjardins was once,' and here he leant forward in his seat, as if imparting some much-awaited secret, 'a parfumerie!'

'A parfumerie!' Fleur exclaimed, her hand to her mouth.

'Indeed, my dear Madame Saint-Christophe Desjardins! A parfumerie, and it could easily be again! Its famous gardens were the source of its fragrance: fields of lavender, sunflowers for oil, it was a delight to the senses!'

'That sounds wonderful,' Fleur spoke with new colour in her cheeks. 'Grandmaman never spoke of such a thing, but we so rarely corresponded.' For reasons, on Fleur's part, of feeling far superior to her country relations but she would not admit that in company, or even to herself for that matter.

'As a boy I remember Madeleine Desjardins was called la Dame Parfumée! And now that title is open for a new successor, Madame,' Captain Merreux said with a twinkle in his eye.

Fleur blushed prettily. 'Well I did used to make my own scent in the city.'

Guillaume, silent until now, spoke in a solemn monotone, 'A fanciful dream, but we have no funds to begin such a venture.' Fleur visibly wilted under the weight of those words.

'That is the other part of my visit,' their guest said. 'I propose an advance for the beginning of this business, if I can be allowed to remain as a silent partner.'

'And recompensed in what way for such generosity?' Guillaume forestalled Fleur's gasp, both in response to the offer as well as the manner of her husband's blunt query. Beau simply watched the whole exchange from his seat with interest.

'One fifth of your profits, after tax. But also with the understanding that you may call upon me for any loans required to expand the business further, if it is successful.'

'And if it is not?'

'Then I will call this a gamble well-spent.' Captain Merreux was not smiling now. 'I am an old man, no longer fit for the sea. I find living on land rather dull, and the only enjoyment I get now is in using my wealth to invest in others, and to see new ventures arise out of nothing. Sometimes they succeed, sometimes they fail, but that is part of the gamble, out of which I gain much pleasure.'

And so the Saint-Christophe Desjardins had gone from socialites, to farmers, to entrepreneurs.

The first thing they did with Captain Merreux's advance was to hire a gardener to expertly tend to the extensive gardens, as without its floral bounty there would be no business. The gardener was called Monsieur Leverte, and he carefully pruned and prepared the gardens to survive the incipient cold.

Beau cleared the outbuildings behind the house of its several years of accumulated rubbish, lain unused since his great-grandparents' death and the closure of the parfumerie.

The house was bustling with activity all winter. Fleur had found a cache of her grandmother's books hidden away in a cupboard, and undertook to educate herself further in the role of parfumier. She was taken by the notion of being la Dame Parfumée, and the thought of being fashionable and in demand once more. It gave her new life and spirit, and she now wept only once a fortnight at most.

In the spring, Beau hired on some help to sow the fields, but he would not leave it to them alone. Even though it took him twice as long and sometimes tried the patience of the experienced hands, his sheer perseverance won favour in their eyes.

Much to the delight of all involved in this venture, the weather was perfectly auspicious and a showery spring led to a brilliantly clear summer. Under the careful ministrations of Monsieur Leverte the gardens were vibrant and their sweet fragrance carried far across the fields. The fields themselves were swathed in purple and yellow blossoms, and it was exactly as Captain Merreux had described to them.

They began to work on the distillation of perfumes in the summer, and the family was able to produce vial after vial of floral essences and oils with Fleur's direction, and that of her grandmother's books. This work kept them busy and industrious, thinking of little else, until one autumn night, their hands scented with the dried roses they were sorting in front of the fire, Beau dusted off his palms and said, 'But where is Désiré?'

Chapter 6

Five more years passed.

Maison Desjardins was a successful parfumerie, and Captain Merreux handled distribution of its scents and essences to the city. The family lived comfortably, though not nearly as extravagantly as they had before.

Beau still worked in the fields himself, but also took his leisure with the Captain and his peers when invited. After hearing Beau's previous enjoyment of hunting, Captain Merreux made a point of inviting his new young business partner to the shoots and hawking on his estate.

He was now four-and-twenty and was being advised to consider marriage, a state which Beau felt himself entire unprepared and unsuited for, and so kept making excuses for why it could not be.

It was late afternoon, and Beau had just returned from the last hunt of partridge for the season, the early spring air still bitter with lingering frost. He sat astride his horse, a hunter from a reasonable bloodline recommended to him by the Captain and his groom, when it was discovered by that gentleman that Beau had been walking the ten mile distance between Maison Desjardins and the Merreux estate. Beau had called the horse Commodité, not being easily taken by fancy, and indeed this mode of travel lived up to his name and was more convenient by far. A handful of partridges were now affixed behind his saddle beside his rifle, where they hung beside well-shod boots in good leather, completing an outfit of modest refinement; he was quite the country gentleman, now, by all appearances.

Beau felt the same sense of surprised pride when he entered his own land and nodded to Marcel and Pierre who were considering the deep mud of the fields with frowns of disappointment. The last of the hard frost had thawed and they had been hoping to begin the first sowing but that would now have to be unavoidably delayed. They had endured some unpleasant late blizzards recently, but were enjoying a clear spell these last two days. The first was spent in waiting for the snow to melt, but now that it had the fields were left in ankle-deep mud. Another handful of clear days should dry the mud, but would delay their already-tight schedule.

'Monsieur,' Pierre called to him, wiping his dirty face with a dirtier hand. 'Who is that?' He pointed down the road.

A horse was coming towards Maison Desjardins, with a figure slumped on its back. While they watched, the figure fell in a slow, boneless drop onto the road while the horse danced nervously away.

Beau nudged Commodité into a quick trot and caught up with the horse to restrain it and tied it beside his own onto the fence which enclosed the fields along the roadside. Then he inspected the fallen man.

To his shock and surprise, the man's face was the mirror of his own. It was Désiré, finally returned, haggard in face, with clothing hung in rags from sinewy, starved limbs. At first his eyes were dull and unseeing, but then they grew bright with recognition.

'Brother! At last!' Désiré cried before fainting into Beau's arms.

The house burst into a flurry of surprise when Beau entered the house with his twin carried between himself and one of the farmhands. Guillaume simply stared from his seat while Fleur dropped her tea cup, which shattered onto the hearthstones. She attempted to direct and assist the men's progress between gasping sobs in such a disastrous fashion that the men eventually forced her to sit.

Fleur perched herself on the edge of the nearest seat, and watched avidly as her younger son, her dear lost child, presumed dead for these long years, was propped up with cushions on the chaise-longue. He began to stir from his languishment, and Beau helped him sit upright.

Five years' worth of guilt and reprisal welled up in Guillaume's bosom as he sat and stared in silence, before he, too, began to weep to see his child returned, a child he thought killed by the permission he had granted for a foolish quest. How many nights had he beat his breast in castigation for that mistake?

They were impatient to hear what had caused his delayed return, and what had made him so pitiful in appearance, but it was obvious that Désiré needed rest and nourishment. After many embraces and words of thanksgiving, they forestalled any attempts he made to speak and had a light invalid's supper of broth and honeyed bread placed before him.

'Please eat,' Fleur insisted through her tears. 'You look so thin! It breaks my heart to see you so!'

'Hush,' Guillaume admonished her. 'Do not worry the boy so with your mother-henning. He will eat, and rest, and be strong again in time.'

Désiré protested that he did, indeed, feel stronger already after some food, but Beau helped him upstairs to the bed they would share again, as before. Despite his claims of strength, Beau could feel his twin's fragility beneath his arms.

The next day Beau woke with a cramp in his shoulder from the unaccustomed folded position he had perforce assumed in the night. When he rose he was careful to not disturb his brother's sleep, which looked uneasy enough without his interference. A sheen of sweat lay across Désiré's brow, despite the cold morning air seeping through the window panes.

The family, by unspoken agreement, did not wake him and ensured their much-cherished housemaid, Marcella, did not perform any noisy chores while he slept. Having spent so long without servants made Fleur in particular extremely fond and kind towards the young girl they finally had the funds to employ. In return, Marcella was a thoughtful kind of young person who sought out ways to calm her mistress' easily frazzled nerves. This day's request did not cause her any trouble, she insisted to

Fleur, and she privately thought that even if it did she would refrain from mentioning it.

By supper time, when the sun's feeble light finally diminished below the hills of the horizon, Désiré carefully descended the stairs.

Fleur caught her youngest child in another fierce embrace, murmuring into his chest, 'I scarce believe you are returned to us!' She tried her best to hide her tears, newly sprung from the feeling of Désiré's protruding ribs against her cheek, but they dampened his shirt, borrowed from Beau's armoire, nonetheless.

They ate a meal of partridge pie, made from the meal of those roast birds Beau had brought home the day before which no one in the family felt able to eat while still in shock from Désiré's sudden return and the mystery of that miracle, while he slept in the room above. After, they retired to the sitting room where Désiré made clear his intentions to speak.

'I went looking for enchantment,' Désiré said, his voice hoarse and small, 'and I suppose I found it, but it was not what I was hoping it would be.' He began to laugh, but his laugh was bitter, exhausted, and soon became a painful cough. After a pot of tea was brought in by Marcella, and a warming cup pressed upon him, Désiré tried to begin his tale again.

'After I left here, I planned to travel to the city with all of my original intentions,' he said, lifting his eyes from his tea cup to meet the gaze of his brother. 'I had hopes that we were not as friendless as it appeared we were, and wished to visit the houses of our old compatriots.'

'Were they as faithless as I had suspected?' Beau asked, his mouth twisted in scorn. It was hard not to feel a sense of betrayal from those youths who professed such lasting friendship in one moment, only to avert their eyes when such a connection was no longer beneficial to them.

'I never got the chance to find out. It did not help that I got lost several times on the way, but before I arrived in the city, I was… waylaid.'

'Waylaid?' Beau lifted his eyebrow at Désiré's hesitation. 'What do you mean?'

'Where you robbed?' Fleur asked, her hand over her mouth. 'I cannot fathom that in this enlightened age a respectable young man cannot travel alone without fear of being accosted by brigands and thieves!'

'Then I must not have looked respectable enough for even the meanest robber to be tempted, Mother, for that is not what happened at all,' Désiré said with black humour. 'No, several weeks into my journey, as winter just began to approach, it was my fate, my gaoler, the devil himself who met me on the road one day.'

'Heavens above!' Fleur cried out.

'What blasphemous exaggeration is this?' Guillaume asked. It did not sit rightly with him for his sons to speak lightly of evil, else it should it make that terrible being cast his eyes upon them, being summoned by such an utterance.

Beau watched his brother and saw that he spoke as truthfully as himself.

Désiré spoke again. 'I do not exaggerate, please believe me. I do not blame you if you do not, as at that time I did not yet know what stood before me. I would not have believed me either. Let me describe him as best I can:

'He wore a green coat and was a rather fine looking fellow, if you failed to see that in lieu of boots he had horse's hooves. The exact features of his face, however, I cannot say, as his visage constantly changed. He looked as it suited him to look in each moment, and it seemed that what suited him was never the same between one minute and the next.

'I could see that this was no ordinary person, so when this being called my name as if he knew me, as the devil does indeed know the names of every sinner, I did stop and address him in return. I listened, and it was clear that he knew my heart and what made it heavy with worry, for he then offered me exactly what I had hoped for. He wished to make a bargain, and I thought myself clever enough to outwit any being.

'He told me that if I would agree to be his servant for five years, then at the end of that time I would have as many jewels and gold as I could carry away with me. I demanded to see proof that such riches were in his possession, and he took my hand to transport me, by some means I never knew, to a chasm where I could see, as far as my eyes could make out, piles of every precious metal and gem known to man.

"'I will do it!" I promised in ignorance, thinking myself very lucky indeed to have met this creature who would surely be my, our, salvation.

"'However," he cautioned me, "if you should perish while in my service, or leave before the five years is completed, then your immortal soul is mine and I will have you for eternity."

'How I scoffed at the thought! I had the bravado of youth, and thought myself immortal. I did not see how I could possibly fail. I had no idea – I did not know anything at all.'

Désiré's voice faltered, and he lifted his hands, grasping emptily at the air, at a thought, at his youthful incomprehension.

'I now was in the service of a creature who wanted me to die. Not quickly, no, and not painlessly. He wanted that death to come as his victory at the end of a long period of servitude, to gain the most benefit from my soul before he claimed it.

'For four years and eleven months I served the devil. Sometimes it was simply that I was ordered to do something seemingly impossible, something which could only be completed through guile and misdirection. Like being told to fill a whole chamber with one single object, so I brought a candle and filled the room with light. Other times, I carried out such hideous tasks which I cannot even describe. I do not wish to describe them. They will haunt me throughout the rest of my life.'

Silence fell in the sitting room, and the cheerfully glowing fire crackled without pity, casting its pleasant light across the scene of such horror without sympathy.

Fleur was afraid to speak, and her lips trembled with barely checked distress. Guillaume was pale and devastated.

Beau spoke. 'What happened? You are here, alive, so surely you won the wager?'

'I did not,' Désiré said, so quietly that his family nearly did not hear the words. 'I learned that the devil would have a final task for me, from which there would be no possibility of completion, which would surely take my life to attempt. This would be how he ensured he would have my mortal soul.

'So on the eve of that day I crept from my sleeping-place – I cannot call it a chamber, I cannot call it a dwelling of any sort, such was the baseness of my existence – but I stole into the devil's room while he slept. Yes, the devil does sleep. I had learnt the ways of my master in those long years, I knew how to move so that he would not notice my passing, and I knew where the keys were kept.

'I did not leave that night, though I cannot describe to you the temptation of freedom. I simply unlocked the door to make ready my flight, readied my horse, reclaimed Honneur, and Mother's ring, though Father's fine clothes were long since reduced to beggar's rags. Then I returned the key, and went back to my sleeping-place and acted as if I had not moved from it all night. Part of me thought that this would be my final act of foolishness in a lifetime's worth of folly, to have freedom in my reach, and then return to bondage. But I still had some small hope that I could effect my freedom with the bargain intact and win my prize.

I knew with those riches came our salvation, and I could not leave while it was still conceivable that I might be able to possess them.

'He called me to him, that next morning, and made his final command. My heart fell; it was as impossible as I had feared, and would be my certain end to attempt. I told the devil I needed time to complete what he asked of me and he left me then.

'And so I escaped. I would not be empty-handed though; I took these,' from within his trouser pockets Désiré drew his hands forth, 'from the devil's stronghold as I fled.'

He opened his palms as slowly as a blossoming flower, and within lay several glimmering, shining jewels which scattered firelight as sparks around the room.

'Oh!' Fleur covered her mouth with trembling hands, and Guillaume's eyes widened.

'What was the final task?' Beau asked, breaking the silence which followed.

'The devil gave me this riddle to perform: to "leap but do not fall through the air, and do not again place your feet upon the earth."'

'That is impossible.'

'Exactly so, unless one were to become a bird, or be a contortionist of the sort who can walk on their hands for the rest of time. I puzzled for a long time before I made my escape, in case I was missing some obvious solution. I could not find one, so I left.'

Beau spoke again. 'But the five years were not finished.'

'No, they were not.'

'You did not complete your service.'

'I did not.'

'Now the devil has a claim on your soul,' breathed Fleur in horror, realisation dawning slowly.

'Which I am certain he will come forth to take when it suits him to do so.'

'No,' his parents breathed in dread.

Désiré laughed. 'As if this were the worst news I could bring you! I fear to tell you, for your sakes, that there is more to my tale. A worse fate, perhaps, than even that which I have revealed.'

Chapter 7

'Worse! How is that even possible? I cannot bear it!' Fleur cried out.

'Strength,' Guillaume told her, taking her hand. 'If our child has lived it, then we can bear to hear its recital, surely.'

Désiré continued, 'I was now returning home through the mountain pass, but a storm threatened to throw me from the crags with winds and driving snow.'

'This must have been the very same storm which covered the fields,' Beau said.

'You were so close, so near, and we did not know,' Fleur's voice wavered. She gripped tightly to Guillaume's hand as Désiré told his tale:

A light had flickered through the gloom and Désiré had followed it, hoping to beg shelter from a local crofter at least. He was now so far from pride as to feel no misgivings about that which he would have once dismissed out of hand as unimaginable.

When he drew near he saw a huge edifice, an imposing castle in the mountains, with its gates invitingly open. The wrought iron was choked with ivy, and the place had a neglected air, so it if were not for the light coming from inside he would have thought it were abandoned. His horse led him into the courtyard, where a stall in an empty stable was lain with fresh straw and hay. Once he tied it therein he approached the castle door to find it unlocked, and it opened to the knocking of his fist. Calling inside gained him no answer, but a fire lay crackling in the hall before which Désiré could not help but stand to dry his soaked and chilled clothing. The mantelpiece was elaborately carved, if crumbling at the edges, with a heraldic griffin rampant upon a shield cast in flickering shadows.

On the table before him sat a feast and, after waiting an appropriate period for the master of the castle to arrive to explain himself to, Désiré, famished from five years' mistreatment, availed himself of the repast with a sneaking guilt that he was trespassing upon someone's fine supper. His stomach filled quickly, and he had care not to partake of the overly rich dishes that might upset his stomach. He then settled himself in a large comfortable chair by the fire, though its fabric somewhat torn and rubbed thin, to await judgement for his boldness, and soon drifted to sleep, warm, dry and fed.

In the morning Désiré was unsettled to find that the master of the castle had never arrived to wake and castigate him, but that the table was cleared from the night before and a simple but hearty breakfast laid out before him. Supposing this to be a sign that his presence was not unwelcome, he sat himself down and ate his fill once more, wondering all the while if he was dreaming.

He stepped out of the castle to find the morning fine and dry for the final leg of his journey home, and crossed the courtyard to retrieve his horse. A large shadow passed over his head, and Désiré's blood went cold to see a monstrous beast soar over him to land in the gardens.

At this point he was nearly certain he was dreaming.

'You will remember the reveries of our childhood,' Désiré asked Beau, 'in which my imagination would call forth some fantastic, hideous dragon to conquer? I found myself now living this fantasy, and uncertain about the reality of what I was seeing. I cannot imagine why else I rushed to meet the beast, how I could have thought I would defeat it, as weak and wretched as I was. But that is what I did, sword raised as if I had the strength to wield it.

'I confronted the beast, shouting, "Begone, dread creature! Leave this place be!" In my mind, at that moment, I felt the need to defend whatever mysterious benefactor had sheltered and fed me. I would not skulk away from danger like the miserable, sneaking thing I had become, no, I would meet danger face to face like a man.'

What stood before him, however, was the embodiment of a nightmare, not a dream. Then it spoke.

'Is this how you repay my kindness, stranger?' she snarled, casting a baleful eye upon him. 'I would have been better served to leave you to the storm's fate, if not for the bond of my oath. I am now freed of it, having given you shelter and hospitality as I am bound, so for this ingratitude I will have my satisfaction and kill you where you stand!'

'I knew not it was you to whom I owed my thanks!' Désiré said in his defence. He suddenly felt the harsh awareness of reality, faced by this being he could have never imagined in his own dreams. She had the body of a lion but the head of an eagle, in a strange and unnatural pairing. Her wings spread full twenty feet across, and blacked out the light from the rising sun. 'I would ask that you spare me, as I have to return home to give my family that which has been hard-earned for their keep.'

'Spare you?' she spat, laughing a terrible laugh. 'Why should I do such a thing, when faced with such insult as a naked sword? No, I will not let you go. If I let you leave here now, you will return with the company of a great many other sword-waving fools. Why on heaven and earth should I bargain with you?'

Désiré spoke to his family of this exchange, and tried to explain what happened next. 'You may wonder at what I proposed, and struggle to understand it. I am not sure I can fully express the various reasons and emotions that brought me to what I offered.

'Having just escaped from servitude to the devil I found myself in two minds. One, detesting myself for the baseness of my existence during that period of time, one day shy of five years. Two, however, was that during my battle with the elements, when I was uncertain if I would live despite my freedom, I felt that death would perhaps be the better solution. I did not, and I do not, know how to face my freedom. I grew used to the life of a slave, and, as much now as then, wonder how to survive any way else.

'So I offered myself as a servant to this beast, recommending the talents I have gained. I promised that if I were allowed to return for a week, time enough to give you the riches I promised to gain in my absence, and then make my goodbyes and apologies anew. I pledged to return, and to ensure no others would follow in my company with whom I might seek to destroy the creature. The beast vowed that any person who appeared, besides myself, would be killed on the spot, and its size and power was such that I saw at once the futility in any attempt to overpower it.

'So this is how I am returned to you, at least for the time being. But I cannot stay long.'

'But brother,' Beau shook his head, 'there can be no question of you returning there. The beast you describe will surely devour you rather than put you to honest work.' He forbore from mentioning the fact that he doubted his brother would even survive the return journey and the labour required at his destination, even after a few more days' rest. Meanwhile, their parents were dumb with horror from this latest story of terror, their mother pale and fainting against Guillaume's chest.

'Do you doubt my powers of persuasion, brother?' Désiré asked, with something nearly like humour in his bleak expression. 'This inhuman creature would have murdered me without a second thought, and yet I convinced it that my worth was higher as a servant than as a meal. I am certain I can do so again, and as often as required.'

'Your brother is right,' their father said, regaining his powers of speech. 'I cannot allow my child to go to such a fate. If someone must be sent to the creature, it must be me. I have outlived my usefulness to this family, I have grown fat, indolent and stupid, it is true,' and here he raised a quelling hand to the beginnings of protest from his family. 'My two fine sons have much to recommend them to the world as yet, so I will take my leave of you all in the morning. At least I will have done one final act of good to you all.'

'Father,' Beau said, 'one of the beast's conditions was that no others could follow Désiré's direction and appear at the castle. She would take you for a doer of mischief and kill you. It must be Désiré, or no one at all.'

'Then let it be none!' Fleur cried out. 'Why should my son, or his father, voluntarily return to such a fate? Not when the beast herself can hardly expect it? What would it do if you simply did not appear at the agreed-upon time?'

Désiré spoke quietly, but his words were clear and unslurred. 'I have done many things these past five years, and many things have been done to me. I have had my freedom removed against my will, and I have been forced by circumstance to do, and think, and feel, unworthy things. I have given my oath to this creature, if only I were able to be reunited with my family again, and here I am. So now I must make honest compensation, and restore my honour. For my own sake, if for no one else.'

Defeated, Guillaume retired for the night, quickly followed by Fleur, feeling helpless to stop their son leaving them again, and this time to an even more certain doom.

Beau sat up, unsleeping, that night. He watched the slow rise and fall of his brother's chest, and the features laid slack from sleep which so closely mirrored his own. Then those features twisted, and sweat beaded upon Désiré's brow. He moaned in quiet anguish, and Beau laid his hand upon his brother's shoulder. Désiré woke quickly, his eyes wide and frantic.

'Where am I?' he asked, feeling his wrists, where faint scars still circled. He was shaking.

'You are home,' Beau said, reading more from the contours of his brother's haunted face in that moment about the truth of the past five years than he had learned from Désiré's own telling of the events. 'You are safe now.'

'Am I?' he asked, quietly, into the darkness of their bedroom. 'Will I ever be, while the devil has a claim on my soul?'

Beau still could not understand so much of what Désiré had said. 'You tried to explain it and, as you expected, I find it troubling to comprehend. Why did you offer yourself as the beast's slave? When you had already endured and suffered at the hands of an unnatural master once before?'

'Sometimes, brother, you cannot help but wish to return to the things that have made you suffer. Maybe because they gave your life a purpose beside itself, or maybe because you think that this is what you deserve.'

'You do not deserve it,' Beau said, and as always he spoke the truth. 'Then answer me this final question: why return when there seems to be no repercussion if you should not?'

Désiré looked at his brother in the darkness, and spoke with quiet certainty, 'I do not belong anywhere any longer. I came to this opinion even before meeting the beast in the castle, and part of me even felt it before I left here all those years ago. I feel as though there is no place for me, no occupation I could ever have, that would fulfil the ideals I have always held about my future. You have made such a success here, it is ever clearer that I have no place here or anywhere.'

'You do have a place,' Beau said.

Désiré closed his eyes again in exhaustion, a sigh rattling in his chest unhealthily. Soon he was asleep again, but now that Beau looked closer, it did not look peaceful. It was simply the relief of unconsciousness.

Beau looked at his brother and knew that he could not return to the beast's enslavement. Désiré had already been a slave once, it had broken him, and almost killed him. A second time would surely be his end.

Beau lay awake in bed, considering the situation. His father's appearance would have inspired murder in the heart of the beast, but Beau's own appearance would gain no such comment, being exactly what the beast expected to see.

He wrote his brother a letter, and in it he wrote the words, *You can have my place.* He left in the early morning, before the colours of the world were yet convinced by themselves. He gathered his belongings, regained his sword, and mounted Commodité. It was not yet sunrise by the time he was set on the road to meet his brother's fate in his stead.

Beau could not say he had always been a good brother, they had been so close that competition for friends and accolades had sometimes split them into opposing factions, but he knew that if he could do something to help his brother, he must do it, as he must help himself. Love for his brother was a certainty, and with that came a sense of responsibility for his mortal person. Going to doom in his place was not really the selflessly martyred act it might appear to another, it was the natural act of one who knows it is the thing to do, and then does it.

Chapter 8

The mist was clearing from the mountain road as Beau approached the place his brother had described, and the sun was now high in the sky above him. Turning a bend suddenly revealed an incredible vista, where all the range was laid out before him in its heights and depths and shadows. Thin snakes of the morning mist remained in deeper crevices, falling down into the valley like waterfalls off a cliff. Nestled into the rock sat the turrets and peaks of the castle, exactly as Désiré had said it would be.

A chill rose up his back as Beau watched a large shadow glide soundlessly over the tallest turret of the castle and climb in twisting spirals up into the thin mountain air. Even from this distance it was clear how massive the shape of the beast was, and as he watched her disappear into one of the rivulets of mist all he could feel was an unfamiliar grip of emotion, that of dread horror. Suddenly his former certainty about this course of action no longer seemed so certain. It soon passed; Beau mastered himself and encouraged Commodité forward.

The gates to the castle were opened, and the horse hurried in towards the smell of hay. Beau dismounted and allowed him to lead the way to the stables, thinking that at least he had seen the beast depart and may have some reprieve before meeting his untimely end. He spent some time in industriousness, being the natural state of his person after the last five years, to relieve his mount of bridle, bit and saddle and to scrub the itch of perspiration from his hide with handfuls of straw. As he was hanging up the saddle cloth, wet and fragrant with horse sweat, on a tree branch beside the stone outbuilding, a shadow fell upon him.

'Why are you here?' a harsh voice roared in his ears.

'I am here to fulfil my oath,' Beau said, suddenly worried that his brother had spoken wrongly about the agreement, that perhaps it did not exist at all. He looked around himself to place the speaker but did not see anything but the dark shadows of the trees.

'I had not expected you so soon,' came the voice again, and then spectre was before him, moving out from the darkness. Even Désiré's luridly detailed story was not enough to prepare him for the being in front of his eyes. Her head, with long, curved beak, stood taller than the roof of the stables and her talons gripped deep into the mud. Her wings shone with hundreds of enormous dark feathers, the longest of which would have stood fully as tall as Beau himself. Her leonine body was furred in tawny, she was deep-chested and lithe as a greyhound. Matts clotted her underside, and old blood stained her feet to the hocks.

Beau took in all that was terrible and strange, but he stood fast and did not blanch as she spoke further, 'In truth I did not expect you at all. You must be even more foolish than I had first thought, to rush so to your own doom and incarceration.'

'When I vow to do a thing, I will do it,' was all he said.

She cocked her head to examine him in turn, with one yellow eye, but it was impossible to see from her expression whether her opinion was favourable until she spoke, 'Seeing you here before me again, I suppose you look a useful sort of person, comfortable with hard labour. Our bargain for your life can remain if you can manage to make yourself invaluable to me.'

'What could you need of me? I would have thought you had servants for the keeping of your castle.'

Somehow her beak replicated something like a snorting guffaw. 'All the servants fled, when I-,' she paused, and then continued, snarling, 'There is no one else here.'

'But the feast, when I-,' he struggled to speak the lie, 'from before?'

'It is the enchantment upon the castle. As I am oath-bound to help all travellers in need on the road, the castle is enchanted to give them food and comfort. It will not do so much for you, anymore. You are no longer a traveller, nor in need. You must make your own comfort, or perish without even my interference. It does not matter to me if you starve.

'Now stop with these tedious questions, and go do something useful! I have not yet wholly decided not to eat you.'

Her tail whipped behind her as she turned and stalked off. Beau turned to the castle and considered the task before him. He felt much more equal to the task than he would have felt five years ago. Though this estate gave him far more to work with than he was used to, from sheer size as much as its state of ruination, so he would have to prioritise immediate needs, and continue as such.

For his own pressing needs, he required only shelter and food. It did not seem too difficult at first thought, but without the castle's enchantments he found that there were no rooms within that were wind and water tight. The rain had gotten into upholstery and mould had spoiled all the furnishings throughout. So for the first requirement of shelter he found which room had the fewest draughts and leaks, emptied it of everything ruined, which was mostly everything inside, and then hunted down whatever furniture was made of the sturdiest materials and required the least attention to be serviceable. In this way he was able to provide for himself a single welcoming room among the wings and turrets of ruin.

Beau felt more at ease in dealing with the second of his needs, being by nature more happily industrious outdoors than in confined spaces. He walked through the gardens and found that many edible plants yet remained from the previous growing season which had been given the freedom to spread, grow tough and choke their neighbours. One raised bed he designated to clear out completely and here he transplanted cuttings of those plants to cultivate a more domestic garden. He was lucky that it was only just spring, and he would be able to do much with the raw material before him.

As for meat, Beau could hunt. In his rummaging around the castle, he had located the gunroom and was now in possession of a fair arsenal of rifles. Beau had not considered bringing his own, for which his perfect hindsight had lately castigated him, so he was inordinately pleased by this discovery. He had assumed, until then, that he would need to rely on his lately-gained knowledge of snares and traps taught to him by the landsmen whose poaching efforts he turned a blind eye to.

By the time the sun had set, Beau had finished his day's labours, and sat himself on a creaking but serviceable chair by the side of his large new bedframe, its four posts carved in reliefs of mythic scenes. By the firelight from the hearth, at least firewood being a resource easy to come by with the splintered furniture scattered around the castle, the figures seemed to move of their own accord. Forked tongues wagged at him, their blank eyes seemingly fixated on his. Beau felt chilled despite the warmth, and settled into an uneasy night's sleep having serious doubts and fears about his present circumstances.

Chapter 9

Beau's fears were no more assuaged in morning when the shadow of the beast's wings momentarily blocked the faint dawn glow from his window. The paper-hush of her feathers was a frightful sound to his mind. They had not spoken since the day before. Though Beau dreaded further intimacy, he refused to allow his fear to be his master.

With a spade in hand, letting the sky lighten above him, Beau could almost imagine he was home, if not for the ever-present bulk of the castle as his backdrop, or the mountains further still. The smell of soil and growing things nearly made him feel content for a time.

'I fail to see how this work is benefiting me. What can a garden do for a beast?' It startled Beau how easily she could sneak up on him, with all her bulk and power.

'Do you eat aught else but meat?' he asked, and as he did so he found himself suddenly aware that her lithe shape was the gaunt condition of a starving thing.

'No, I only eat meat, like any other primitive and Godless carnivore. And I am wondering now if perhaps your only use is as such a meal.'

'I can provide a better meal than the one I would make,' he assured quickly. 'I have seen the tracks of several rabbits through these gardens. It would benefit both of us to catch them.'

'Rabbits are quick,' she snarled. 'I have not yet tasted one.'

'Then you shall have one today.'

As the sun had not yet fully risen above the trees, Beau hoped that the crepuscular creatures would still be active above their warrens. In a sheltered bit of trees he had seen the tell-tale signs of a run, fresh scat and recent digging so he knew they were near and hoped to catch them at their grazing. He made his way carefully, downwind, with a rifle in his hand. A chill grip on his throat remained as he crept forward, feeling that his very life was in the balance. It choked him with dread as he saw the ground was empty of furred inhabitants. He must have already been too late, or been too obvious in his approach. He could not shoot a rabbit for the beast, and so his life may become forfeit if her hunger grew too great for her to bear his living presence, when his death would mean a full belly.

So his continued life must become worth more to her than a single day's meal. If he could feed the hungry monster, that may be the only way for their bargain to be useful to her.

A deep, steadying breath calmed him and he recalled his practice of snares, which should hopefully bring reward with the use of a tempting bait, such as a small pile of new lettuce shoots gathered carefully from his new garden. Beau hid a good distance away behind the cover of a dense patch of bracken to wait and watch for the moment to pull the loop taut, his heart beating so loudly in his chest that he felt certain no rabbits would emerge, surely hearing the noise even below-ground.

It was a long wait, or so he felt, knowing that his very life likely depended on the outcome. He began to imagine with morbid helplessness what manner exactly the beast would use to eat him. If she would simply fall upon him with gaping maw, or dash him to the ground first with her talons. Perhaps take him aloft and drop him.

Movement stilled his terrible thoughts, and the cautious head of a brown rabbit extended out towards the snare's bait. Its whiskers trembled as it smelled the air, but detecting nothing but an easy meal moved forward a hop. And then another.

'Would you prefer it skinned and jointed?' he asked, and was pleased to interpret surprise in the space of the hesitation before she answered him. She likely expected him to fail, and he was glad to disappoint her.

'I never bothered before, having not the means to do so.'

'But having the option now, what is your preference?'

'If you can do it quickly,' she snapped. 'I grow less patient with every moment you wield that bloody knife, and would be careless in what exactly I would be grabbing if I was forced to help myself.'

Beau had automatically stripped the inedible guts from the carcass, and then made short work of removing its head, skin and feet. The rest was quartered roughly, and he found himself suddenly uncertain of how to present it to her. If he was cooking for his parents he would use a fine porcelain serving platter, and if he were feeding his horse he would toss hay upon the ground. The beast was neither a human eating civilly at a table, but nor was she a dumb animal in a paddock. Neither method seemed appropriate, so Beau found a rock of a good size and height nearby where he laid out his offering with care – but also quickly.

It seemed that barely seconds passed before the rock was bare again, with only blood staining its surface to indicate that anything had been left there.

'Good, but too small,' she muttered. 'I am still hungry. I will have to hunt today after all.' And she took to the skies, casting up clods of dirt from her talons and whipping the wind into a frenzy with her labouring wings.

When the beast later reappeared it was growing dark, and the trees were throwing long shadows on the overgrown lawns. An early spring murmuration of starlings startled out from the grass and filled the air with chattering alarm. She landed heavily, scoring troughs out of the earth while her sides heaved, head lowered and beak agape. Beau set down his hammer from his efforts at mending the paddock fence, where Commodité had now fled to the furthest corner. Her eyes were closed, but then opened suddenly to fix him in her stare.

'What makes you stare so?' she growled. 'I begin to think you are in fact a daemon, here to plague me further into my own personal hell.'

'I take it that the hunt did not go well?'

'Damn you!'

'Then you will be especially glad of my efforts today,' and he gestured to where a large flat section of peeled bark had been laid as a platter upon which a half dozen prepared rabbits were lain. They remained in silence while she tore into the offering, and Beau took his hammer back up again. His back was to her, and he did not turn when the harrowing sounds of her beak snapping bones ceased. It had seemed that she had left, as so long passed with no words spoken or threats made, but for the sensation of being watched by a malevolent presence.

'Thank you.' It was a quiet voice quite unlike the one he had been learning to be accustomed to in their short acquaintance. 'Though I still have not yet decided if I should just eat you and be done with it.' That was more like what he expected. Beau twisted his torso around to reply but she was already disappearing into the black shadows between the trees.

Their days began to take shape, with Beau rising just before dawn to catch some animal unaware, and leave it in a discreet but obvious place for the beast to break her fast with. He would then set himself to whatever task he had given himself that day, clearing rubble from rooms or scouring all the kitchen's pots and crockery back to a useable state. Mostly he spent time in his garden, and tended carefully to the plants which now flourished with the incipit warmth of summer. Slowly the castle was becoming more habitable, and even more slowly he began to find himself no longer dreading his interactions with its solitary and monstrous resident. He even began to get bold enough to ask her questions.

'How long have you been here?' he asked one morning, while she finished a brace of partridge.

'My family have lived in this castle for ten generations or more,' she said. 'I was born here.'

'Ten generations? There have been more creatures like you?'

'There is only one of this creature here before you; I am the product of cursed fate, not natural design. My late father was the Marquis de Beaumont, my late mother his beloved wife Lunestra, and I their only daughter, thought to be late but still very much present. My father's family line can be traced all the way back to the Aedui people, but that, and much beside, has ended with his death.'

Beau stared, horrified, as the truth of her situation began to dawn on him. 'You mean to say that you are – you were – human?'

'I am nothing now,' she rasped. 'But yes, you are correct. I was once, until the cruel trick of destiny gave me an exterior to match and house my rotten soul.'

'How could that be?'

'The fell work of sorcery. But enough! I cannot speak of these things – I will not! I have made a point of forgetting, and I will not let you force me into remembering. I would rather crunch your bones in my talons, and rip your flesh asunder! Do not forget that you are here at my mercy, man.' And the last word sounded like a curse as it was uttered from her beak, bitten off and bitter.

But Beau was feeling uncommonly bold and no longer cared to choose his words carefully. He could see that there was a truth he was beginning to uncover before him, and so he spoke without thinking, for once in his life, and said, 'Well that explains why you are such a poor hunter, at least.'

The beast reared back her head, beak agape and aghast. Her hackles rose alarmingly and she began to pace, cutting ribbons out of the ground with her every turn. 'And who are you to pass such judgement upon me, to criticise and comment on the nature of this monster before you? When I could snap your neck, I could peel the skin from your flesh, and eviscerate-'

'Yes, yes,' he interrupted, unmoved and unaffected. 'That is all well and good to say so. I am sure that you are physically capable of doing all these things, but I am wondering about the likelihood of it when it seems you are struggling to keep yourself fed on the dumb animals of the forest.'

'Well, I-'

'And it would seem to me,' he went on to say, 'that you actually do need my help after all. You are only just beginning to fill out around the ribs and look less of a starving thing, and only due to my kindly gifts.'

'I have managed just fine for years and years before you came along!' And still she paced, tense and spitting with rage.

'Perhaps you have survived, yes, but not well and not thrived by any measure.'

'I would like to see you do as well, in the circumstances! This cage of flesh, this prison, it is entirely cumbersome and unsuitable!' She stopped and stood kneading the mud beneath her talons with suppressed emotion.

Beau cast an appraising eye on her form. 'Well I can see that your weight is certainly impressive, but the counterbalance of those wings should surely carry you well.'

'They are entirely too long, and I am incapable of any sort of swift pursuit, when quarry takes me between the trees!'

'Ah,' he nodded. 'Well that is the issue. Your feathered form is more of an eagle, while your remainder is that of a lion, and thus is not resembling a hawk whose shorter wings allow for greater agility, and whose long tail counterbalances their twists and turns. Your apparent design is for soaring aloft as if on sails, and then plummeting upon unaware prey from on high. Or even driving it like a sheepdog harries sheep, to fall from crags and cliffs. Have you tried to observe other winged things like yourself, to see how they are successful?'

'I have not,' she said, and her hackles had finally smoothed down somewhat. It was clear that she was struggling to speak aloud her failings, and so with effort she admitted, 'I fear that I have only survived this long by monitoring the passage of livestock through the mountain passes, and scavenging like a vulture upon whatever hapless brutes fall to their own demise.'

'There is no shame in finding the advantage in opportunity,' Beau said. 'An eagle will not hesitate to do exactly that, and they are known as the most regal of all the raptors, flown by only emperors. And as the lion is called king of the savage jungles, he will also fight the jackals of the savannah for a fallen carcass. Both your halves are equally disposed to this method, and so it is no wonder that you have turned to this as a natural consequence.'

'And as for the other, unseen, part of me?' she spoke with quiet savagery. 'The part which, as a girl, grew squeamish at the sight of a dead bird in the garden? Who would not touch it, and shrieked until some servant came to remove it from my sight? What of she, in this equation of parts?'

Beau fell silent at last, not knowing what to say apart from, 'I thought we were not speaking of that.'

'No,' she agreed. 'We are not.' And she turned and left, her tufted tail lashing the air.

Chapter 10

Beau spent the night sleepless, tossing and turning with newfound knowledge sitting undigested in his mind. He had not thought that the beast's form was anything but her natural state, although unnatural in itself by the formation of it. He had thought of her as one of those magical beings, like the secretive enchanters of the world, who was scarce seen but on the outskirts of the world. It had not occurred to him that this was something imposed upon a human girl, and against her will. It did not sit right in his thoughts at all, and he was suddenly filled with pity and sympathy for her situation, and wonder for how it came to pass.

He also realised that here was the first person, if 'person' was the correct way to identify the beast, he felt at ease with. His awkwardness seemed gone in her presence, and it was unaccounted for.

In the morning, Beau waited in the customary spot in the garden where usually his offering would have been laid. Instead of such an offering, he had a plan.

'I will teach you how to hunt,' he said when she arrived, 'using your innate talents and strengths.'

'But why,' she started to protest, but his boldness from the night before was still running through his veins and he would not hear it.

'Well if you do decide to eat me, after all, you would be left in a bit of an unfortunate state again. Far more worthwhile for you to learn to provide for yourself properly than rely upon my efforts.'

'I hardly plan to eat you if you are providing such easy meals for me on a daily basis. Surely this would only place your position here in jeopardy if you stop being so invaluable to me in such a way. Why would you wish to do such a thing?'

He shrugged, making a rare gamble. 'Maybe I am just becoming tired of hunting for such a lazy monster who cannot even catch her own rabbits. Maybe I would rather be eaten after all.'

She growled, but he ignored her.

'Come,' he shouted over his shoulder, heading into the forest. 'We are wasting the best part of the day.'

The canopy hid the emerging sunlight from illuminating the forest floor, but even so there were some obvious tracks which Beau could follow, even despite the thickening summer undergrowth. Behind him, the beast had folded her wings into her sides tightly but still struggled to fit between some of the more narrow spaces. Beau could feel her frustration like a palpable force, until finally she wielded a taloned paw and threw bracken and brush aside with a crash.

'Well that was the very picture of stealth,' he spoke mildly.

'I cannot do this! You ask too much of me!'

'I do not, and you can. Or at least, you could if you just found a bit more patience.'

She snarled but she did stop kicking at the branches around her like a furious, cornered cat and stood there, chest heaving, in the dappled sunlight.

'Good, now we will just have to wait until all the animals decide to return to this place. Come, we will go around this outcropping here, and perch ourselves above the valley. It may take a while,' he added, 'as it was such a lot of noise.'

'Fine,' she spat the word at him, glaring.

Beau settled himself in the crook of a tree branch, and folded his arms across his chest. He closed his eyes and wriggled into a more comfortable position. 'It helps if you stand still. Pacing is noisy. We will have to wait all day, at this pace.'

'I am hungry now!'

'That is something you should have thought about before you lost your temper. If you had only stayed quiet you might have already been eating by now.'

She growled low under her breath and curled her long body up, unhappily, at the base of the tree, folding her wings neatly and with only the flicking of her tail to betray her mood. Beau watched the sky above, where the branches parted far enough to leave a wide blue field. Clouds passed in steady streams, though they were too well sheltered to feel the wind that moved them.

'Oh,' he spoke, breaking the silence. 'I realise now that I do not know your name.'

'What use would my name be to you?' she grumbled into the loam under her belly.

'Well just now I was about to say, "Oh, look," but had no name to address you by. There is a wild hawk above us.'

And just visible in the trees above there perched a grey bird with white barred breast, its orange eyes regarding them with suspicion. With a shouted call, high pitched and angry, it burst from its place to disappear into the deep forest beyond.

'I was called Yvaine,' she said. 'But that was a lifetime ago.'

Beau accepted the silence that her words brought, felt it not his place to break it.

'And not that I care, but it occurs to me that I never asked your name either,' she spoke a few minutes later. 'I suppose it is only fitting that I know how to address my servant.'

'Beau. My mother named me Beau.'

Yvaine snorted. '"Handsome". What a motherly choice of name.'

The passage of the wild hawk seemed to signal for the forest to begin to come alive again. First, daring songbirds began their chorus, then the rustling of small rodents in the leaf litter. Beau kept an eye on the valley below, scanning for any likely opportunity.

The direction of the shadows slowly changed, and the morning was nearly nooning before his sight caught a glimpse of dappled fur.

'There,' he spoke, low and even. Yvaine said nothing, but he could hear her limbs re-arranging into a ready position. 'When I say the word you jump down onto it, and aim yourself well.' It was a fine young buck, pawing through the low foliage for choice grazing.

She was all tense muscle, her wings half-spread and ready.

'Now!'

Her descent was instant, and her aim was exact. She fell upon the buck's neck and broke it with her sheer weight.

'Excellent!' he grinned, sliding his way down the loose rock and exposed roots of the drop, to land beside her. 'Well done,' he praised.

Yvaine quickly turned to him, her beak bloodied and eyes bright with bloodlust. A growl escaped her gape, low and threatening.

Beau fell back a step, suddenly reminded of a hawking trip with a friend's newly trained bird. She had an untameable disposition, even with long bouts of manning, and prone to tempers and fits of misplaced aggression. And so when finally she was allowed to catch her first kill in captivity she grew possessive and lashed out at her falconer, catching him full on the face with her feet. He had been lucky not to lose his sight, and had released her that same day with his mind set on trapping a less violent hunting companion. This memory was strong, and Beau in flawed hindsight wished that he had been a bit more circumspect in his approach, and had treated Yvaine with the care required in such a precarious situation. Perhaps she would eat him, after all.

But the moment passed, and Yvaine dropped her beak back down to her meal. She stripped the meat from its bones with no delicacy at all, and snapped the joints to discard what she had finished. Soon all that was left was a pile of steaming entrails in a bed of bones, a head and hooves.

'I do feel much better,' she spoke, using one bloody paw to scrape morsels from her beak. 'Though it is such a messy business.'

Beau had recovered his tongue by now, and so suggested she avail herself of the stream nearby. He watched her ducking her whole body into the water, flapping about like a songbird in a dust bath, and reminded himself not to fall too much at ease with her. The knowledge that she had once been a girl had lulled him into a false sense of safety. Yvaine, whatever she had been, was now a violent, wild creature. She was a beast, with a beast's nature, and he had better not forget again. He was spared this once, but may not be a second time.

He also though that however much he wished for a simple life, he would never again be in possession of such a thing. His life was now entwined with this wild, angry being, and the only thing he could rely on was his own power of survival. At least his last five year's education had prepared him for this. Beau could not help but think that if he had encountered this situation while he was still a gentleman of means, he would likely have perished by now. He was so far from a place of normalcy that it was unrecognisable to him. He was the captive of a monster, and his life was not his own.

Chapter 11

Désiré woke, started coughing and then found that he could not stop. This was not new, having come upon him in fits and starts ever since that night, one of the nights he would not speak of. There had been so many nights that he had not expected to wake up in the morning. But this was not one of them, for once.

He was home, or near enough what home could be. His physical childhood home in the city may not exist any longer, but his family's current residence was the nearest thing. And he was there, at long last. He just needed to catch his breath.

The phlegm was choking him, but he struggled to get the air into his lungs to clear them. This weakness of his body frustrated him and often kept him from sleep, awake with the fear of suffocation. Not that he minded much, his dreams were fragments from the last five years' worth of waking nightmares. At least when he was awake he could control what memories he relived and which he strove to push aside into the very furthest dark corners of his mind.

Like his brother's sacrifice.

Désiré had stirred that morning to find no resistance on Beau's side of the bed where his arms and legs were stretching. At first he revelled in the space and the comfort of the whole bed to himself, and he drifted off into another spell of oblivion. But later he woke again with a feeling of dread in his ague-tightened breast, and he shivered. He was suddenly fearful of the lack of companionship, the space beside him which he had so recently enjoyed was now a cause for uncertainty.

Telling himself to stop being so foolish, Désiré dressed and descended the stairs. He expected to find his brother at breakfast, or in the fields at least, but before him was a different scene. Their mother and father turned reddened eyes towards him.

'Désiré, mon cher,' Fleur said softly. 'He left this for you.'

The note she handed him was written in his brother's hand, he knew it well, but it told him an impossible thing.

'Why would he do this?' he asked, genuinely baffled.

'Because he is your brother,' Fleur said, but then she needed to turn from him to press her handkerchief to her face, well-used.

'Yes,' Guillaume agreed. 'Beau did this because he is Beau. There is not a member of our small family that does not owe him their very lives and livelihood.'

Désiré had to leave the room, there was too much to bear from the tears of his parents and the weight of the letter in his hand, and so he fled into the morning sunlight. The early spring air had been cool, though bright, and while mild enough he found himself trembling like a man palsied. Beside the house sat a log store, and he sat himself abruptly on the bounty of wood spilling out from inside.

How could he do this? These were the first thoughts echoing inside him. *How dare he?* It seemed that no matter how far he had gone, or how much he had seen, Désiré would always be at the mercy of his brother's insufferable goodness. It was simply too much to bear, this burden placed upon him. Knowing for ever more that he was the instrument of his brother's doom. Knowing the sacrifice he made in his place. Désiré would never be able to forget it, and neither would their parents.

He knew that they would look at him and wish for his brother, the good one, the honest one, the responsible one. Just look at what his brother had made here, this thriving business. He had not known what to expect on his return, but this was certainly not something he had predicted. A part of him had always fantasised about his triumphant arrival, spilling his bounty of gold and jewels at his parents' feet, and his brother embracing him in approval. But it had not happened like that at all.

It would have not been so bad if he had been able to gain overflowing pockets of imaginable riches, which would surely have served them all for the rest of their lives. It would have not been so bad if he had kept his health intact, but weather was so unpredictable. And so he had come to them half-dead, and nearly a beggar, and he had some few small gems that seemed so precious once but now seemed so tawdry, so insufficient.

Désiré could not live with such a burden for the rest of his life, he needed to somehow redeem himself. All these were thoughts that plagued Désiré, and more, while he struggled to catch his breath during the long nights of planning and healing since that inauspicious morning. He now waited for the fit to pass, but knew that this weakening of his body, like his feelings of guilt and responsibility, and the state of his soul, were likely to be conditions of his life henceforth.

Unless he did something about it.

Chapter 12

The next day, Beau took it upon himself to sort through the pantries in the kitchen. Most of what was there was decayed to dust long ago, or devoured by mice and rats and other pests. Only a few wax-sealed containers remained with anything inside, but their contents would more than likely kill him. He removed everything from the pantry and took the remnants of broken containers out to the refuse heap.

As he tossed in a sack which would have once held flour, he sighed.

'I miss bread,' he thought aloud to himself, distracted by the domesticity and so accustomed to working alone that sometimes his own voice was his only day's company if Yvaine was not in evidence. 'Bread, crusty and warm, with a strong, hard cheese.'

'Bread?' Yvaine asked from behind him, as if summoned by his thoughts. He had not realised she was nearby, and blushed that she had heard his inane musings. 'I can barely remember the flavour. But I remember the smell was intoxicating, though I cannot be certain of what it was.'

'If I only had sound flour and yeast, I would be able to bake bread for you to recall the smell,' Beau offered.

'If indeed this wretch of a form can even process smells,' Yvaine grumbled. 'I find the world very flat, in that regard. Sight, foremost, and sound besides, I am far beyond what I once observed. But I do not believe a beak is designed for smell, particularly if one spends much of one's time cavorting in the clouds.'

'Nonetheless,' Beau hazarded to press the point he had been considering for some time, 'perhaps there would be a way of obtaining some supplies beyond what I can grow or hunt here?'

'And where would be the point in that for me?'

The thought took Beau aback. He had not considered his query from that point of view, so he temporised, 'Well, I suppose that unless your physical person could tolerate something besides the raw meat you have until now subsisted on, there would be very little benefit to yourself. Have you tried a cooked meal?'

'And who indeed would have cooked for me? Spirits from the forest? Some good and kindly fairy, who felt the urge to practice her domestic cookery for a monster in the mountains?' Yvaine snorted her disdain.

'Indeed so,' he agreed, about to leave off the discussion but she continued, 'I have never known a wild beast who could tolerate cooked food,' she continued. 'So it would follow that I would be equally unable to do so.'

Beau thought for a moment, then spoke, 'Only, let us remember that you are no wild beast, and your previous state may have some influence on your current one. Not to mention that while certainly a natural creature may have such demands on their digestion, you are no natural beast of the wilds. I dare say no person alive has seen your equal, and even if others have existed there has been no scientific study to explore what culinary options may be available to you.'

'And so, what then? Do you propose an experiment upon my person? To feed me this or that and see what follows?'

'Why not?' he asked boldly. 'If you wished to attempt it, that is.'

'I suppose indeed it does not matter to you if I grow gravely ill, or perish from the effort. So of course you would be happy to begin such a task, if either outcome benefits your cause. If I, having enjoyed and tolerated finer cuisine, thus enable your own culinary position to improve. Or, if being poisoned and perish, you have your freedom once again. Pardon me if I fail to see my own benefit from such an experiment.'

Beau shrugged, 'You are not wrong. Only, if your current state being so detestable to you, means that an improvement, however risky it could be, would give you a higher satisfaction with your own self, perhaps that risk would become acceptable.'

'Meaning?'

He gave her a level look. 'Meaning – if you hate being a base and carnivorous beast so much maybe being able to enjoy finer cuisine would help you to reclaim your civilised state, and so, your own esteem of yourself. In that perspective, would you not prefer to accept a small risk to your digestion?'

'I will think on it.' And so, she turned and stalked off into the forest, her tail lashing behind her.

For days nothing more was spoken on the matter, but Beau continued in his improvements of the kitchen and clearance of the pantries, more out of a need for activity than any actual hope in the success of his arguments. He soon managed to clear the kitchen hearth and restore the state of its great ovens.

Then one day, Yvaine appeared and she when said, 'I have been thinking of what you spoke of,' they both knew what she meant. 'While I can see the merits of your argument, I cannot subscribe to it wholly. I do wish to improve myself, for my own sake. However I cannot say that the idea of cookery has any appeal for me. I enjoy my raw meals, and while I shudder to admit it, the taste of life escaping my prey, the hot blood and the enjoyment of the chase is preferable to any long-remembered fragrance of spice or seasoning or cookery.

'I am a wild thing, though yes, an unnatural one and not found to exist outside the realms of my cursed state. I cannot change that about myself, and I would hope that you do not press me further to attempt it.'

'Of course, I only-'

'I am not finished,' she admonished. 'As I stated first, I do see the merits of your argument for self-improvement and civility. As such, I have decided that if you wish to procure such goods for your own enjoyment, I will not prevent you. And I have in the castle holds some great funds of money and jewels to assist your efforts. While I do not believe I will ever be able to be tamed, or domesticated, like some pet, I will attempt to be a more civil fiend, and hope that we both find some greater peace in that. I would like to learn how to be good, and civil, and polite, as I never even was as a human. And perhaps I will not hate myself so.'

Her speech done, Yvaine left. But where she had stood lay a leg of venison, bloodied and torn but well-sized, her gift to him.

As Beau cooked himself a fine meal of stewed venison in the castle's kitchen, he considered what she had said, and the passion with which she spoke it. She did truly hate herself, in her current state. This knowledge made him feel a considerable, and surprising, empathy and sorrow on her behalf. Beau had never been one of those youths who was so confident in himself that he crowed to any and all over his minor achievements, but he had seen what he was capable of with clear eyes and respected that which was respectable. He had never known self-hatred, and only the merest of self-doubt. To find a creature, and that creature a human girl, no matter her current form, who was so immersed in replaying and reliving her faults and failings enough to hate herself was beyond his understanding. Yvaine was not so terrible a villain as she thought herself, to his eyes she seemed no worse than any of the spoiled children he had grown into adolescence with in the city, only the size and shape of her making those tempers far more violent than otherwise would be. If Beau could play any small role in helping change her feelings, to let her see that which was beginning to become clear to him, then he would happily do so.

Chapter 13

Having decided to obtain some foodstuffs that Beau himself could not otherwise get, he was suddenly confronted with the logistical trouble of arranging a delivery where no merchants would be normally passing through. At his family's townhouse in the city it had been as simple as collaring a local cheesemonger or baker plying their wares on the street, or calling into a nearby store front if none could be otherwise found. Even at Maison Desjardins there were other farms, dairies and millers that they could prevail upon to make such an agreement with. In the end, Beau realised that he needed to ask Yvaine where the nearest town or village might be so that he might have some idea of direction and distance required to find such a purveyor of goods.

'My parents had agreements with the local grocer, Monsieur Defeuille in the town of Princemont, about a half day's journey from here, on a horse or cart. They came weekly with supplies, and respected our family so never cheated us or gave us poor quality. Why such an expression of defeat when I am here helping your cause so graciously?'

'I cannot exactly be your captive here and still go to this town to make these arrangements. I will have to forget this plan, and try to see what other crops I can grow here instead.'

'Nonsense,' she scoffed. 'You will go and return within a day, if your horse is not as useless as it looks, cowering most of the time and then prancing about like a parade pony when it is not, and we will not consider this foray as a breach of our agreement.'

And so it was that Beau left the castle, when he had not believed such a thing would ever happen again, and Yvaine watched him go from high aloft. She did not think that she would mind him leaving, as she had spent so long alone, but her heart was in her throat as she watched him ride away. It was a risk she was taking in hoping he would indeed return, though he gave his word that he would, and she found that the gamble played on her mind with fears and doubts, from the moment his shape left her far-reaching sight through the mountain pass.

Her day was spent hunting, and then soaring the mountain thermals, what would normally give her pleasure and distraction, but the hours seemed to drag on endlessly. Although the castle was out of sight, but for the turrets above the tree tops, it looked empty without the knowledge that Beau was toiling somewhere within, silently and stoically at work doing something or other. Yvaine sighed, and rose higher into the clouds, one part of her wishing that he would break his promise and leave her alone to her violent temper and dark thoughts, and another part feeling that she may perish if she were left alone once more.

It was dark when Beau arrived back, and Yvaine was perched like some living gargoyle on the eaves. She watched his shadowed figure approach, watched him stable his horse, and listened to him speaking to the brute as he stripped it down and saw to its needs. She wondered if he only spoke to her from a similar placating necessity, or if he truly enjoyed her company. It was hard to imagine that he could, given her bestial form. What enjoyment could she give, when most of what she said to him was rude, or violently meant?

With a shake of her fur and feathers, Yvaine opened her wings and glided silently to her place of rest, to forget about her complex thoughts.

Meanwhile, Beau took himself to his chamber and considered the reaction of the town to his sudden appearance among them.

Princemont was a small town, but made into a busy centre of commerce by the simple fact that all the other surrounding villages were even smaller. It was a pretty town, featuring the slate roofs the area of Le Morvan was known for, set amongst gentle countryside and edged on one side by the forest, where the land gained sharp altitude up into the mountains. That was the direction Beau had taken from the west. Down the main thoroughfare of the town there were shop fronts lined one after another, and most of the townspeople seemed to be either buying or selling when Beau arrived there at midday. He dismounted out of courtesy once he entered into the busy streets, and led Commodité on foot beside him, keeping a tight rein.

He was given searching looks as he passed, this being a small enough town that its people all knew one another by name, and even most of their neighbouring villagers, so it was clear that he was a stranger. This was made even clearer by the mount he was leading, as Commodité was of fine hunter stock. None of these people could have likely afforded a horse like it, even with a lifetime of saving funds. Only a few mules and cart horses of dubious lineage clattered placidly down the street. Beau's own horse, seemingly affronted by their common origins, made only further efforts to stand out in comparison, curving his fine neck and picking up his shining hooves sharply.

Soon enough, though too late to save Beau from being the object of many stares and whispers, he sighted the store front labelled as Defeuille the Grocers, Purveyor of Fine Goods of Quality. The rumours of his presence had outpaced him, it seemed, as soon it became clear that this was his ultimate destination the door opened smartly on his approach and a portly man in a pristine apron came out to greet him.

'Monsieur!' he called to Beau. 'Welcome, traveller to our small town, how may I be of assistance?'

'Well,' Beau began, eyeing the crowd that had begun to form, and not as discreetly as they thought they were being. 'I would like to have a regular delivery sent to my current residence.'

'Aha,' the man nodded, a wide grin stretching his face beneath impressive moustaches, and opening an arm to draw Beau closer to his shop. 'Very well, might I inquire where this residence may be? Then we can begin to sort out arrangements that may suit your needs.'

'The old Beaumont castle, which I believe you once had dealings with before,' but Beau's words drifted off into uncertainty as the uproar around him grew in volume and intensity.

'Beaumont castle?' one woman shrieked to her neighbour.

'The cursed place!'

'That monster! Is the beast no longer there?'

It seemed the whole town was holding its breath awaiting a response from him, so Beau answered to the crowd at large, bemused and hesitant.

'Ah, yes. She is still there.' Which sparked an explosion of voices, all speaking at once.

'Come, come, monsieur,' Defeuille drew him away. 'Let us speak in peace.'

Beau hesitated again. 'My horse,' he looked worriedly at the excited crowd, whose shouts and violent gestures were making the poor animal's eyes roll as it sidled nervously about.

'Garçon! Take the monsieur's horse, if you please!' The grocer snapped his fingers towards one of his young assistants, a boy with a mop of hair and his own apron somewhat less pristine and askew across his waist. 'That boy is a bit of a fool, I will tell you,' Beau was told conspiratorially, 'but he is a good hand with the cart horses. I wish he were only so at ease with the customers, then he would be a fine apprentice!

'But yes, let us discuss your request and see what arrangements could be made.'

Beau outlined what he was hoping to obtain, and his wish to see the goods delivered monthly.

'Yes, yes, monsieur, that is fine enough. Only,' he held up a warning finger, 'I cannot in good faith send any of my usual delivery drivers up that mountain pass, they being all young men with families who would feel they were going to their doom. No, I must do this myself.'

'Thank you, but I do assure you that your passage to the castle will not put you in harm's way,' Beau began to say, but Defeuille's hand came up to forestall him.

'The other condition, which I feel most strongly about, is that I cannot deliver to the castle.'

'But you just said-'

'I said I would do it, and I will get the goods to you, but I will not deliver them to the castle itself. I will not, I *cannot*, it is too painful for an old man with a long memory to lay eyes upon that accursed place, that site of such misery. No, I simply cannot.'

In the end, Beau had to agree that the man could deliver the goods to the bend in the mountain pass just before the castle came into view, and that Beau himself would meet him there for each monthly delivery and take the goods the rest of the way to the castle himself. Having made that allowance, Beau felt no compunction against bargaining harder than he would normally have to get his order at a reduced cost, for his own labour in delivering it. He knew that there was a cart and harness on the estate that he could, with only a bit of work, get into serviceable order. Commodité, being a vain animal unused to serving in such a way, might complain about being put in harness but this arrangement would get the job done for the short distance required.

'Very well,' Beau said, and they shook to seal their negotiations.

There had been a moment on the road back when Beau had considered why he was voluntarily returning to his captivity. His horse had spooked at some imagined shadow in the darkness, and he had stopped on the track and suddenly become aware of his freedom. It would have been easy to pass the turning to the castle, head west and towards his parents' villa. But something stopped him, had nudged Commodité onward carefully and had steered him towards those ivy-laden gates.

Now, staring at the ceiling above the bed, he wondered what it was that had moved him so. What could have drawn him back to his prison willingly, apart from the fact that he had given his word to do so. But then, having given his word he could not imagine a situation which would make him break it. It was simply not in his nature.

Chapter 14

Their lives had a certain routine which Beau found himself very comfortable within. He rose early, now with the help of candles purchased from the grocer, to begin his self-appointed chores and make his daily war against the creeping rot and pestilence that had taken hold of the castle in its years of ruin. When the sun began to lighten the horizon, he was often out in the forest with Yvaine while she hunted, giving advice and direction depending on the terrain, weather conditions and wind. Later, he would return to his homely tasks, unless a delivery of goods from town was due.

It was the latest such delivery, and Beau was helping load his order from the back of the grocer's cart and into his own, Commodité stamping in equine fury at the uncouth work he had been reduced to. From his esteemed beginnings as a prized mount, paraded around town or sometimes out on the hunt, to this newest indignity of cart horse, it was not to be borne and he made sure to make his feelings about this perfectly clear.

'Whereabouts are you from, originally?' Defeuille asked, filling the industrious silence. 'I can tell from your manner that you are no local, and if I am not mistaken I would say you hail from the capital.'

'Yes,' Beau said, surprised by the question. 'I was born in the city, and lived there until the summer I turned nineteen. Misfortune had changed my family's circumstances, so they now reside at Maison Desjardins to the west of here. We have started there a parfumerie, with the bounty of the gardens and lavender fields.'

The older man nodded in acknowledgement of that worthy business, and then asked, 'Have you heard anything of them since you came to your current calamities?'

Beau shook his head, chagrined, 'I have not.'

'If you would like, I can ask about town, see if any of our delivery drivers have heard aught of their present circumstances, if it would set your mind at ease. You seem a good, honest boy, and I feel my heart moved to pity by your situation.'

'Thank you,' he said, and meant it. 'That really would put my mind at ease, indeed.'

Defeuille waved his good-byes as he drew his cart off back down the road, and Beau returned the salute before coaxing his horse to head back to the castle, one disgusted step of a dainty hoof at a time.

Beau had some daylight left after storing his goods in the kitchen pantries, newly swept and made tight against both weather and pests by now. He decided to continue his exploration of the further reaches of the castle which he had not yet attempted to reach, in particular its towers and turrets.

It took him some time to discover the means of ascending those heights, but eventually he found a door he had not seen before. It revealed a tight spiral staircase, leading him upwards towards the heights of a turret. Several small, empty rooms twisted off at regular intervals, covered in thick carpets of dust and misuse. Beau assumed the turrets must not have been used in some time, and expected to see nothing but a pleasant view at the top. He was surprised to find, once he reached the summit, that the room it led to was anything but deserted.

This was in fact the only inhabited room in all the castle, though its present occupant was away, flying across the valley. Beau could see her distant shadow from the wide open doorway which led to the parapets beyond.

Beau trod carefully around the heap of mattresses in the centre of the floor, arranged into some sort of a nest, over which several torn blankets had been thrown. A few trinkets, surely prized possessions of their owner, lay scattered against a wall. One well-handled doll, a heaped dress made of fine fabric, a sparkling array of jewellery. A very large looking glass had been placed at the furthest corner of the room, smashed.

Suddenly Beau felt very much like an intruder, just as if he had entered the private chamber of a gentlewoman whose acquaintance he might have met in the usual way, at a dinner or through friends. The impropriety of standing within the intimate resting place of a person he had only just met, even if she was not a person in the strictest sense, made him blush. He was only glad that Yvaine had not been here to be imposed upon, and that his intrusion would remain unnoticed.

He thought that it did explain where she slept at night, and what arrangements she had made for her own comfort. For some reason he had thought that she kept to the forest at night, but of course that did not make sense. As a natural creature she might have abhorred the restrictions of an indoor dwelling, but as she retained her memories of her past human existence it only made sense that she would seek the familiarity of encircling walls and the belongings and furnishings which could give her some small comfort.

He was about to descend the staircase again but a shadow blanked out the light from the doorway. Beau's heart was in his throat as her voice boomed out.

'What are you doing here?'

'I am sorry,' he hastened to speak in some way that could explain his unintended trespass. 'I had not realised this was your chamber. I would never have intruded.'

'But you have.' She stalked across her nested bedding, cataloguing her possessions with a measured eye.

'I have not touched anything, I promise. I was just about to leave.'

'After you had had a good laugh, you mean,' and she began to take pacing steps forward. 'What monster needs a doll? What beast needs a dress?' Closer and closer she came. 'It is a miserable existence that I live, why could I want such reminders of my past self, the self I wish to forget?' They were nearly nose to beak and eye to eye, her neck craned to meet his gaze.

Beau swallowed a lump of fear. He had ignored her threats for long enough that he had begun to think they were not true. Standing so close to her he saw the talons, the tearing edge to her beak, and her hate-filled look.

'I would never laugh at your pain,' he said, with all the honesty he truly felt, hoping it would carry the meaning through his words. 'I do not laugh for such reasons.'

She stared at him, through him. Her yellow eyes never blinked. Her beak was agape and panting, issuing a terrible smell of blood and pain.

'Go,' she said. '*Go*!! Leave my sight, I do not care to keep you any longer! If you remain for one minute more, I *will* eat you, kill you on the spot, rend you limb from limb, eat your succulent flesh, cast your entrails from the parapets, leave your liver for the crows and jackdaws to peck and let your bones rot and bleach in the sun!'

Her words echoed terribly in his ears as Beau ran down the spiral staircase, tripping up on his own feet time and again within the tight space.

He fled out into the hallway and from there out into the night beyond the castle walls. He did not pause long enough to consider gathering his few belongings, only threw the bridle on Commodité, who snorted and would not stand still, making his owner curse aloud, in reaction to the fear and impatience he could smell in the air. Beau did not even bother with the saddle, and simply jumped up, bareback, and spurred the animal on with his heels. Commodité bolted, eyes rolling, out of the ivy gates.

Beau kicked his horse more cruelly than he would have otherwise contemplated, making the poor creature gallop towards the sunset. It was too much to ask, having interrupted Commodité from his slumber, rousing him unexpectedly and in such a manner, and then this headlong flight into the darkening night. When he skidded and bucked, nostrils flaring, Beau knew it was only what he deserved. He landed hard on his rear, though it could have been his neck, having gone straight over the horse's neck, with no saddle or stirrups to gain purchase for his legs over such a slick-furred back.

'Now, now,' he tried to calm his horse, though he was badly shaken himself. 'Now, now. I should not have done that, but you are alright,' Beau kept talking calmly and inanely as he checked Commodité's limbs and hooves for any lameness, worried that he may have caused some great harm to befall him from a twisted ankle or worse in the twilight, where hidden hazards on the road would have been too shadowed to see. He sighed, relieved, when he found nothing, and regained his saddle but Commodité continued to prance in place, snorting alarm, and would not walk on. 'What is it? What do you smell?'

And then he heard it, the howling of wolves drawing near. It seemed that he had fled from the maw of one dangerous beast only to be caught by another. He groped at his side, but of course he carried no sword, no rifle, to defend them with. The smell of equine panic and his own fear must have been a heady scent on the wind, and Beau took a couple of deep breaths to steady himself and accept what fate might come.

It was pointless to try to flee, with his horse already made incapacitated by fear. Running on foot would be even more pointless, even if he had been inclined to desert the poor creature who would not have even been out on the road just now except for his mastery of him.

Eyes glinted at him from the trees, drawing near. Beau's hands caught up the reins tightly and he saw, as his horse backed in anxious circles, another, and another pair of eyes, surrounding them.

Chapter 15

It had now been several months since Désiré's arrival, and since the incarceration of his brother. Not a day had gone by that he had not worried, helplessly, that his brother had already perished in his stead. Not a day went by that his guilt did not consume him. But it was every minute, with every throb of his heartbeat, that Désiré felt the cold dread of his own danger.

The months of regular meals, warmth and cleanliness had improved his health enough that he was able to finally contemplate carrying out his plan. He had been going out riding every day for the last fortnight, for increasingly long spells, to build himself back to travelling strength again.

'Désiré,' his father called to him before he could leave that morning. 'Do you remember that we are expecting Captain Merreux shortly? He will want to see you, I am sure.'

'Oh,' he paused, his hand on the latch. 'I suppose I can wait until later for my ride, then.' He sighed quietly, frustrated by the necessity of changing his daily habits. Their patron was a tiresome individual, he thought, and unworthy of all the scraping and bowing which they were reduced to on his visits. But he waited nonetheless, though he took no efforts to hide his impatience while they sat in the sitting room awaiting his arrival.

When at last the carriage pulled up outside the house, Désiré stood perfunctorily. The Captain entered the room in his usual way, with a grin and a bow to Fleur, and a handshake for Guillaume.

'How are you feeling, my boy?' the man addressed him, too-familiar.

'I am well, thank you, Captain Merreux,' Désiré replied, a touch cold in his address.

'I am glad to hear it, glad indeed!'

They seated themselves with cups of tea and Fleur's rose scones which she had perfected over the years of her son's absence, and to his surprise to see her performing her own cookery.

'I am glad we were able to meet today,' the Captain spoke after first complimenting his hosts on their fine repast. 'There are some troubling figures which I wished to discuss with you.'

'Oh?' Guillaume asked, his brow furrowed with concern. 'What figures?'

'Profits, as always,' the Captain said. 'It is always profits, or the lack thereof. I fear, in our case, it is the latter.'

Fleur and Guillaume exchanged a worried look between them. Désiré spoke the words they would not, 'How bad is it?'

'It is bad, my boy,' and Désiré could not help but bristle at this address, 'In the last year interest in scent has begun to diminish. There is a new wave of pragmatism rising around us, and a disdain for that which is unnecessary and frivolous. There is an odd tension in the capital, and people are made anxious from it. Anxious people do not care about perfume.'

Guillaume hesitated before asking, 'So what do we do? What happens next?'

'There is really nothing we can do, I am afraid to say. And in the circumstances I am sorry to say that I must do something deplorable. I fear that I will be forced to rescind my patronage. And with it, those funds which I had lent under different circumstances. Too many of my business interests are folding at once, and I cannot sustain my livelihood otherwise.'

'But Captain!' Guillaume half-rose from his chair in alarm. 'You had promised those funds would be considered a gift in the event of our venture failing!'

Désiré felt his heart sink. He was not sure if he could still carry out his plan if his family were in crisis, but he could not bear his existence as it was.

'I had given my assistance in a time of plenty,' the captain was saying, 'with the hopes of being generous. Sadly the times are changing, and I find myself unable to be as generous as I had hoped. It is not personal, my dear friends, it is simply business.'

Désiré could have cheerfully murdered this man who would place his family's livelihood in such peril, as well as casting inconvenient doubt on his plan to reclaim his soul and its eternal salvation. He could not leave, but he could not stay and await his doom in this helpless fashion. It had made him bitter, snappish as he ever was as a flippant youth, and fearful. Fear was his ever-present companion. He had no escape in dreams, and no relief in daylight. At any moment the devil could appear before him, claiming that soul which was his.

No, Désiré vowed anew that he would not, could not, live in fear any longer, even if by seeking that fiend he was going to his own death.

Chapter 16

Beau saw his death approach, and it did not take the form he had come to expect. Just when he was about to give in to his fear, it seemed Commodité reached the same conclusion and burst into renewed action with an equine shriek.

They now flew back down the mountain pass towards the castle, a last, frantic act of survival in the direction of the doom they had just escaped. Beau thought he might see the harrowing shadow of wings overhead, so that they were pursued from above as well as behind.

Commodité's gallop quickly brought them near, and then past, the iron gates. Now they thundered down the pass towards Princemont. Beau could only hope they would find salvation in the town, and that the wolves would be too wary to enter such a press of humanity.

They had outpaced the wolves for a time, but now Commodité slowed, sides heaving and breathing hard from nostrils which flared as he tossed his head in distress. The pack had been patient, calculating. They had known their prey would soon tire, and were ready.

From their right, one was boldly encroaching. Beau felt horribly helpless and exposed on his mount's back in that moment, but Commodité found a last reserve of energy. He bolted into the trees on the opposite side from danger, crashing through the bracken and low-hanging branches which slapped Beau across his face and arms. He made himself as low in the saddle as possible and trusted Commodité's instincts to direct them.

Then, the branches no longer battered his body, and Beau looked up to see that they had exited the forest and were now dashing towards a fence that he had only just enough time to brace himself for as the horse bunched his hindquarters and leapt over it. They were now in a field, with a faint winking of light from the windows of a nearby farmhouse in the distance. A cow lowed in alarm somewhere in the darkness.

Beau could feel Commodité's sides betray a trembling in the horse's limbs. He had come to his final reserves, and could run no longer tonight. He was no endurance hunter, this horse, he was used to a sedate life. Even his regular sport had been curtailed in these recent months at Castle Beaumont. This field and its bovine inhabitant would be witness to the final moments of Beau Saint-Christophe Desjardins and his fine steed, and there was nothing any of them could do about that fact.

Death was certain, it stalked them from all sides. It had no mercy, only hunger. It grew ever-nearer as shadows within shadows.

Then, inexplicably, it stopped.

The air around them exploded. A wind suddenly stirred the air. The wolves yelped and whined in pain. The cow called urgently, then was silenced. In the darkness, Beau could not see anything but the suggestion of movement and struggle and fleeing shadows.

It went quiet. The only sound was the stirring shush of leaves from the forest's edge, and a distant clamour of dogs from the farmhouse.

'You should not have done what you did,' a nightmarish voice spoke from the darkness. 'But I was, perhaps, hasty.'

'Oh, Yvaine,' Beau cried in relief. 'I have never been happier to see another than I am to see you here, now.'

'Yes, well,' she stumbled on the words harshly, 'I am here. I am glad that I could,' she managed an approximation of a human's cleared throat, 'help, well, yes.'

'Do you still want me gone from the castle?'

'No,' she said in a new, quiet way. 'I do not wish that.'

'Then I will come back presently,' he said. 'I may be some time returning, however, as I fear my horse has exhausted himself. I will dismount and walk him back carefully, as he has been through much trauma tonight.'

'Then I shall meet you there,' Yvaine said. 'As I am certain my presence will do him no good in reclaiming his senses.'

Before Beau could answer, she was gone. It was true, her scent on the air would keep Commodité on edge, but he found that he wished her company regardless.

Chapter 17

'I used to laugh at others in pain.' She sat before the hearth of the castle's hall when Beau finally entered. Her tail curled around her body like nothing more than a poised house cat upon the faded, intricately woven rug. 'Just as I accused you of doing. I was a terrible person who loved nothing more than to revel in another's pain or sadness. I was a gossip, a schemer, a hateful person by all accounts. So forgive me if I assume all others have the same failings as mine were once.'

Beau once again found himself not knowing what to say to her on the subject, and his response was almost automatic. 'I thought we were not speaking of this.'

Yvaine sighed, 'Well, I suppose we are speaking of it. I suppose that as I promised to become civil, my redemption must come from admitting my past sins.

'My parents were the best of people, and I was their only child. I cannot blame them for the attention and liberties they gave me which caused me to grow lazy and spoilt. I expected others to attend to my whims and fancies and gave back no thanks for it. I harassed the servants, and I spoke hideously to my parents, and thought that the world was there to provide nothing more than a diversion for me alone. I never had to alter my behaviour for anyone, or anything. I was a beast even then, even if I looked like a girl.

'We were all meant to go visit a neighbouring dignitary, whose son was intended as a match in marriage for me. I did not want to go and do my filial duties, and marriage seemed like the worse fate designed to force two people into captivity, beholden to one another. I did not want to be forced to bend for another's sake, so I refused to go. My parents went alone and had to make their apologies for me.

'There was a terrible storm one night, and a bedraggled traveller tried to seek shelter at our doors. The servants asked me what they should do, and I told them to refuse. The traveller insisted on seeing me, and again sought shelter, begging in person at my feet. As I had never before had to care for another's troubles, could only see the inconvenience to myself and refused again.

'But the traveller then cast off her bedraggled appearance and revealed herself to be an enchantress, travelling in disguise. She stood in her shining glory, and cursed me then to have an exterior to match my bestial nature. I changed, and the servants all fled in terror. She also lay upon me the oath to take in any stranger who finds themselves in need in the mountain passes, which I have spoken of before.

'I had, at first, thought it was some nightmare and spent days in denial, trying to live like the girl I knew, pretending nothing had changed. When my parents returned I went to greet them as I would have done, but they screamed in fear of me and fled. I pursued them through the woods, trying to make them understand and see me for what I truly was, but then maybe they did in truth. My own parents looked into my eyes and only saw a monster. They saw their own death approaching, and chose to end it on their own terms instead. My sweet mother and my strong father, who I never fully appreciated in life, chose death rather than face the horror that was their own daughter.

'I knew then that I was indeed this beast, this form I was housed in, and not a girl any longer, and could not carry on like I was a human being. I began to live a wholly brutish existence: feeding when hunger provoked me, sleeping when I tired, and then I realised that this was not actually much different from how I had been before, having never stayed my wants for any other person. I knew that it was exactly what I deserved.

'So I want to tell you that I am sorry for how I spoke to you, and I am sorry for this temper I struggle so much to control. I would like to be better, and to be a better person than I have been, and have ever been.'

Beau was struck dumb at first, trying to ingest her horrifying tale. When at last he could speak again, he said, 'I do not believe that you deserved this fate, no one could. You have suffered more horrors than any living soul should have to suffer. And for my part, I am sorry and ashamed for my intrusion into your privacy. I would never have trespassed if I had known what it was I was trespassing upon.'

'And how could you have known? I do not blame you for it, and I do not think you are the sort of person would have done so with malicious intent. It takes a person with poor qualities to know what sort of failings to look for, and thus I knew from the beginning, or almost, what sort of person you really were.'

'How do you mean "almost"?' he asked, noting her particular phrasing.

'I was not sure, when we first met. You spoke too well, I was suspicious of your intentions then. But since you returned, to start your captivity, you have been faultlessly honest. And if *I* am to be honest, that is one of the reasons my temper has always been so inflamed by your presence. Your goodness sometimes seems to mock me. You are perhaps too good.'

Beau laughed. 'If we are being honest, then let me correct you on that score. I am not honest. I am a schemer and a fraud.'

'How do you mean?' she asked, puzzled and wary.

'That stormy night, that bedraggled traveller who bargained with you for his freedom. That was not me.'

Yvaine was still, she could have been a beast cast in bronze, but for the intensity of her stare.

Beau swallowed, and continued. 'The one you met was my brother, Désiré. He is my twin. He had spent the last five years as a slave to the devil. I could not let him return to you, and to slavery once again. It would have killed him to do so, so I took his place, knowing that you would mistake me for him. I am not as honest as you think.' And he awaited her judgement.

'You are almost worse, an even better fool than I thought. How could you think that your actions could have lowered you in my esteem? You took your brother's place to spare him, as the captive of a hideous beast for a lifetime of servitude at the whim of an inhuman creature. And you think yourself a worse man for this action? I think you are hardly to be believed, except that you are as honest as ever a man has been and to be trusted with the truth of his words. Even in your dishonesty there is only the best of selfless intentions. My poisoned soul is at once disgusted and at the same time filled with jealous admiration.'

Beau did not have a reply to this, so merely stirred the embers of his burgeoning fire in the hearth and lay several logs to catch flame. Soon the shadows were forced to retreat from the light, and dancing flames revealed Yvaine in flickering ebbs and tides. Beau could now see that her sides were scored, some of the cuts deep and weeping, while others crusted over. Her feathers were frayed at the edges, some tipped at their ends, and her cere was bloodied across her nostrils.

'Are you not in pain?' he asked.

'It is not much.'

Beau could not be so dismissive of her wounds, especially after hearing such a story of pity that had moved his heart so deeply to sadness on her behalf. He made makeshift bandages with lengths of rag, and cleaned her wounds with well water boiled over the fire. Yvaine closed her eyes when he applied the warm, damp cloth to her wounds, and hissed behind her clenched beak at the worst of it, but refused to cry out or complain.

When Beau was done, Yvaine said, in a quiet, tired voice, 'I will just stay here by the fire for a moment and rest.' She lay her head down with exhaustion.

Beau nodded, feeling much the same reluctance to leave the warmth of the hall to seek his own bed. He settled back into the comfortable chair he was sat in and was soon drifting off to sleep, unaware that this was the same chair that his brother had slept in on that stormy night which had sealed both their fates.

Charles Petit-Laurent had thought the dogs had scented a fox but the chickens were unmol ested, scratching contentedly in the dirt of the farmyard.

'What the devil did you hear?' he asked the dogs by the fire, but they twitched their ears and lolled their tongues, happy to be addressed but entirely without answers. Their master knelt to give them an affectionate tousle, now wishing he had risen from his bed in the night to investigate when he first had heard their warnings, after all.

With a grunt, Charles stood. He was getting old, always tired and his back and knees ached him terribly. There was a time when he had kept flocks of a hundred head of sheep, but he no longer had the stamina, and all his herding dogs were as aged and limping as he was. His farm was now just his chickens – and Précieux.

She was as precious to him as her name, as with all his last savings he had bought her to be the saving of his farm. Précieux was a Froment du Léon cow, in calf, and would provide him with golden butter once she calved in the spring. He dreamed of that golden butter, how much he could sell it for in town, and how the housewives in Princemont would gather in droves to buy it for their table.

Charles was now pushing his rusting wheelbarrow towards Précieux's field, piled so high with fragrant hay that he could not see over his load, trusting his knowledge of his land to direct him. He had worked this land all his life, and his parents before him, and their parents before them. He had thought in the bitterness of autumn that he might have to sell up. But that was before Précieux, before a chance meeting at the winter market had given him new hope.

He set down his wheelbarrow, and gathered an armful of hay, whistling to her. She was normally quick to grab hungry mouthfuls before he had even thrown the hay to the ground, but today her great head was not there.

The hay fell in soft drifts.

Charles stared across the field. Dark bloodstains glittered like jewels in the frost.

Chapter 18

Morning dawned, glittering with dew and innocent of the terrors from the night before. Beau woke with a neck cramped from his awkward position, opening his eyes to see the hearth rug bare and the hall empty, no hide nor feather of Yvaine in sight. He assumed that their argument and tense words were forgotten, and went to his endless task of reclaiming the castle as a hospitable space. It really was too much work for a single man even over an entire lifetime's work, which it might well be.

Nothing else was spoken about the conversations they had had, or the revelations Beau had revealed about his brother's identity, and his own. He spent a lot of time with Commodité, in remorse for their misadventures, soothing him and spoiling him with late apples found on the branches despite their falling leaves.

'There are some promising tracks leading off that way,' Yvaine said in greeting, nodding with her head. 'Shall we go hunting?'

Beau snatched up the satchel which he had designated as a game bag, and slung it across his chest. He took his favoured rifle in its case and crossed his chest with its strap. Thus prepared, they slipped through the trees together, as silent as shadows. Yvaine had improved her stealth on foot in the forest, practice and a better diet being excellent tutors. Her ribs no longer protruded so, and her hips no longer had a sunken look to them. Her very coat looked healthier, shining tawny gold in the filtered sunlight from above. Her feathers, apart from the damage from that terrible night, were a glossy and vibrant deep brown-black.

They did not speak in the forest; it was not necessary. Their pursuit was a singular effort, and the merest of glances or gestures conveyed enough meaning for the task. They had worked out several effective techniques over their time together, and had become well used to it.

Today Yvaine flew up to the heights of a strong tree while Beau circled far downwind. On an unspoken signal, he took up his beater's club, a bit of sturdy branch, and flushed up several ungainly game birds who burst, chattering, from the undergrowth.

Beau's heart leapt in response to Yvaine's well-timed leap, her outstretched talons grabbing the birds in mid-air and falling upon them on the ground to their instant demise. Beau left her one to satiate her immediate blood-lust, but gathered the rest in his game bag to prepare later. They were only small, but they could at least dull the edge of her hunger.

'That did not feel very sporting,' she said, panting only a little.

'Perhaps not. Would you like a greater challenge?'

'If there is one to be had.'

'If you are keen to try, we can see what can be found further into the valley.'

They continued deeper into the woodlands for an hour or so, until they reached the point where the trees began to thin. Beau held up his hand, but he need not have bothered. Yvaine had seen the pair of grazing buck elk before he had, and had begun to plan her trajectory. She slinked back into the cover while Beau lay still, purely witness to this hunt and not a participant.

Beau could not see where she had disappeared to, but the next he sighted of her was as a soaring shadow far above. Cleverly, she had hidden her ascent in the heights of the tree tops, but now, she was falling like a stone. The elk scented the air, but were not yet aware of their danger. It was almost too late by the time they spooked and bounded across the valley, cut off from the safety of the trees by the direction of her approach. The elk tried to shake her pursuit by twisting and turning in their run, but Yvaine was tenacious. Her wingbeats ploughed through the air, buffeting the tall grass like a tempest, and she gained on them.

Suddenly the elk split, and went in separate directions. Using her predator's instinct she followed the smaller and weaker of the two, gaining on it ever more. Her shoulders bunched, and then her feet shot out and caught the hindquarters of the animal while it kicked and bucked, trying to free itself. Beau hurried out and ran to get a clear view. Yvaine was stretched out across the ground, her feet gripping tightly and not to be shaken off. But she also could not move forward to dispatch the elk in her current position.

Beau quickly slipped out his rifle from its case and took a couple of deep breaths to steady his hands. He sighted down the length of it, and did not hesitate beyond to check that his shot was clear. It rang out across the valley, frightening pigeons from the trees, but the elk lay still, its head bloodied and blank-lidded.

'Was that more like it?' he asked, grinning.

Yvaine panted, her chest heaving with effort as she began to right herself. 'Oh yes.'

'That was a beautiful flight,' he said. 'It was a pleasure to watch.'

She craned her neck with pleasure at the compliment. She did not believe she had ever been so proud to receive one, nor felt herself deserving to do so, before. 'Thank you. Now we will both eat well tonight; there is plenty to share,' she said, striving to be generous in her satisfaction.

Indeed Beau was able to create a venison stew using the last of his barley and bread, glad to be receiving a delivery from Defeuille the next day.

However, when he saw the grocer, the man told him some unpleasant news.

'I have word about your family,' he told Beau, wringing his hands in distress as he descended his cart. 'I have it from the butcher, who sends meat up that way, that your brother, you do have a brother? Yes, well, he has disappeared and no one quite knows where to.'

Beau shook his head in dismay while the grocer continued, 'I see this worries you, and this is where I am sorry to tell you but the parfumerie is lately in debt to Captain Merreux, and that man, while generous in his lending, is utterly ruthless in collecting his debts. Your parents are in a very tenuous situation, it is said, and they may lose Maison Desjardins outright. I wish I did not have such ill news to pass along to you, I already pity your situation so greatly, I really do, and do not wish to cause you more pain.'

Beau felt the very bottom of his stomach drop with a sudden sickness. 'Thank you for telling me, I must find a way to go to their aid.'

'Could you not escape your dread captor? Or would you be maimed to attempt it?' Defeuille spoke, shaking his head in concern as he began to unload the cart of its goods, and pass them to Beau.

'My situation here is not so filled with horror as you must suppose,' Beau said, accepting a sack of flour. 'Yvaine is no daemon, for all that she cannot see it herself. I am sure I can appeal to her growing sense of humanity.'

The older man froze in the process of passing him the next sack, and potatoes rolled out onto the dirt of the road. His face was pale as he turned it to Beau. 'Yvaine? What in heavens are you using that name for?'

'Yvaine is the name of the beast,' Beau spoke slowly, taking the potatoes from the older man, surprised by his reaction. 'Or, I should say, was her name prior to the transformation which left her as she is now.'

'Yvaine is the beast? The Marquis de Beaumont's own daughter?'

'Yes,' Beau nodded. 'Why? Was that not known?'

'No,' Defeuille was beginning to regain his colour. 'We had all assumed, and been told, that the beast had come upon the castle and murdered each worthy soul it found therein. Only the servants escaped, telling stories of its terrible size and fearful visage. But it was Yvaine?'

Beau had to tell the whole story as it was related to him, though feeling like nothing so much as a gossip as he did so.

'Yvaine, that poor girl,' Defeuille said with quiet sorrow. 'I knew her as a tempestuous child. Always stamping her small feet, but I could not resist handing her a small gift from my cart when her disapproving chaperone's back was turned.' He shook his head and his face was fallen, and Beau felt sorry to have burdened the older man with this unwelcome news, even as he had received the same. He left the man to his thoughts as he was left to his own, trying to think clearly about what he had just heard about his family's position.

He had been worried about this from the start, uncertain of how long Désiré could be counted on to stay and take on Beau's role as manager of the parfumerie, to be relied upon to maintain the business he had worked so hard to build. Désiré had been changed by his five years' trial, that was clear, but he could not have been changed so much as to have become another person entirely. Désiré would be Désiré. And he had never needed to be responsible before.

Beau wished with all his heart that he could have – what, never come to the castle? Never known Yvaine? He could not wish that, it was not true. But if only he could have relied on his brother, and been able to know that their parents and their livelihood were well-kept. Or to have been able to do both things at once, to have known Yvaine, to spare her from her solitary existence, and also take care of his parents and run the parfumerie.

Suddenly Beau knew what to do, if only Yvaine would agree to it.

He was full of uncertainty, unsure about how to approach the subject and when it would be appropriate. But Yvaine took that out of his hands.

'You seem distracted,' she commented when they next chanced to meet. 'What are you thinking about?'

'I have had news about my family,' he began. 'And it worries me.'

'What is it? Has something happened?'

'My brother, Désiré, has disappeared and it seems no one knows where he might have gone. And meanwhile, the parfumerie has fallen into debts without proper management, which is my own fault for abandoning them. My parents have never been very good at – well, I had spared them while I was home.'

'But you are here, and now your brother has left them as well.'

'I would never ask,' he began to say.

'But you must ask,' she interrupted. 'They are your parents and they are in need.' She fixed him with her yellow eyes. 'And you must go to their aid. If my own were in need of me-,' but she found she could not finish the thought. 'So you must go.'

'Taking care of my parents and the parfumerie is no temporary situation,' Beau tried to state delicately. 'I could not be there and also your captive servant.'

'Then you are no longer my captive, and I release you from your oath to me. I will not keep you here while you are needed elsewhere for such a worthy purpose. Your goodness shames me into self-awareness of all my flaws, into realising how a person should act, and am now able to see that it is right to do so. Only, do not ask me to watch you leave!' And she burst into sudden flight.

'Yvaine!' Beau called after her. 'Wait!' Only he did not get to finish, to tell her that he intended to come back, only that he hoped to bring his parents here with him. That his work on the castle had meant that there were several hospitable rooms now, and more nearly so, to house his family. The gardens were even more extensive here than at Maison Desjardins, so the parfumerie could be relocated as well. They could all be happy here together, and Yvaine need never be alone again. He wanted to say all that, and more, but had not been given the chance.

He waited, hoping she would return, but true to her word she did not appear to wish to be present for his departure. He saddled and bridled Commodité, the combined breath of both brute and man whitening the air in plumes around them, mingling together.

'I will go and return,' he told the pricked ears of his horse, which flicked in his direction in attention. Commodité heaved an equine sigh at being dragged out into the cold, and it not even being an expected delivery day, but was placid enough.

They headed off at a sedate walk out of the gates. The ivy had some time ago turned red and fallen in drifts to carpet the ground with a dark, foreboding stain. They turned west, and soon disappeared from the sight of the castle.

Yvaine had lied, she was not yet an honest enough creature to have kept her promise to herself. She could not spare herself the pain of seeing her only friend in the world leave her, and she felt the crushing weight of loneliness press upon her, now seemingly doubled from its long absence in her heart.

Chapter 19

While Beau was heading west, towards home, and Yvaine was dwelling on her sorrow in the castle, there were other happenings occurring from an unexpected direction.

In the town of Princemont, there were men meeting for a dread purpose.

Charles Petit-Laurent stood. 'I am glad you came,' he said to the eight men before him. 'I did not know what else to do, but I know you all, you are my neighbours, and some of you are even my family: cousin Gerard,' that man nodded, 'and Henri, though I still think my sister married you because you resembled her favourite goat.' They all laughed, and jostled that man good-naturedly. 'I needed to tell you all, because rumour is never reliable, what happened on my farm several days ago. It changes everything.'

'Tell us Charles,' said Martin the chandler, a large man with wax burns over his big hands and arms, 'as you say, we have only heard rumour, but what we have heard deeply concerns us.'

'As it should,' Charles said, all humour now gone from his face. 'Put as simply as possible, to be clear on the facts, I will tell you what I discovered that morning. My cow, who you know I pinned such hopes on, was disembowelled in the night. It cannot have been a natural creature.'

'Not even a wolf?' Henri spoke, rubbing his beard. 'We heard that there were wolves near the town that night, others heard them not far from your farm, yipping and howling and making an awful nuisance of themselves.'

'Would a wolf leave this behind?' Charles asked, and now he brought out the proof of his claim. It was a feather, broader across than even Martin's wide palm and as long as a child's arm.

The scene erupted. The men told each other, 'I told you so!' and anecdotes which had been dismissed as wild ravings long ago were now dragged out for fresh examination.

'What will you do, Charles?' one man asked.

Charles shook his head, 'I do not know. I do know, however, that my livelihood has now been destroyed, and all hopes of keeping my farm from ruin are gone.'

'That beast should pay,' Martin frowned.

'Yes!' the call was answered around the room.

'I have long suspected,' began Old Jules, and the rest of the room quieted to hear what he had to say. He was the oldest man in the town, once a scholar, and much respected. 'I have long suspected that the Castle Beaumont may still contain all the coffers of the late Marquis. Indeed, the beast shall pay, but what good is more bloodshed? Rather to sneak in, take those riches, and then your farm, and your livelihood, will be saved, Charles.'

'You speak wisely, as always,' Charles said, 'but if we leave the beast alive then what happens the next time it happens upon our town? Are the castle's coffers deep enough to rebuild all of Princemont, should it come to that?'

The rest of the men nodded, while Old Jules looked grave.

'We have never before been in danger,' that old man said. 'In all its years at the castle, nearly as long as some of you have lived, and in that time the only casualty is a mere cow?'

The men all went silent; they knew that the old man had gone too far.

'A *mere cow*?' Charles said with great emotion. 'I suppose it is all nothing to you, just a dumb animal, which you care not for, so what does it matter? But what if next it were your shop, your home, your wife, your children? We have been in danger all that time, we just never knew it! And now we know, so must do something!'

'We must protect ourselves,' Martin said.

'And our families.'

'Our farms, and businesses.'

'We cannot afford to let the beast live!'

'Else it ruins us all.'

Old Jules spoke again, but he knew his cause was lost, 'What of the boy?'

'The newcomer, you mean?' Charles asked.

Old Jules nodded. 'What if he should be there, as he seems to be a companion to the creature?'

Charles frowned, 'Then he is an unnatural creature himself, for no ordinary human would surely keep the company of such a thing, capable of such horrors.'

The frenzied shouting from the back room had gained the attention of the proprietor, who sent his oldest boy to slip in unnoticed and find out the cause. The boy was now watching the proceedings, wide-eyed, from the shadows.

'We will march up to Castle Beaumont,' Charles said, standing straight and tall, ignoring the pains in his back, and hardly feeling them at all for the passion he felt in this moment, 'and we will finally do what we should have done so long ago, when first we knew of its presence – we will kill the beast!' He then met the grey, clouded eyes of Old Jules, 'And any who aid it!'

Charles did thank the old man, inwardly, for his information about the castle's riches. After the deed was done he planned to help himself to what he might find inside, just for honest compensation, he told himself.

The watching boy felt a cold grip of fear in his chest, and he swallowed with great difficulty. Garçon helped his father in the pub at night, but during the day he was Defeuille's hapless assistant. Quietly as he had come, he slipped away and into the street to go and warn the grocer. If the mob were targeting anyone who has aided the beast, then it was no small stretch to believe that they might target Garçon's acerbic but kind employer who travelled within reach the castle every month. He could not let that happen.

Even if Defeuille was not harmed in the violence, they were speaking of doing harm to the man with the fine horse. Garçon was certain it simply was not right for anyone to go about rampaging and threatening people, even though stories of the beast in the castle had made for vivid nightmares while Garçon was younger.

His feet skidded on a film of ice on the muddy street as he raced to the grocer's shop front, and knocked loudly on the door to Defeuille's upstairs apartment. When no answer was forthcoming, he knocked and knocked again.

'Enough, enough!' Defeuille bellowed, opening the door. 'What is the meaning of this late intrusion – Garçon? Is that you?'

'Yes, sir, and I have something to tell you.'

When Garçon had finished his tale, Defeuille clapped him on the shoulder and sent him back to his father's pub, sworn to not reveal what he had heard.

'I will deal with this, you go and be safe tonight.'

Garçon did as he was instructed only he could not help himself, he told one other person what he had heard that night.

'It will be alright,' his mother said, but her face was lined with worry. Madame Houblon patted her son on the arm distractedly. 'It will all be set right, at long last.' Garçon was not soothed by her words, but was put back to the task of assisting his father and the thoughts which followed him were soon waylaid by work.

It was times like this that Defeuille felt his age and the restrictions of his portly figure. He also wished that the beasts in his stable were built a bit more for speed than their plodding endurance. Nevertheless, he hoped that he could reach the castle in time.

The road was difficult in the dark, and his cart horse was being uncharacteristically stubborn in his traces, frightened by the odd hour and the shadows plaguing their path. Defeuille could at least feel assurance that if he was struggling, so would the other men be, even if they were younger and fitter they would be travelling on foot.

The horse tried to slow and stop when they reached the usual bend in the road where he met Beau to deliver his goods. It took a few minutes of coaxing and some harsher treatment that normally he would have allowed, but soon they were approaching the castle gates.

The castle was an imposing hulk of stone, even seen through the darkness it took his breath away, as he stepped down from the cart. Then he gasped anew as a terrible voice addressed him.

'Who are you, and why are you here?' A towering shape loomed in the darkness, the impression of wings and a rasping breath that did not escape from any human mouth. He had to hold on tightly to the cart horse as the animal cried out in fear.

'I am Defeuille, Yvaine,' he made himself speak normally. 'I do not suppose you remember when I used to give you sweets from my cart as a child, ma chérie?'

She was silent for a time, then spoke, 'I do remember.'

'Then please listen to what I am about to say. There is a mob coming, men from Princemont, who wish to see harm to you and Beau. You should rouse him at once so I can pass this along to him as well.'

'He is not here.'

'What? Has something befallen him?' And suddenly Defeuille did not feel so sanguine about addressing the beast before him, even if he had known her as a child she was so far beyond what she had been that he did not even know if she valued human lives any longer.

'I let him go. He is going home to take care of his parents.' Then, quieter, 'It was the right thing to do.'

Defeuille felt a wash of relief, followed by a strange admiration of this creature, this beast who was the girl he knew, who looked so terrible but spoke so justly. 'But then you are quite alone here. You must leave here, you must fly away!'

'No. I will not leave. I see no point in trying to escape my fate, when I know it is what I deserve.'

'No, child, no, you do not deserve this. Please, will you not go?'

'I will not.'

'Fine, then I will stay and help you fight.'

'No, I cannot allow that. I know my own life is not worth much, so I cannot ask, or allow, any others to sacrifice theirs on my account. I could not bear it.'

'But I cannot leave you.'

'I do not care what happens to myself now, it does not matter.'

'It matters to an old man, and it matters to Beau, can you not see that?' She was certainly as stubborn as the girl Defeuille remembered, and he frowned in frustration.

'Beau is gone. I will never see him again, not in this life,' and she laid down her monstrous head, defeated by the sorrows that plagued her.

Defeuille mounted the seat of his cart once more, 'Very well, then I shall go and find him at Maison Desjardins. I am certain that he will come to your aid and you will see him again. I just hope it will not be too late.'

'To his doom, if he does,' she spoke softly. 'Better if he is too late.'

Chapter 20

The journey to Maison Desjardins was uneventful, but for the dusting of snow laying as a light carpet on the road before them. The world was still and quiet around Beau and Commodité as they made an even pace through the mountain pass and then beyond, into flatter, more fertile country.

The track was soon laid out, familiar and alien at once, leading to Maison Desjardins whose chimneys smoked invitingly. Approaching through the snow, heavier now, Beau could only notice that it was quiet, too quiet, to be the hive of industry he had left behind, even for the time of year that it was now. Where was their gardener, Monsieur Leverte, pruning the shrubs and trees back for winter? Where were Marcel and Pierre? They should be performing any one of a hundred wintering duties of maintenance to the equipment, the places of storage or the machinery itself used in the production of their perfumes. This weather would not have been enough to prevent their industriousness.

Beau stabled Commodité in his usual stall, but he need not have been particular. Every stall was empty, and the space normally filled by the plough horses looked even larger from their absence. Their harnesses were also gone, the traces and heavy collars not hung from their usual nails. If it were not for the smoke rising from the chimneys he would have thought the place abandoned entirely.

A strange feeling of trespass made Beau hesitate on the doorstep, and knock politely instead of letting himself in. After a moment, the door swung open with feeble light and warmth to reveal his father.

'My son?' Guillaume asked in wonder. 'But which of my sons are you? Come in, I cannot see you well enough.'

Beau stepped over the threshold and continued into the sitting room where Fleur stood at his entrance.

'Beau!' she exclaimed, throwing herself across him. 'We thought you were lost to us for good.'

'But then we had thought your brother lost before he was re-gained to us,' Guillaume said.

'Then he left us again as well,' Fleur spoke into her son's shoulder.

'I am sorry you have been left alone by us both,' Beau said, gripping his mother tight before releasing her. He helped her sit on the chaise longue, her pallor telling him of her weakness. 'But tell me, what has happened here? Where are the groundsmen? Even little Marcella? Have they all gone?'

'We could not afford to keep them,' Guillaume said, shaking his head.

'I heard that the captain called in his debts, then, is that true?'

His father nodded.

'What of the jewels Désiré brought? Surely that was enough to cover the debt?'

'Not quite enough, I am afraid,' Guillaume sat himself with a heavy groan, massaging his knees. Beau looked at him, and suddenly realised that his father was an old man. It shocked him.

'I wish it had not been so,' he said.

'We know,' Guillaume said, and his words were soft and rueful.

'And Désiré?' Beau asked. 'Did he say where he was going? And to what purpose?'

'He would not say.'

Fleur clutched her shawl about herself, 'He would only talk in riddles and nonsense. I have wondered if his servitude to the devil had driven him quite mad!'

'Hush,' Guillaume admonished.

'But, please tell us, how did you escape? How are you here, returned to us at last?' Beau's mother clutched his hand fiercely, possessively.

And so Beau sat with his parents and explained his sudden arrival had been prompted by the news he had received, which was now confirmed by his own eyes.

'She just let you go?' Fleur asked. 'However did you convince the beast of such a thing?'

'She needed no convincing,' Beau explained, but that required further explanations. Soon he found himself telling his parents the whole story of his captivity, from his initial dread to his slow understanding of Yvaine's true nature and history. They were appreciably as shocked by the revelation as he had been, and then moved by her determination to improve, a decision which had led their son back to them. Or at least one of their sons.

'So you see,' Beau spoke, 'I feel torn between the responsibilities of my life. To yourselves, firstly and always, but also to this individual. I had a plan which I had intended to discuss with her before my departure, but she did not stay to hear it. Instead, I would ask it of you first, and then address it with her on my return.'

'Your return?' His mother's shaking hand gripped harder on his own. 'You will not leave us again, surely?'

'No, I will not leave you. I give you my word that I will not abandon my family again,' it was a promise born from his guilt and his uncertainty. 'Let me explain my scheme to ensure I can see out both of my responsibilities, and please hear me out.' And he outlined what he had been thinking.

His parents looked at one another after he was finished.

'I do not know,' Fleur said.

'Neither do I,' Guillaume shook his head.

'It is a lot to ask, for us to share quarters with a beast. Even if she was once a girl.' His mother's face was still pale in the dim firelight.

His father's mien was hardly less grey. 'We cannot make a hasty decision on this matter. Please, give us some time to consider it.'

Beau nodded, accepting that this was a large thing to be asking of his family, who had never spoke to Yvaine, and had only heard Désiré's eldritch description of her during one of her moments of temper.

He left them to discuss it themselves, while he went outside and began to see what tasks he could apply himself to in the meantime. There were quite a few things he could see that had been left in disrepair since the landsmen had been dismissed, so he was happily busy, if not somewhat distracted by the knowledge of his parent's discussion and what their decision would mean for him, for Yvaine, for all of them.

At periodic intervals his mother would bring him out meals or refreshments, which he heartily appreciated. But each time he would give her a questioning look, and it was answered again and again with a negative shake of her head. They had not yet decided.

When the shadows began to lengthen, a motion caught by his peripheral vision made Beau look up from his work. A cart, driven in haste, was pulling up their remote track. That fact alone was unexpected, as they were not on a road leading to or from anywhere, but then as it neared Beau recognised the cart and its driver. Defeuille was coming in all speed to speak to him.

Beau met the cart as it pulled up in front of the house, and he offered Defeuille his hand as the old grocer tried to heave himself out.

'Beau!' he spoke, his breath in gasps. 'I have to tell you!'

'Come inside, please,' Beau helped the man into the door, leaving the cart horse in its traces for now. He would see to it as soon as he saw the grocer situated comfortably and once the reason for his unexpected appearance had been made clear.

'Mother, Father,' Beau addressed them as he showed the older man into the sitting room. 'This is Monsieur Defeuille, a grocer from Princemont.'

'Princemont?' his father asked, incredulously. 'That is some distance away, indeed.'

'I had to reach you in time, Beau,' Defeuille spoke fervently. 'There is a group of townsmen marching on the Castle Beaumont! I already tried to warn Yvaine, but she would not listen. She does not care if they come, in fact I think she would relish an end to her suffering. She would not let me stay to help in her defence either, so I came here hoping to reach you with enough time that you could do what I could not!'

Beau felt the colour draining from his face.

'Can the beast not defend herself well enough against a crowd of men?' Fleur asked, bewildered by their urgency.

'If she put her mind to it,' Defeuille answered. 'Yvaine could at the very least simply fly away, which is what I hoped she would do when I went to warn her. But she is in a black sorrow, she does not seem to care for her own mortality any longer.'

Beau said to his parents in anguish, 'I promised I would not leave you again.' He had given his word, and those words were tearing him apart.

Guillaume spoke to his son, beside whom he felt so insignificant, saw his torn conscience and was determined to ease it. 'You would not be the man you are if you did not go. Though it pains me to send you back to the place I had until late considered your grave, you must. The promise you made to us can wait until you have seen through your more urgent responsibility. Your mother and I are well, we are in a poverty very much of our own making, and not for the first time, but we are well. This girl, trapped in a monster's body, she needs you more than we do, and she may be in truly mortal peril.'

Fleur clung to her child for a few shuddering breaths, she never seemed to be able to hold on to them for long enough, unwilling until the very last moment to release him. She turned from him to hide her tears while Guillaume drew her to his side.

Beau left, again. He felt like he was always leaving, lately.

Chapter 21

Madame Houblon sat in her parlour, above the main room of her husband's public house. She was straight and still in her seat, a high-backed chair covered with simple but pretty floral fabric, she had made curtains to match which she now drew back from the window to look down at the street below. The stillness of her body belied the turmoil inside of her.

The words her son had spoken had filled her with dread. It had been so long since she had considered the sole resident of Castle Beaumont, but now she could not think of anything else.

Everyone had agreed she had married well, and Timothy Houblon was a good husband and a good man. But he did not understand why she refused to talk about her past, and why she sometimes had nightmares. His life was a simple one and so long as the seats were occupied, his rooms were full and the casks of ale were not, he was happy. But she was not happy.

There had been some pleasures in her life, it was true. Her wedding day, and night. The birth of her son. Watching him grow into the ungainly but sweet youth that he was now, kind to animals but tongue-tied with people. The smaller delights of a good meal or a bolt of fine fabric to furnish their home.

However, a higher concern always sat in her mind. An awareness of debt. One that she had incurred twice, and both times by what she did not do rather than what she did. The time she should have stayed, and the time she should have spoken.

From where she sat, Madame Houblon could see as a group of men left the pub and spilled out into the street. They walked with purpose towards the gates of the town and, watching them revel with one another, laughing and japing with grim amusement, made her suddenly stand, filled with determination.

She could not make this lie of omission any longer. She had to speak, and speak the truth. It might save a life that night, and redeem her own.

Chapter 22

Beau tried to coax his horse into a faster pace. He did not risk a true gallop in descending darkness, with the sun setting behind them so that only the merest pink still glowed on the western horizon. There were some hours of the journey yet before them, but a fast trot would see them over more ground for a time. He would let Commodité walk again soon enough, and alternate gaits as often as he could. He had learned from their misadventure with the wolves to pace their journey sensibly.

He just hoped he would not be too late.

With all his heart he wished that he had been able to tell Yvaine of his intentions to return before he had left. If she had known that her loneliness was only going to be a temporary state, then perhaps she would have not felt so self-defeating. She might have listened to Defeuille, and fled from the castle to await the mob leaving in disappointment.

If only he had had the chance to tell her how he felt.

How did he feel? It had been a creeping sensation, one that snuck into the back of his mind, unaware. From fear and horror turned to companionship and pleasure. He enjoyed spending time with her, hunting in the forest. Even her sudden tempers were friends of his; he esteemed her fierceness, her wildness. Having left her side made him understand how much he missed her and how much he looked forward to spending his days with her. How his heart leapt and his face broke out into an unintended grin when he saw her silhouette across the sky.

Beau had never understood Désiré's sighs and his tears, his hilarity and his sobriety, those hallmarks of his easy passions and flexible affection. These strong emotions were like another language to Beau, he could hear the cadence, the unfamiliar consonants and vowels being spoken, but the meaning was lost to him. But now it seemed that he had suddenly gained the understanding, that he had finally woken, fluent. Knowing Yvaine, and now being on the cusp of possibly losing her altogether, stirred something inside his breast that threatened to overwhelm him. He could have sighed and wept and rent his clothing enough to upstage even his brother's dramatics.

He hoped, and prayed, that he would get there in time.

If only the road was not so long, so winding. If only he could, against all sense and better judgement, spur his horse into an unwise gallop, and spur him onwards and onwards, ever faster. So he could reach her before the mob of unkind men could do her harm.

Sudden anger filled him, left him gasping with rage. How dare these men threaten Yvaine! What had she ever done to the town of Princemont? Yes, her visage was fearful, and her distant form often seen above the valley, but she had never ventured close to any town or village, for she feared them even as they feared her. It was simply unfair that she should be targeted for no crime apart from proximity, and the appearance of a monster. She was no monster on the inside. These men, marching towards the castle with bloodshed on their minds, were the villains of this story. They had no cause but fear and misunderstanding, the worry of what might be rather than what was.

If only he were there now.

At least the moon was on his side, she was well-risen and nearly full in the darkness now spread thick above him and lighting the road ahead. Her pallor cast a subdued glow over the mountains, made the tall pine trees shine with their glittering needles, made the shadows stark in contrast.

When at last they reached the final stretch, Beau cast off the remainder of his caution and nudged Commodité into a brisk canter. He could not contain himself any longer, he needed to be there, and now already felt too late.

There it was – there was the castle up ahead. Its turrets and walls cast palely against the dark trees and clear skies, lit by the moon's glow. Raised voices carried across the still air. They seemed to be shouting, but whether in victory or dismay, he could not tell. His skin felt cold, but it had nothing to do with the chill night air.

Then a shot rang out, and all went silent in its wake.

Chapter 23

While his brother was running headlong towards Castle Beaumont, Désiré was looking for the devil.

Many times in his months at Maison Desjardins he had asked himself how he would find that fiend, but in his heart he knew that the devil was waiting for him, looking for him. All he would need to do was make himself known, and the devil would surely find him, if it pleased him to do so.

Every day since his escape, Désiré had asked himself why the devil had not already found him. Why he had not stopped him at the time, and how he had gained his freedom at all. He then remembered the grand speeches of his lord and master, those times the devil crowed over some long-planned victory. The devil was a gentleman of refinement and, like a nobleman sipping a fine vintage he had allowed to age in his cellars, he enjoyed most those delayed pleasures he could appreciate when the time was exactly right.

In short, Désiré had escaped because the devil found his soul all the sweeter from allowing it to be so.

He would not allow the devil that satisfaction any longer.

When he could not sleep at night, which was often, Désiré planned. He imagined the scene countless times, facing the devil – what would he say? How would he outwit the devil? His silver tongue had gotten him out of, and into, countless childhood adventures, but he could not find the right words, the right argument, there in the darkness of his brother's bedchamber. His bedchamber, he should now say, as his brother was surely lost to the beast.

The devil may not want his soul, after all, as dark and flawed as it was.

Désiré had walked long and aimlessly, first on horseback then on foot when he was forced to sell his mount in order to buy meagre rations when his own were reduced to crumbs. He was not too proud to lick up every morsel, at this point, and to sleep on the cold ground, bundled in in blankets and a moth-eaten fur he had haggled keenly for.

He heaved himself upwards and upwards through the mountains so that the pass below soon disappeared out of sight. It seemed that he had walked for an eternity and that his feet were no longer belonging to him, as so little feeling remained in them. While the sun was setting he found himself on a precipice from which he could touch the silken chill of a waterfall above, which glistened and danced in the gathering gloaming. It fell from the impossible height into a rocky pool below, making white foam rush and swish madly, stirring the water like a nymph's hand.

Across the countryside, bright fire touched the fields and forests setting them alight with colours so brilliantly orange and red that the eye was drawn towards them unerringly. In the lee of the mountains lay deep shadows, unbearably dark next to such lustre. The beauty of the scene heartened him, made his chest swell, his chin lift and his back straighten. This was his country, he was his own man and he would decide his own fate.

'Master!' he called into the wind. He waited. He would know what to do when the time came.

Chapter 24

Charles had never felt so important, so listened-to. He was starting to have a secret thought, which shocked him mightily, that Précieux may have served him better in death than she may have in life. She may have lived to calve, then perhaps died from the process. She may have survived calving, but then sickened later. Or may have survived and lived for a long time, but perhaps her milk would not have flowed as well as he had hoped, or the butter would be not as fine, or as popular, as he dreamed.

Now he marched beside the men of his town, shoulder to shoulder for a common purpose. They would do this brave deed together which would be sung about for generations, their heroic tale perhaps going as far as the cities, where noble folk may hear of their adventure, and lay plaudits upon them and even patronage.

The mountain pass was carpeted with snow but they kept warm by moving with quick, determined steps. Their certainty warmed them likewise with an internal fire, though knowing that each step forward could be bringing them closer to their doom. They were many men, but the beast was an unnatural creature, and they did not know how easily they would overcome it. Each man held what weapons suited them best.

Martin held the long, curved metal bar with which he hooked candle wicks out of their molten wax vats. Henri and another shepherd clutched their crooks. Others held sharp pitchforks, long-handled awls and axes. Charles had a shotgun but only two shots, the last of a valuable box of ammunition normally used to dispatch foxes. He would use them with care, uncertain of the outcome of their use on a much larger creature. He would have to aim well.

Only Old Jules did not join them out of their gathering in the public house, to no one's surprise.

The castle sat dark and ominous above the treeline, looming larger and larger as they grew closer and closer. The moon was bright, all the better to illuminate their way as they had chosen not to carry torches lest the element of surprise be taken from them.

All those careful thoughts were banished from the minds of these men, however, when they entered the castle gates.

'I had expected more of you,' a voice spoke in the darkness.

'Who is there?' called out one of their party.

'Surely you know who I am, if your intentions are what I think they are.'

'Are you a companion of the foul beast?'

A terrible laugh issued forth from a source they could not see.

'Show yourself, stranger!' cried Charles. 'Let us know if you are friend or foe!'

'If you insist,' the voice rumbled. The shadows moved, impossibly, terribly, detaching from the gloom within which it had lain.

The men fell back a step. She stepped into the moonlight, sleek and dangerous in the silver glow, deep wells of black shadow in her plush feathers and bright reflections glinting off her talon points. She was a creature of dark and light, soft and sharp.

'I see you have finally recognised me,' Yvaine said. 'Perhaps you did not expect the foul beast to be capable of speech? Yet I am, and here you are, seeking to kill me though you know not the first thing about the creature you have sought.'

'We know what you have done,' said Charles, his face white but set in determined lines.

'Oh? And what have I done?'

Charles looked at the monster, and she looked back at him. He felt his insides tremble, but he would not back down. 'You killed her,' he said.

'Who?' Yvaine was genuinely puzzled.

'Précieux! You struck her down where she stood, and she had done no harm to any living soul. For no reason, for no purpose, you killed her and while she was heavy with pregnancy!'

'What on heaven and earth,' Yvaine reared her great head, 'are you speaking of, man? I have done no such thing to anyone.'

'He means his cow,' a nervous voice spoke, when it was obvious that some further clarity was needed.

'Oh,' Yvaine said. 'Oh! The cow in that field? All of this,' she raised a talon with near-human exasperation, 'over a cow?'

'She was not just any cow!' Charles shouted. 'She was going to save my farm, and save me! I had such plans for her, but now I am ruined!'

Yvaine looked down at the aging farmer. 'A cow is a cow,' she said. 'It is ridiculous to go to such lengths to revenge a-'

She never finished the sentence.

Chapter 25

'Yvaine!' cried Beau as he burst through the ivy gates with Commodité's hooves kicking up puffs of snow. He forced his horse between the men and their target, shoving aside the smoking barrel of the foremost man's weapon.

'What have you done?' he demanded of the townspeople, seeing Yvaine laying prostrate on the ground.

'Justice!' cried the man with the shotgun, raising his fist to the heavens, about to give an impassioned speech.

Yvaine heaved herself to her feet with awkward grace. 'This one tried to kill me over a cow,' she said mildly, shaking herself, flexing a wing where several primary feathers were broken and bent from the flight of the bullet. 'Luckily my instincts are truer than his aim. But you should not have come.'

'Of course I came,' Beau said, his breath still coming hard from exertion.

'It was not really about a cow,' another man spoke.

'Why-ever should you have?' Yvaine asked. 'I released you from your servitude, so you were free.'

'It was really more about what the cow represented, you see.'

'I had tried to tell you before I left,' Beau tried to explain. 'Even free, I did not choose to be forever gone from your side.'

'The cow could have been one of our wives, perhaps,' the man continued to attempt his explanation.

'If you had been careless enough to leave your wife alone in a field at night, then – but enough about this damned cow!' Yvaine snarled to the man, who fell silent. 'You have it all wrong in the first place. It was the wolves who killed the creature, I did not touch it.'

'But this feather!' Charles held up his prized proof.

'Was shed from the exertions of fighting the wolf pack – did you really mean that?' she turned to Beau suddenly. 'You would wish to be here?'

'Of course,' Beau said.

'You cannot have us believe you are entirely without blame or bloodshed on your, um, hands,' a large man said. 'All of us at Princemont know your history.'

'And what history is that, then?' Yvaine snapped.

'You killed the Marquis, his wife, and their daughter.'

'No, she did not,' spoke a new voice. A middle-aged woman stepped into the scene, and she was gasping to catch her breath.

'Madame Houblon?' the men asked, perplexed. The pub land-lord's wife was the last person any of them expected to see at Castle Beaumont that night.

'Yes, you know me by that name now, but many years ago I was known simply as Eugénie, and I lived here at the castle as Yvaine De Beaumont's maid.'

Yvaine landed with an ungainly thump on the ground beside the woman who could not help but draw back in fear, as suddenly as a bewildered woman finding a seat.

'Eugénie?' she asked, incredulous. 'Is that really you?'

'It is, do you not remember me? After all, I resemble myself more than you do now,' Eugénie said.

'What are you talking about?' Charles was beginning to lose the attention of his men, and his patience. 'What is this?'

'This,' Eugénie gestured to the beast beside her, 'is my former mistress. This is Yvaine, the Marquis De Beaumont's daughter.'

'How can that be possible?' the men asked, mutters breaking out between them.

'Has the woman gone mad?'

'Maybe drunk too much of her husband's homebrew?'

'I was there when it happened,' she replied, giving them each a stern look, drawn from that place inside every woman who has endured motherhood which, when cast upon them, turns even the hardest of men into truant little boys. 'I admitted the enchantress into the castle, and I saw her turn a young girl into a monster. I am not proud to say that I fled immediately after.'

The men were still looked sceptical, and one spoke out, 'Why did you not speak before now? It seems convenient that this explanation has turned up out of nowhere.'

'Convenient?' she asked, turning on him. 'It was not convenient at all for me to leave my home in the middle of the night and make my way into the mountains alone in the dark and in the snow. It was not *convenient* to think, with every step, that I was walking to my doom, to be devoured by the beast as just punishment for my betrayal. No, do not speak to me of convenience!

'It was shame that stayed my tongue, though it was not right that I did so.' Eugénie now addressed Yvaine, 'It was not right, and I am sorry for it. I would suffer the travails of my journey here a hundred times if it would gain your forgiveness. Do you,' she visibly gulped, 'do you wish to eat me, then?'

'Eat you? Why-ever would I eat you?' Yvaine shook her great head. 'You do not need to absolve yourself of this – this betrayal, as you call it – as in truth I spent all of my days, until recently,' her eyes catching Beau's in the moonlight, 'lost in self-pity and self-hatred. I did not think of your absence as a betrayal, or even thought of it at all, as I was not a creature capable of imagining loyalty, or love, or trust. It is only now that I see these emotions. You may feel badly for not doing it, but I now feel badly for not even thinking it possible. I was a beast even before I became one in the flesh.'

'You were a spoiled child,' Eugénie wiped tears from her cheeks with impatient hands, 'but you were just a child. A better companion would have understood that, and stayed to help you after your transformation. I do not blame you for your tempers and tantrums, though you were a terrible fiend of a girl!'

Charles watched this exchange with a feeling of growing dread. He had lost Précieux, and now he could see he was losing his chance to avenge her, and to gain retribution and compensation for her loss.

'What are you doing?' Martin hissed from beside him.

'I just, I need-,' he shouldered his shotgun.

'We are finished here,' another said.

'There is no need to-'

Hands reached for his weapon, and the beast in his sights turned to see her danger.

'What is going on?' the beast demanded.

'Enough of this nonsense!' shouted Madam Houblon.

Charles grappled with his neighbours, his friends, but were they his friends after all? How could they listen to this story, how could they believe it, and take the side of an inhuman daemon instead of one of their own?

Another shot rang across the night, startling an owl into flight.

Chapter 26

The devil came for Désiré, he did not have to wait long. The sun had disappeared below the horizon, but from the high peak there was still light casting a wide net across the sky.

'Are you so eager to relinquish your soul to me?' the devil asked.

'Why would you think that my soul belongs to you, Master?'

The devil frowned. His hair was black-brown and his eyes were blue as the cold, emotionless sea.

Désiré continued speaking. 'I am now, and always, your obedient servant. I have done everything you have asked of me and have never failed.'

'It has been most entertaining,' the devil said, 'to watch the lengths you would go to. Never before has a servant of mine been so willing to debase himself for gold. Never have I seen a man with such gifts as yours for persuasion and guile. I will enjoy your soul.' His hair was now golden waves, and his eyes green as new leaves.

Désiré flushed with mingled shame and pride. 'But my soul is not yours.'

'You left before your service was complete. Your gifts are great, but they cannot change what has happened.'

'I asked for time,' Désiré said, 'and time you have granted me with no conditions upon it. I never left your service at all, Master, and I am now ready to complete your final command.'

The devil stared. His hair was red flames, and his eyes black as smouldering coals. 'I will have your soul!' the fiend hissed, flickering a forked tongue from between his lips.

'Not in this life.' Désiré smiled and jumped into the falling water beside him.

He leapt but did not fall through the air, and his feet never again touched the earth.

Chapter 27

Beau carefully lowered himself to the ground, holding his bloody thigh. He had waved off Madam Houblon from assisting him before she departed, as the wound was thankfully shallow, but it still pained him somewhat. Yvaine paced with contained rage and distress. Beau could not shake a sudden feeling of horror and foreboding, but surely their danger was past? And yet, something bothered him. He felt a sudden overpowering of emotions he had not known he was capable of, heightening every awareness of his senses. It was like a part of him that was halved was now whole, and he looked at Yvaine with overwhelming feelings he could not parse.

They had both just survived death. Beau had never felt more alive.

They had both been incredibly lucky that the man with the shotgun had terrible aim, but the man himself was lucky that Yvaine had her rage in check. It would not have lasted long, so after that last shot, Eugénie had harangued the men long and devastatingly enough for them to take hold of their revenge-seeking fellow, and to forcibly remove him from the scene. They had left together to return to their homes, no one satisfied and no one pleased with the outcome of the night. Eugénie gave Yvaine one last, searching look, and followed the men.

'You are hurt,' Yvaine said to Beau, becoming still, her head drooping to brush the snow-dusted earth. 'I had told myself I would never let any harm come to you, especially on my behalf. I wish you had not come.'

'I am barely hurt,' Beau said, making himself stand with only the smallest wince, wishing his utmost that he was able to convey the thoughts and feelings rushing through him. Yet he could speak only awkwardly, 'And, for my part, I am so very grateful I got here in time. I had to come.'

'Why?' she shook her head in disbelief. 'Why would you bother? Surely you were revelling in your freedom, so why return at all? Least of all to come to my aid when I have been your captor for so long, keeping you against your will when your family have been struggling without you.'

'Because, despite everything, when I returned home I realised that my life was lesser from your absence,' he spoke softly and with fervour. 'I could not, I cannot, imagine a world in which your life is extinguished, where I would never get to see you again.'

'You cannot mean that.'

'Do you know me as a liar?'

'Of course not, but I-,' she stumbled over her words. 'I did not think, I did not expect-'

'Do you so belittle your own value as to be unable to believe that someone could esteem you so?'

But they both knew that she did, and that knowledge saddened Beau to the core of his being.

'While for my part,' she said, quiet and uncertain, 'I am certain that you are the only friend I have had in the world. The only bright spark in the eternal night of my heart, and without you there was only the darkness.'

Beau smiled and reached out to her. She froze, fearful and with painful sadness. His wide palms lay warm on either side of her scored withers, and he gathered her neck into him. They were illuminated by the pallid moon who gazed fondly down at the unlikely pair, the air sighing around them. Yvaine exhaled with the release of years of sorrow, loneliness and self-hatred, and curled her forelegs around this fragile man as carefully as she could. Her wings furled out to mantle over him with possessive jealousy against the world at large. Beau felt the soft touch of feathers to his cheek, the sharpness of talons pricking ever so lightly at his back.

'I love you, Yvaine,' he said, and never had such words been spoken as honestly and with as much emotion as in that moment. 'You need not be left in the dark again.'

'I love you, Beau,' she said, and only by speaking did she know that it was so.

The soft wisp of feathers on his cheek softened further into silken waves, and the talons' sharpness retreated to delicate finger tips. They fell together, both insensible from pain, from relief, and from an unexpected arcane magic suddenly loosened upon them. They fell together, and knew no more.

Chapter 28

Thalassemia rocked back and forth, back and forth, with a rhythmic creak. This had been her mother's rocking chair – or had it? No, it was her teacher's. Or maybe it had always been here. The memory was all wrong, but the chair was comfortable, so she sat and rocked and watched as the sun set over the lake. There were things she must discuss with the moon tonight, so she awaited its appearance in the sky.

Her cottage was a castle, and the lake and its surroundings were her realm. From the open doors of her sitting room she could see it all, and she did not care that the wind had carried drifts of fine snow across her carpets earlier in the day. There was a mirror on the table beside the chair, and Thalassemia picked it up to ease her tedium. The old woman looking back at her was not the person she remembered. She had been beautiful once, feared and respected. Kings had come to beg at her door, offering her gifts and favours in exchange for her talents.

That seemed so very long ago, but then she could not be entirely sure.

The moon rose and cast its glow on the lake. Thalassemia smiled a crooked smile and set her mind, though it was crooked too, to the work required. She and the moon had much to discuss.

Then it happened. The old woman felt it, and it felt like a spring which had been pulled taut was finally released.

'Who was that?' she asked the moon, but it did not reply. 'Fine, I will do this without your help, you cantankerous orb.'

Rock, rock, Thalassemia sat and thought, following the thread of that sprung spring. Which of her spells had just been broken? She had not been expecting any, and had not been for some time.

Here it was, and the image in her mind was a rampant griffin. A griffin? It felt familiar, but she could not place it. There had been a girl, a storm and a commission fulfilled. Who had asked for that one? There was some Duke or Earl, she could not keep all these self-important men straight, even when her mind had been less crooked.

'This is not right,' Thalassemia informed the moon who still watched her, unblinking. 'That was done too long ago.' Her thoughts twisted and rambled, but she remembered in fragments. It had been an enchantment which she had charged according to a timescale of a week, two at the most. It should not have lasted as long as this.

'I must check the ledger,' she said, frowning. It pained her to move from her seat, but this was a question which needed answering.

From a shelf, Thalassemia pulled one of several thick leather-bound books. She blew the dust from its pages and set it on a lectern to turn the pages with impatient fingers. Her late master had been insistent she keep written records of every magical working she performed, as well as contracts with her clients so that they could not later dispute the results of what they commissioned. He told her it would help her remember when the magic turned her mind. She thanked him in her thoughts while she searched for the spell in question, though she found that she could not even remember his name.

There it was. Twenty-two years ago the Duke of Nièvre paid her with three hundred livre to enchant Yvaine de Beaumont. The ledger continued in her careful hand, 'The Duke wishes to teach this girl a lesson of tractability so that she will acquiesce to marry his feeble-minded son, as her parents cannot control her.'

Below those words she had written in a smaller, scribbled note, as she often did once her clients had left, ruminations of a more speculative nature concerning their intentions, 'He hopes to gain through marriage, and with the incipient death of the Marquis and his wife [arranged?], ownership of the mountain pass to create a toll upon its use. Usual love-declaration countermand. Parents expected within the week.' It was all written down, all clear and straightforward. But why had the spell only now been broken?

Thalassemia sat back down in her chair with a sigh, and rocked back and forth, back and forth. Her thoughts soon dissolved into turbulent mist, as they often did. Creak, creak, back and forth. This had been her master's rocking chair.

It began with a scream.

Beau was barely conscious, but he could hear the noise around him. It was shrill, terrible and a voice he had never heard before. He opened his eyes.

At first he thought it was snowing, but it was not nearly cold enough. Nevertheless, the air was full of dancing motes of white, drifting down to settle around his body. He picked one up and realised it was feather down. As his awareness expanded it became clear, and strange to observe, that the ground was covered in feathers. It was like some explosion had happened, like the impact of a shotgun hitting a pheasant in flight only multiplied a thousand-fold.

PART II: Mortal

Chapter 1

There had been some magic wrought upon the pair of them, that much was clear. Where drops of Beau's blood had soaked into the earth beside where he lay, red roses had sprung up lush and fragrant. He could feel the barbs of their thorns through the fabric of his trousers and hose, pricking and catching his skin. Where he had been wounded there were now petals in place of blood, and the bullet hole was now a rose bud. He plucked it from his skin but felt no pain.

And as for Yvaine, it was clear to him that she was that very young woman in distress and plumage. For who indeed else could she have been? Like the beast, her body showed evidence of habitual starvation, though lately less so, and her ribs and hips protruded from beneath her mud-caked skin. Her appearance was so shocking and feral that Beau felt no embarrassment at the sight of her naked body, which was in itself a shock to his principles.

She was twisted away from him, but soon turned. This was the face of Yvaine, the mortal, the human, the girl, and she was beautiful. Her eyes were clear and sharp in an angular face, her nose aquiline and her cheekbones prominent, while the teeth inside her mouth were ever so slightly crooked – and it was all beautiful and it was all perfect in its imperfection. Down to the very shade of her hair, which was the colour of those glossy brown-black wings his eyes still sought on the horizon, in a tangled spill of lank and greasy strands. The feather-down clung to those filaments while the larger feathers lay in a casual sprawl across her shoulders, drifting down to collect about her knees, upon which she knelt.

'My God,' Beau could not help but utter aloud. 'What has befallen us?'

With great trembling effort Yvaine gained her feet, and swayed to grasp at the trunk of a tree. Her fingers gripped tightly to the uneven bark, digging in painfully to her tender skin. It was all familiar and all strange to be in this body.

'What have you done?' she whispered, finding her tongue in her mouth uncomfortable and alien. 'What have *I* done? This was what I had once dreamed for, but have since forgotten was even possible.'

'Yvaine?' Beau did not know if he should go to her, so remained where he was. She was still the feral creature he knew, and he must tread lightly.

She was issuing forth a long groan of self-recrimination, but stopped and spoke to him, 'There was a way to break the spell, which I had thought impossible. To gain the love of another, and love in return. It seemed a cruel jibe, an unreachable goal only left to torture me with its possibility. My parents were supposed to have fulfilled this charge, but I have told you what befell them.

'Now it has been fulfilled, but I am not sure if I am glad of it.' Yvaine looked at Beau and asked him, 'Are *you*? Can you love this person as you have loved the companionship of the beast she was?'

Beau spoke with quiet honesty, 'I would love you in any form, so long as you remained yourself within it.'

'And if being human makes me soft, and my violence and rages, your old companions, become no longer?'

'Then I will love you softly.'

Yvaine's vision, now so poor and narrow, became blurred and stinging as tears filled her eyes. They flowed over her cheeks and dripped warm onto the skin of her chest and arms as she wept into the tree at her side. She had so many unshed tears to make up for.

Beau now stepped forward, cloaked her in his jacket and pulled her gently to him.

'You speak such words which I had never imagined being spoken to one such as myself,' Yvaine said through her tears. 'But I fear them even as I rejoice in them.'

'What are you afraid of?' Beau asked, not understanding.

'I am afraid of everything; I find myself overwhelmed by emotions which I had not been aware of for years. I am afraid of who I am now, and I am afraid of you, your love, my love for you, what it all means for both of us.'

'You need not be afraid of me. I will never hurt you. I promise to never leave you alone again, and never to let any harm come to you.'

Yvaine looked at him, eyes still streaming with tears, and said, 'No one can, or should, promise such things to another. I do not know myself any longer, and you do not know me as I am now. We do not know how to love each other anymore, and I will not hold you to promises made in ignorance.'

Beau pulled away in startled refusal. 'In ignorance of what? I believe that the being which I came to know and love is still this person here before me. I wish only to do and be that which is best for you, and what can keep you from the loneliness which nearly overcame you.'

Yvaine gently untangled herself from his arms. 'When you left me it was for a noble purpose, and one which has not yet been discharged, I wager. My loneliness is my own burden to bear, you have enough of your own to shoulder.'

'I should have found a way to tell you what I intended before I left,' Beau said. 'I had a solution which would allow me to at once care for my parents as I should and also remain your companion as I wish. If you were agreeable to it, I would have them come here to live with us.'

Yvaine smiled wanly. 'And so I would have in-laws before ever being wed? They would be happy living in a dreary, dreadful ruin of a castle?'

'I am making improvements on it every day.'

'And then what, we all live here until the ends of our time here on earth?'

'If that should that be your wish.'

'I do not know what my wishes are – how can I, when even my very limbs are unfamiliar to me? I do not know myself, nor my mind, nor my heart.'

Beau looked down at her, finding it strange that he should be looking down, and could understand. 'Then what would you have me do? I am happy to wait and let you reacquaint yourself with yourself.'

Yvaine nodded, thinking, 'I need time, yes. And you must return to your parents in the meantime, they will be missing you again, and must be thinking the worst if Monsieur Defeuille had been talking of mobs and terror to inspire your return to me.'

Beau had to admit the truth of that.

'Return, if you should still wish to, after settling them well in some fashion, and I will be here.'

'My return to your side will be the constant wish of my heart.'

Chapter 2

When Eugénie arrived at Castle Beaumont she was glad to have been forewarned about the state of her former mistress. Yvaine was in the South Tower naked and filthy, wrapped in foul-smelling blankets in a heap of old mattresses like an animal in her den. Her face was streaked where tears had run dirt clear off her skin.

'May I dress you?' Eugénie asked quietly and with some hesitation, having come prepared with several plain garments. Yvaine nodded her assent. The older woman first wielded a damp washcloth like a fencer with his sword, and attacked the layers of grime upon the younger woman's skin.

'Ouch!' she hissed with pain as Eugénie tried to tease snarls loose in her hair.

'I am sorry,' her former maidservant said, 'but you are in such a state!'

After Yvaine had been scrubbed pink, her hair yanked and pulled until finally the comb could pass through unhindered, and a pottage sat on the kitchen hearth bubbling to itself, Eugénie considered herself victorious.

'Now mind you,' she told her charge, pointing to the stew pot, 'to eat that by sundown. Give it the odd stir, so it does not stick to the bottom.'

Yvaine nodded, but she was distracted and only half listening to the older woman.

'I'll be back tomorrow,' Eugénie said as she wrapped her shawl over her shoulders. 'I must get back to make Monsieur Houblon *his* supper, or else I'll never hear the end of it.' She paused at the threshold of the door, and said, 'He does not know I am here.'

The words penetrated Yvaine's thoughts and she looked sharply at Eugénie. 'He does not?'

'I have not told him what has transpired and the state of your current form, nor told anyone for that matter. Your young man was very clear on that,' she said.

'Why?' Yvaine asked.

'He is protecting you,' Eugénie said. 'Can you not see it?'

'He is too good,' she said softly. 'I do see it.'

Eugénie turned to leave again, but Yvaine bid her wait once more.

'Please, could you give this to that foolish man with the cow?'

With surprise, Eugénie accepted a weighty purse. She looked searchingly at the drawn face of the girl she once knew. She did not really know her at all anymore.

Yvaine was caught up in her own thoughts, and did not see the look of admiration on the older woman's face. If she had, it may have strengthened her spirits, for she still could not see how anyone could love her, in either of her forms.

The next day, as promised, Eugénie appeared again. To her dismay, she found Yvaine still cloistered in the tower, and the stew pot burned black on a hearth of cold ashes, its contents tar.

'I suppose it has been mere days,' she thought to herself. 'I must give her time.'

As she had the day before, Eugénie tried to restore some signs of civility to Yvaine's appearance, combed her hair out and again left her with supper on the hearth.

'You must eat,' she told Yvaine with concern, but the girl barely showed any sign of hearing. It was becoming clear that some days Yvaine would not speak at all, and others only rarely and in response to some provoking comment. When she did speak she was mournful and self-pitying, but Eugénie sighed and told herself, 'I must give her time.'

Eventually the days passed into a week, and still the young woman was barely speaking and barely eating. Eugénie had had enough of seeing Yvaine waste away before her, too lost to her own thoughts to stir herself out of her torpor.

'Here,' she said, handing her former mistress a wooden spoon. 'I will show you how to make coq au vin. It was my mother's recipe.'

208 | Arielle K Harris

After a moment, when Eugénie's breath was held in uncertainty, Yvaine pushed herself free of the chair she had occupied all morning and stood to accept the spoon.

The next day saw a change in Yvaine's engagement with the world around her. Eugénie began to impart certain lessons that she felt Yvaine's education had not covered, much to her current detriment.

'As a woman living on your own,' she said, 'you would be well-served to manage your own household tasks, such as the particulars of cooking, making and mending garments, spinning wool into serviceable yarn, cleaning, and laundry. You will not have anyone else to do it for you, and I cannot be here always.' In this way, Eugénie's long-standing guilt, which lingered still, could be somewhat assuaged by the hope that she could do some good for her former mistress.

And so Eugénie came, and went, and Yvaine found that the days were often blending together. Sometimes Eugénie would put tasks before her, and Yvaine would be one day holding a needle, or the next a spindle, or a wooden spoon, or a broom. Mostly what she was doing was learning how to be herself again, in her mind, her spirit and her heart, but the physical work helped focus her thought.

The domestic education she was undergoing, while frustratingly menial, also helped her fine-tune her control over her hands. They were so flexible and sensitive, Yvaine would sometimes, unthinkingly, bruise them by using them too harshly and hitting them off of objects, using them like the talons she once wielded. Her feet were sore from walking barefoot, but she could not bear the feeling of shoes confining them. She would rather trod on a hundred pointed stones, or through ankle-deep snow, to than feel the pinch of leather boots wrapping too-tightly across her toes, pressing her flesh together unnaturally. Clothing was binding enough, though she was grateful to Eugénie for providing her with these garments, as well as the cast-off boots which had been worn by her son many years before, when his feet were roughly the size hers were now. She wore them only when necessary, but never complained about the discomfort when she did, at least not in Eugénie's hearing.

Being a human was taxing, she was realising anew, particularly as her mind was often interrupted by insidious thoughts and emotions which she had no control over. As a beast she had been easily overridden by her bloodlust and hunger, but now there was so much all clamouring for her attention at once. Fear, loneliness, and frustration.

And guilt.

Yvaine tried not to remember the hurt on Beau's face, his beautiful face – how had she not seen his beauty before? – when she told him to leave, even though it was for the best of reasons.

These thoughts came to her most when she lingered by the red roses in the courtyard. Despite the changeable weather they remained as vibrant and red as the day they had sprung from Beau's blood. She had a strange superstition when looking at them that so long as they were hale and healthy so would be their progenitor. Yvaine needed to walk the grounds often, feeling too claustrophobic if she remained indoors too long.

On one of her first such walks, Yvaine heard a clamour in the trees which her human heart first recoiled from, but her bestial soul, that fierceness which still remained, lent her a predatory instinct which she followed. This was how Yvaine discovered Commodité; he had caught himself by his loose reins in the undergrowth and could not break free. He was in reasonable condition for all his panic, and the length of time he may have been held in place, though it was clear that he had grazed the ground bare within his reach, so Yvaine led him back to the castle where she stripped him of his trappings and gave him a good rub down as she had watched Beau do on many occasions. The horse was not at all settled to be near her, she found with interest, wondering if he somehow sensed what form she had lately taken. After caring for his needs she turned him loose into the paddock and made his care and feeding part of her daily routine, wanting the return of his horse to be her gift to Beau on his return.

Yvaine's dour moods improved further when she discovered a shelf of books which Beau must have carefully recovered from the ruins of the old library. She revelled in her old much-visited friends within those pages, and took to having a book under her arm most everywhere she went while wandering the castle and grounds.

The final important discovery was the gunroom. Eugénie was not entirely approving of the zeal with which Yvaine took to hunting, but if nothing else it ensured that the girl could now provide her own meat as she was proving to have some skill with its use. Eugénie had never felt it right to mention the difficulty of her household cost in providing meat for both her own table and Yvaine's. Luckily Monsieur Houblon never looked closely at his household costs, and let his wife manage their house-keeping, or else the ruse would have been discovered from that alone. She knew that if she asked Yvaine that her former mistress would have quickly agreed to payment, but it was Eugénie's remaining guilt which stopped her. She still felt that she had only begun to make amends.

Yvaine was becoming more practised with the rifle every day, and returned one morning smiling and victorious with a fine cock pheasant she had shot well through its head. She had gained some skill with a knife, and was pleased with how easily she had been able to field dress the bird as well. While contemplating her various accomplishments she passed Beau's roses, as she did every day.

Only now they were wilted, casting petals to the ground.

'Something is very wrong,' Yvaine said, and she knew in her heart that it was so.

Chapter 3

After leaving Castle Beaumont, Beau knew he had several things to attend to so he had turned eastward rather than west. It was a long walk into the town, and he missed Commodité greatly. He took a winding route through the forest, where the snow still lay in shadowed places. Elsewhere it had begun to disappear as they began a patch of thankfully milder weather.

It distressed him more than he thought to think of his horse coming to some calamity but he could not find him. Eventually, he had to stop searching or else he would have no daylight left to complete his errands in town.

For the first of these, he went to the tavern and spoke at length with Madame Houblon. He left there cheered, feeling pleased that he could ensure Yvaine would not be entirely friendless and alone, at least. But he was not entirely at ease, and found himself sighing as he continued down the main street and its slate-roofed buildings.

He sighed that he had agreed to return Maison Desjardins, because now he must do it. Beau knew that this was the correct course of action, and knew that his parents would be desperate to hear news of him, and what had transpired in the night, but he sighed nonetheless. He had never before felt so divided between two opposing actions: the thing which he must do and the thing he wished he could do. Never before had he even seen that there was an action other than the correct and necessary one, but now he saw that there were so many other choices he could make. Other avenues he could take. He just needed to decide on one.

In searching his heart, Beau saw that he needed to be alone, to push his body hard and to think without distraction. He felt irrationally claustrophobic of the mountain pass, so wondered if there could be another way. It seemed so irresponsible of him to take himself off on an adventure, when so much was going on around him, but for the first time in his life he felt the need to be selfish, to give in to emotions and thoughts that normally his brother embodied. He felt like a whole person suddenly, both the thinking and feeling sides at once, and wondered how it were possible when his whole life he and his brother had shared between them these two parts.

However, before he could begin his journey west by any route, he had one more task to complete. Beau called in at the grocer's, though knowing Defeuille would be very unlikely to have returned so quickly. And indeed within the shop there was only the wide-eyed youth, Garçon, whose eyes grew even wider when he perceived the figure of Beau entering, and alone.

'Is all well with my master?' the youth asked in haste. 'Is he not with you?'

'Defeuille will be traveling back presently,' Beau assured him, 'but we did not journey together; I rode ahead.'

'And-, well -, what -,' Garçon stumbled over his words, until at last he found his tongue and leaned forward with conspiratorial zeal. 'What happened? Does the beast live?'

'Yes,' Beau said, but he would say no more on the subject. 'Could you thank your master for his assistance in that matter when he arrives?'

The boy nodded.

'And a further favour,' Beau said, 'if you would have a spare ledger, or something like, upon which I could write two letters?'

Garçon did as he was asked, and Beau set down his thoughts between two missives, one to Defeuille himself, relating the state of things in spare words and vague specifics in case it should be read by other eyes than his, as indeed his apprentice looked too keen for discretion. And the other letter he addressed to his parents to assure them of his safety and his intention to travel back to them by foot, should his journey take longer than he expected and its delivery occur before his arrival. He found himself relishing the prospect of a challenging journey, and the time it would give him to think on the way. He just needed to discover what route might lend itself to this goal.

When he handed the two letters back to the grocer's apprentice, Beau thought to ask this youth, being a native of this part of the country, about his current predicament.

'Is there any other way one might travel west from here, apart from the mountain pass? I have an adventure in mind.'

Garçon considered it, and replied, 'There are some small villages you could travel by, going north of here and then west. First the village of J—, then M—, then L— and finally B—, but after B— there is no way around the forest. To continue west one would need to go straight through its centre to the other wise, but from there lies easy farmland, at least.'

So Beau travelled as he was directed, and in the final village of B--, when the villagers understood his intention to travel further west into the forest they tried their best to warn him off his path and told him of the dangers within. Many of their men had entered, they said, but seldom few returned and never the most handsome of them. But Beau would not hear it, and ignored their warnings as the superstitions of country-folk.

When they could not dissuade him, the villagers pressed gifts of food and warm clothing on him before letting him travel onward. He was much obliged, and could only thank them all profusely for their kindness, touched by their generosity.

But, for the part of the villagers, they thought that they would never see this beautiful stranger again, and hoped that their kindness to him in life would prevent his haunting them in death.

As he left the village, Beau watched for the position of the sun and set off correctly to the west. This stretch of forest, however, was far denser than the woods around Castle Beaumont or Princemont, and it did not take long for the sun and sky to become wholly obscured by branches, even though bare of leaves. But Beau did not despair, as he remembered a boyhood lesson that postulated that moss would only grow on the northern side of a tree trunk, and oriented himself by the evidence of that theory instead. He travelled thusly, and stopped occasionally to refresh himself with his gifts of food, rationing it carefully as he could lest the journey grow long.

The forest grew ever denser, ever thicker, and ever darker, until Beau found himself surrounded by trees whose bark was entirely encircled by moss. At last he thought that perhaps turning back and reorienting himself would be the wisest course, but it had come to pass that Beau could not identify which direction he had approached either.

The darkening of the trees around him was not entirely caused by the density of the foliage, as the sun had begun to set on his predicament. Had he been a child of this countryside he would have known not to enter the forest lightly, or to at least leave behind a trail to follow back again. But without this knowledge or foresight, Beau realised that he would have to spend the night in this unwelcoming forest.

It would be only the first of many.

Chapter 4

Beau had never known true hunger before. He had known inconvenience for a meal that was not available when required, so that his gratification must wait, and he had known more recently the need to ration food and make little last for a long time, but he had never known honest starvation when simply no food was obtainable at all. Here in the forest he addressed that ignorance, and felt himself well-informed but not particularly grateful for that education. The gifts he had received from the village of B— had run out some days prior.

There was, at least, plentiful water in the streams and pools which latticed through the undergrowth, and he was lucky that the winter was progressing mildly and tamely, though the wind tasted sharp and bitter with threat upon his tongue. Beau drank deeply at each source, sometimes needing to break a layer of ice to do so, to fill his belly with something, at least, and felt that he had never tasted any liquid as sweet as this water before him; not even the finest champagne in crystal compared to it.

This poor diet was not enough, however, and Beau found himself close to fainting by the side of a fast-flowing stream, his mouth parched and his stomach empty, his hands shaking and red with cold.

'Are you quite well?' came a voice which creaked like dry leather.

By the side of the stream, an aged crone was casting her fishing line into the water.

'I am lost,' Beau spoke through cracked lips, wheezing with the effort.

'How deeply unpleasant for you,' the old woman said.

Beau stumbled to the edge of the frost-covered bank, and fell upon his hands and knees beside the water's edge.

'I would not drink from this stream, if I were you,' the crone spoke again.

'Why not?' Beau asked, breaking the ice which lay over the water's surface at the water's slow-moving edge.

'It is well known that a witch lives nearby,' she said. 'Any who drink from these waters are lost to her enchantment.'

'I am just so thirsty,' Beau reached his hand below the cold water.

'I did warn you,' she said.

Beau drank deeply, and the witch smiled.

Chapter 5

'But you have no idea where he could be!' Eugénie followed Yvaine into her bedchamber, where the latter was hastily gathering her few mortal possessions into a bag. 'How do you propose you find him?'

'I will find a way. For surely such a man of noteworthy beauty will not have gone unremarked through the country.' She had filled a purse from the castle's treasury so that she could travel easily through the countryside, and also to incentivise the memory of its people.

'Only if there is someone there to see him. What if he is far from people, or in a direction you do not predict? It could take you a lifetime of searching to find him, and by then perhaps he will no longer need your help? And not to mention that this determination of yours is entirely predicated on the state of a damned flower!'

'He is in danger, I just know it.'

'Roses wilt! It just happens, regardless of the condition of the people we care about. It signifies nothing. They should not have bloomed in the winter at all, for that fact, so it is no wonder they have perished in the frosts.'

'These are no simple roses, they do not act in the normal way of flowers elsewhere. There is magic at work here, for how else would they have been in full bloom and, yes, in winter, for these past three weeks?'

'Yvaine,' Eugénie said while catching the arm of her former mistress, a plea in her eyes.

Yvaine met the pleading gaze of the older woman, and placed her own hand on top of hers. 'I am going.'

'At least let me give you these,' Eugénie said, pulling a wrapped parcel from the pouch she carried back and forth with every visit. 'I had planned to give them to you at Christmas, but I feel you will certainly need them now. I hope they will make your journey easier.'

Yvaine unwrapped her gift, and within lay a pair of fur slippers. 'You made me a gift?' She was so touched, so moved, that she could not speak for a long moment.

'They should not bother you so much as boots do, and do not stare at me so, of course I noticed, but will keep your feet warm and dry in the snow. You certainly cannot be journeying barefoot at this time of the year!' And then the older woman hastened to turn her back and wipe her eyes, before her tears should be seen and betray her.

'Eugénie,' Yvaine said softly.

'At least let me accompany you to the town where I will be able to give you some food for travelling, which you shall surely need.' The older woman turned back briskly, all business again.

'Very well,' Yvaine agreed, a tiny smile on her lips which even her mouth did not really believe was happening.

And so Yvaine and Eugénie made their way to Princemont, leading Commodité alongside them, though the dread of the younger woman rose ever higher with every step taken closer to the town.

Eugénie could feel the tension in her former mistress, and spoke. 'No one will know you, here, or have reason to suspect that you are anything but a mere maiden, though a stranger to them. We will say that you are my niece, should anyone ask, but I doubt that they will. They all still think that the beast is in its castle, still a creature and not a girl, thanks to Beau, and will have no suspicions. Your young man knew what he was about.'

'He is not *my* anything,' she said, but she felt pained at the very mention of his name.

When they arrived at Princemont, as Eugénie had predicted, no person there gave her a second glance, apart from the usual curiosity given to a stranger in a small town. More people looked at the fine prancing form of Commodité, showing away with himself as usual, than either of the women with him.

Within the tavern, Eugénie bustled around the kitchen gathering together food for the journey. 'Where will you go first?' she asked as she did so.

'I suppose I will try asking in the town if anyone has seen him, and his beauty will have ensured people will remember him. If indeed strangers are so uncommon here, one with eyes like his – what?' Eugénie was smirking at her.

'Who are you speaking of?' came a young male voice, as a youth had entered the kitchen unnoticed.

'Ah, Garçon,' Eugénie said, greeting him warmly and at the same time slapping his hands away from the croissants she was wrapping. 'Hands off! These are not for you!'

'Maman, do you mean to be asking about the whereabouts of that man who until lately lived in the castle with the beast? I cannot imagine who else you could mean.'

His mother looked up at him, 'Why, do you know aught of him?'

'He came to the grocers some weeks ago, and happened to ask directions from me, as well as some other favours,' he said, puffing his chest with importance, inviting them to question him further.

'And so where in heavens did you direct him, child?' his mother asked.

'He wanted to know a way west avoiding the mountain pass,' and at those words Yvaine felt a quiet sort of torment, feeling that he must have sought to travel in such a way to avoid her. 'So I told him of the way north to J—, then west by M—, L—, and B—.'

'That way does not go fully west enough,' Eugénie said, frowning in thought.

'I did say that he would need to go through the forest to go any further west,' Garçon protested. 'He was content with that.'

Eugénie delivered a sharp blow to her son's head, making him cry out. 'You fool! How could you send a man, especially one who is a stranger to these parts, through the forest in the winter? Did you desire him dead? There are surely more simple ways to accomplish that task if it was your intention, and if not then you are a fool indeed to think it would not be so!' And she sent him out of the kitchen and out of her sight, rubbing his sore head as he went.

'Is his death so certain in the forest?' Yvaine asked, wide-eyed from this exchange.

Eugénie sighed and met her gaze with a troubled expression, 'If not death then certainly something near. But at least you know now where to look for him, though that blessing may be small. The forest is wide and deep, and I fear that even knowing he is within may still prevent you from ever finding him therein.'

Chapter 6

As soon as Beau's lips had touched the water, things had gone very strangely indeed. He now found himself lying in a narrow bed within a warm cottage, its walls draped with hanging tapestries and a clutter of objects in every corner of the room. The objects themselves were bizarre and wonderful, some made from precious metals and fine jewels, a golden spindle here, and a silver sword there, while yet others were ancient and rusting.

He was quite obviously in the keeping of a witch.

A frantic squeaking sounded from within a glass jar, and Beau saw that trapped within it was a small mouse with a crooked tail. He lifted the jar, and gently turned it over to release the mouse onto the floor, where it soon scampered out of sight through a crack in the wall.

The door handle moved, and the door opened.

Beau was able to keep himself calm and unaffected in appearance, when the witch entered the room, but his heart pounded a frantic staccato within his chest. She did not look terrible in appearance, actually rather average and unremarkable, but he could sense his danger as she approached.

'Who are you?' he asked.

The witch laughed. 'I am your future, your past, and your present, dear one. I am the warm glow of sunrise, and the last sigh of death. I am eternal. But you may call me Pyometra; it is a name that will do as well as any other.' Then she leaned towards him and hissed, 'I sicken the cats, you know, and turn their insides black and oozing.'

Beau recoiled from her breath in his ear, its unasked-for intimacy, and asked, 'Why do you have me here?'

'No need to thank me,' she said. 'I saved your life, and what a *pretty* life it is, indeed. And now it is mine.'

With that, she exited the room. Beau lay back and began to plan his escape.

It seemed clear that it would not be as simple as walking out of the cottage, but the first thing Beau did was try the door. He was not surprised when it would not open, but he was surprised indeed to find himself flung into the opposite wall to crash among the clutter. To his shame and disappointment, he lost consciousness and when he next awoke he was laying atop the bed once more.

The witch was standing nearby laughing, to herself or at him, he did not know which for sure.

'Foolish boy,' she said. 'As if I would let you leave me, when I have so lately got thee.'

'What will you do with me?' and as he asked the question, Beau felt a chill of fear. He had not heard many stories of witches capturing men, but what he had heard was never pleasant. He now wished he had listened more closely to the warnings he had been given in the village of B—.

'Such an impatient youth, so bold and full of vigour. His eyes are like coals, and his hair like ashes, I will have him dancing before spring!'

Beau gritted his teeth, and asked again 'What do you want with me?'

'I want to brush your hair,' she said, laughing again. 'And dress you like a king, and you will be a king of my kingdom, and all you see will be yours – though you and yours will be mine, of course.' She looked at him with scrutiny and then he was dressed inexplicably in satin, lace, gold and jewels. The witch clapped her hands in delight. 'Exactly so!'

Beau ripped a bauble from his chest, and cast off a heavy necklace from around his neck, 'Enough of this! I am no plaything!'.

'Oh indeed you are not, my love,' the witch said. 'You are far more than that, I can see it clearly now as I did when first I laid eyes on thee. You are my beloved, and I will be beloved too, in time.'

He laughed himself in response to that, and was pleased to see the witch frown. 'Beloved of me? I scarce believe that capturing me against my will is grounds for a romance.' Then those words reminded him of a different captor, in a different time, and he despaired that he would ever be free to return to that one who was indeed beloved of him.

'You will love me soon enough, one way or another,' the witch said. 'Am I not beautiful? Am I not kind, to clothe and feed thee?' Indeed the witch was fair to look upon, but Beau did not trust his eyes to tell him the truth when there was magic so clearly at work around him. 'Let me show you how good I am, and you will love me.'

A table then appeared before him with a white cloth laid across it, and set with silver plates and cutlery. It was overflowing with all kinds of roast meats, stews and steaming breads.

'Eat as much as you will,' the witch said with a smile. 'But eat within the hour, as the table will disappear by the time it elapses.' She then left the room, leaving Beau with the feast before him.

Beau knew, however much his stomach churned and pained him, that he must not eat this enchanted food else he would be lost to the witch. It was all he could do lay back down on the bed and to turn to face the wall, but even then the smells tormented him. He stuffed the lace of his sleeve into his mouth to grind his teeth upon it in hunger and frustration, and waited until the hour finally elapsed and the table disappeared.

If indeed my only escape is in the finality of death by starvation, Beau thought, *then at least the witch will not have won.* He now thought that he understood much of what his brother had spoken of in the darkness of their shared bed that night, which at the time he did not comprehend. He wondered what Désiré was doing now, and then felt ashamed that he had not thought of him sooner. Part of him felt as though his twin was near, and with him, and had been since before the start of his foolish journey through the forest.

He lay in bed, feeling helpless and hopeless, dressed in foolish finery and with an echoingly empty stomach. It was rumbling so loudly that Beau almost did not hear the noise at the foot of his bed.

Chapter 7

Scratch, scratch, came the sound.

Scratch, scratch, once more.

Scratch, scratch, a third time, so that Beau knew it was no accident. He turned to look, and was bemused to see a mouse staring at him from the floor beside the bedpost, and realised it was the very same mouse from before with the crooked tail. To his further amazement, the mouse carried an object towards him and lay it beside the bed within reach before dashing off again. Where it had been was now a small cluster of berries.

When it reappeared it was carrying with it a hunk of bread. Then a third time, with a piece of cheese.

'Is this some trick of the witch?' Beau asked himself aloud, but the mouse replied with squeaks of indignation. 'So this food is safe to eat, and I will not be lost to her enchantments?' It indicated that this was so.

Beau picked up the meagre offerings, but to him it tasted better than any feast. He thanked the mouse, though feeling somewhat strange conversing with the creature, and then fell asleep. His dreams were lurid and bizarre, full of grotesque characters and scenes of anxiety and danger.

He awoke feeling no more rested than he had before he slept, but his did feel somewhat better from having had his few morsels of food.

When he woke he did not know whether it was day or night, as the darkness in this part of the forest was all-encompassing. He peered through the windowpanes, which were well-covered in frost which obscured his sight, but Beau did not attempt to see if the windows would open to admit him. It seemed safe to assume that any obvious means of escape would be unlikely to bear fruit.

When the witch appeared she looked at him with expectation, and when a moment had passed with no words spoken by either of them she narrowed her eyes.

'May I go outside of this room, and stand out of doors?' Beau asked. 'I am fearful for my sanity if I remain here much longer, so enclosed by walls.'

The witch said, 'I will need to bind you to allow it, my new beloved, to keep you safe and near.' No sooner had she spoken those words than golden chains encircled Beau's wrists and ankles over his absurd, and now wrinkled, clothing. Another chain wrapped itself coldly around his neck, and it stretched out to the hand of the witch who could now lead him like an unruly dog.

Any thoughts Beau had entertained of escaping during this outing now disappeared, but his hope was to at least see how the rest of the cottage was arranged, and where the exits lay.

As she led him through the doorway, Beau could see that the next room was a kitchen with a large, open hearth. It was equally as cluttered with strange objects as the room Beau was locked in. A shut door beyond must be the sleeping place of the witch, he presumed, passing by its door-frame. The witch then jerked his chain when his steps slowed, and he hastened to make a quicker pace as she led him out of the cottage.

Frost crusted the earth below him and his footsteps creaked underfoot as he shuffled out as best he could within the confines of his chains.

'I will leave you here with the wind for a short time,' she said, and Beau's heart leapt at the thought of a chance finally coming for his escape, but then she wove the golden chains around a strong tree trunk and they formed an unbroken circle. 'I have work to do,' she said. 'I must talk to the crows, and speak to the trees, and they will give me their council.'

When she had disappeared into the thick undergrowth, Beau first turned his attention to his chains. The golden metal was thick and un-yielding, and the chain links solid and held fast. Even if he were to free himself from his tether, he was still hobbled and unlikely to go very far or very fast.

So Beau sat heavily on the frosted ground, not caring that the bottom of his trousers, frilled and gleaming, were growing sodden and chilled. This was such a strange predicament and this conclusion, coming from a young man who had spent half a year in the company of a young girl changed into the form of a beast, was certainly no understatement. He could not escape, it seemed, though he would keep trying. And if he

236 | Arielle K Harris

failed? There was no one who knew his whereabouts, and no one would be looking for him.

Even if someone had known, who would have been able to save him? His parents were unsuited to such adventures, and his brother too well suited to his own. There was only one other that he knew, and he found himself fantasising about her wingbeats. He could imagine so vividly that he almost felt the turbulence from those vast feathered sails – but then he recalled himself. Yvaine was no powerful creature any longer, not taloned and hissing and imposing. In his mind's eye he could see her small, wan face hidden by its greasy mane of hair, her fragile limbs and delicate skin.

Beau could not expect Yvaine to come to his rescue, not the beast and not the girl. He may be captive of the witch for now, but he would keep his wits about himself and look out for the first chance of escape when it might present itself.

That night, once again, the witch called forth her enchanted table and left him to fill his belly with its tantalising dishes, but once again Beau turned his back and waited until it disappeared.

Scratch, scratch, came the scratching sound.

Scratch, scratch, again.

And *scratch, scratch*, a third time, after which Beau saw his new acquaintance, the mouse.

As it had the night before, the mouse gathered some small morsels of food into a small pile at the foot of Beau's bed which he accepted with grateful relief. This time, having more control of his appetite, he shared titbits with the mouse in a sense of camaraderie. The mouse made a surprisingly formal bow in return before scampering back through the crack in the wall, leaving Beau even more bewildered than before.

Chapter 8

The next morning the witch once again gave him a careful scrutiny in expectation, but was once again disappointed in what she had seen. Beau asked leave, once more, to be allowed outside and spent the day as the one before and was tethered to a strong tree.

'Listen to the clouds, my beloved,' the witch said to him. 'They will tell you secrets, but you must not tell another soul, not even the tadpoles in the stream, what they tell you.'

'Oh indeed,' Beau agreed, having grown tired of the witch's strange proclamations. He had some time ago come to the conclusion that she was completely, utterly mad.

'I once again need to do my work,' she spoke again, 'and must leave you for a time. The crows told me much, and the trees as well, but now I must consult with the stone and slug and yew and finch. It is a big working I must do soon, and you will see it then, my beloved, what the product of all my endeavours has been.'

Beau did not like being left alone with his thoughts, as they turned to despair quickly. It was some relief to be out in the cold wind and the damp earth, and not locked in that room, but he wished for nothing more than to have his limbs and body freed. He would have sprinted into that forest as quickly as a stag, and even if he were to remain lost and starving for all the end of his days he would have considered his state a blessed one.

Strange that he would think so after enduring captivity, which he had been willing to prolong had circumstances not changed everything. But he had never truly felt like a captive at Castle Beaumont. He was certainly a captive here, chained and kept against his will.

On that third night, Beau once again resisted the enchanted table's fare. He lay on the bed and picked at the frayed lace on his sleeve, now lank and greying from wear.

The door flew upon, and the witch appeared.

'Aha!' she cried, pointing a long finger in his direction. 'I knew that you have been resisting me, I could tell by your eyes, your breath, and your unchanged heart.'

Beau sat up quickly, 'I, well, I just finished. It was very good.'

'And my beloved now lies to me,' she said. 'He lies, and not very well at all. But I will change his heart, by force if I must. I have finished my work, and now I am ready to cast aside the veil of this world and to make my will be done.'

Beau tried to speak, to ask what she meant, but he could not move. The witch reached into her pocket and brought out a handkerchief that was dripping red with blood. From within lay nestled several small organs atop a scattering of leaves.

'Heart of crow and heart of finch,

The ties that bind and tear and pinch.

Heart of frog and heart of fish,

He who is beloved of a witch

Make her beloved of him too,

Leaf of ash, and birch, and yew.'

The witch tipped the contents of the handkerchief in her mouth, and swallowed.

'My beloved, how dost thou feel?' she asked.

'Very well, my love,' Beau said. 'And all the better now that you are with me.'

By the foot of his bed lay a small pile of nuts and a single small apple, but Beau did not see it. His eyes, heart and mind were clouded by magic.

Chapter 9

Yvaine travelled through the villages on foot, having left Commodité in the hands of the youth Garçon who promised to look after him as penance for having directed his master on such a foolish journey in the first place. She followed the trail of Beau's recent passage and found that he was well-remembered by the people who lived there. To the comments offering concern about her passage alone through these wild parts, she told them that she was the sister of the beautiful man in question, and that they had become separated on their journey. As such she was able to explain her questions about his whereabouts and also ensure her appearance of propriety.

However, at the final village of B——, the last bastion of civilisation before the encroachment of the forest and its total claim of the countryside, Yvaine was confronted with the dilemma she had not wanted to consider until this point.

'How on earth shall I find him in there?' she asked herself on the very outskirts of the village, looking into that green space and feeling very much as if it were looking back at her. It was suddenly clear to her how vast and dense the wild places were in this part of the country, and obvious to her that an aimless search would bear no fruit.

She went back to the interior of the village and into the small tavern that was also its inn and its stables, and housed the communal oven where the people would leave their uncooked loaves in the evening before to collect, baked and steaming, the next morning.

'Good day, my dear,' the innkeeper's wife said as Yvaine entered the common room, cleaning tankards beside her husband the innkeeper who was tending to the casks. 'Are you looking for lodging?'

'I will not be staying so long,' Yvaine said, 'or so is my intention, at least. I will be going west from here to seek my brother who must have passed through your village and into the forest not too many weeks ago.' By now the lie slipped easily off her tongue, and she did not even blush to speak so.

'Your brother?' the innkeeper's wife repeated. 'Is he, by chance, an uncommonly handsome man?'

'So you have seen him,' Yvaine spoke, and her words were so wry that the innkeeper laughed.

'I suppose you must be used to hearing that, mademoiselle,' the innkeeper spoke, 'having grown from a child with such observations. Do not take it to heart, my dear, as you are very pretty yourself.' His wife gave him a pointed glare, which he coughed and shrugged off.

'Oh,' Yvaine said, suddenly awkward, 'thank you.' She could not remember anyone commenting on her appearance before, apart from her mother with her biased maternal eye. It was somewhat unsettling, she decided, and she did not care for it at all.

The innkeeper's wife then turned to her and said, 'So you are seeking your brother? Yes, he left here some weeks ago, though we have often worried about his journey. He would not be counselled to change his course, no, he had to leave immediately and directly west through the forest.'

'Yes,' Yvaine agreed. 'He was particularly set upon that route. I was hoping to discover what path he might have taken in the woods, and how I might set about catching up to him.'

The innkeeper's wife gave her a look filled with pity. 'My dear, there are no paths in the woods in these parts. I could not direct you with any certainty, nor could anyone in B— as we simply do not enter the woods.'

'No one?' Yvaine asked.

'Betimes,' the innkeeper spoke with lowered voice, 'our young men have gone, in the past, to prove their daring. And, long ago, it was a favoured spot for huntsmen to make their trade, as the forest is full of deer and wild boar and fowl. But too often our men, especially those who were fairest of face, simply never returned. No one goes into the forest any longer for fear of what might befall them.'

'You would be safe enough,' his wife said, 'with a face like a kicked badger.' She spoke the words with a straight face and laughing eyes.

'One of these days, woman,' he replied, 'I will go into the woods willingly, just to escape your sharp tongue!'

His wife laughed, and carried on her cleaning. This was obviously not the first time they had had this particular repartee as Yvaine watched with wide eyes and some amusement.

'I am very sorry, mademoiselle,' the innkeeper said, remembering her presence. 'We did warn your brother but he would not heed the danger. I wish we could be more helpful, but not a man among us would enter that cursed place.' He then heaved the cask onto his shoulders, and disappeared down into the cellar.

The innkeeper's wife drew near to Yvaine's side and spoke to her in a lowered voice, 'Indeed, not a man among us would go, but there is a woman.'

Chapter 10

'A woman?' Yvaine asked, keeping her own voice quiet.

'Forgive me for not speaking up earlier, but my husband is a foolish man – an honest fool, but no less foolish for it. He does not like to hear of her, nor would he like it should he learn that all the game on our table and in our cookpot comes from the product of her trade. Her name is Diana, and she is the huntress. You must wait, however, until this evening when all the village men come to drink my husband's ale and get senseless together. When he is so occupied, and unlikely to notice my absence, I shall take you to her.'

Yvaine nodded and agreed to wait until that evening. While she waited, the innkeeper served her a stewed fowl which Yvaine paid for generously out of her still-heavy purse. She had brought too much, she realised, but had not known the cost of things, never having needed to know such a thing when she was a girl, and even less as a beast.

When the village men had gathered together in the common room and began to get boisterous, the innkeeper's wife caught Yvaine's eye. They left together into the cold night, and soon exited the boundaries of the small village.

248 | Arielle K Harris

'She keeps a cottage far from all others,' the innkeeper's wife spoke as they began to follow the line of the forest to the north. 'And I cannot blame her for that. The men both fear and desire her, and that is not a good combination. From what she has told me, she even sleeps with a knife beneath her pillow and has had to use it.'

Yvaine did not have any words to speak in reply to that, but the older woman chattered on about this and that, seemingly needing no input from her, as they approached the glow of a lit window ahead. Dogs barked as they drew near, wood smoke hung heavy and fragrant in the night air above the cottage. The innkeeper's wife knocked twice on the door.

'It is Mira,' she called out as she knocked. 'I do not wish to be greeted with steel,' she said to Yvaine in explanation.

The door opened, and the woman who stood there made Yvaine stare, and then blush to be caught staring. She could not help it, though, so remarkable was the other woman's appearance. She was taller than any woman Yvaine had ever seen, though not mannish in the slightest. Beside her stood two enormous wolfhounds who stood at tense alert until their mistress dismissed them with a word of command.

'Sorry to disturb you so late, Diana,' the innkeeper's wife said when they were admitted into the cottage. Its interior was warm and furnished with fur and antler and the smell of leather and dog fun. 'But this is, Yvaine and she is a traveller to these parts who needs a guide through the forest to seek her brother.'

'You wish to go into the forest to find your brother?' the tall woman asked, fixing dark eyes on Yvaine's face.

'Yes, my brother,' she said, and as she spoke those words she knew that the other woman could see that she was lying. 'He entered the woods some weeks ago, and I know he has come to harm.'

'If that is so, he must already be lost to *her*, and there may be no helping him.'

'Her?' Yvaine asked. 'Who?'

'The witch,' the huntress spoke with venom. 'That she-daemon herself.'

'Is it really true, then?' the innkeeper's wife asked with wide eyes.

'I have seen her myself, though only briefly. She takes her tithe of men and what she does with them I cannot say, but they never return home again. Your brother is likely dead.'

'Then lead me to his body, and the witch herself, so I may revenge his death.' Yvaine asked, feeling suddenly chilled with foreboding.

'I will not go seeking this sorceress on a whim,' the huntress said. 'It means pitting oneself against dark magic and that is not a thing to be done lightly.'

'I do not ask lightly,' Yvaine said.

'It is winter, besides,' Diana continued. 'It would be madness to attempt this even with a party of experienced hunters, all of whom familiar with the dangers of the forest. To take you would require that I take on the roles of both woodswoman and nursemaid, and I simply do not care to be responsible for your life in that way.'

'Then I will not hold you responsible.' Yvaine countered, but the huntress was still shaking her head. 'Fine, then I will compensate you sufficiently to set your conscience at ease.'

Diana looked at her sharply and asked, 'How much?'

Yvaine tipped out her purse onto a table. 'However much this is, it is yours if we should succeed in finding my brother, alive or dead.'

The pile of coins sat in an inviting heap and the huntress measured it with keen eyes. 'To be paid up front,' she tried.

'Half now, half when it is done.' Yvaine held out her hand. The other woman hesitated for a moment longer before reaching out her own, and they clasped on the bargain.

'Very well, we will leave at first light and you may sleep here tonight so that I do not need to fetch you in the morning,' Diana said.

Yvaine nodded, and scooped half of the coins back into her purse, leaving the rest on the table.

The innkeeper's wife watched the exchange with open mouth, and Yvaine could almost hear her trying to work out how much she could have charged for the stewed fowl in light of the money she had just seen handed over so casually. Yvaine felt in her pockets for a collection of coins she had held back from the negotiations, and pressed them into Mira's hand.

'Thank you for your help,' Yvaine said. 'I honestly did not expect to find such generosity in strangers.'

'Good luck in finding your beautiful brother,' the innkeeper's wife said with a warm smile and a full palm before leaving the huntress' cottage. She considered it not to be a bad night's work, after all.

Chapter 11

Yvaine had spent a warm night huddled in a pile of furs by the hearth of the huntress' cottage, joined by the massive dogs who tried to spread across her body with sharp elbows and knees. She was obviously sleeping in their accustomed bed. Diana woke her at the first hint of dawn with a strong hand clasped on her shoulder.

'We had best leave quickly,' she said. 'There is a long way to go.'

Yvaine did not argue, seeing that she would be often conceding to the greater wisdom of the other woman so had best accustom herself to this way of thinking early on.

'You should be wearing boots,' Diana said, looking at Yvaine's fur slippers.

'I cannot abide the feeling of such constriction,' Yvaine said. 'These slippers are all I can bear to cover my feet with.'

'Whyever is that so?' the other woman looked at her askance. 'Are you addled somehow?'

'I suppose you might say that,' Yvaine said, unwilling to explain further and Diana simply gave her a searching look.

'We shall see how well you fare in them, I suppose,' she continued, 'and how long shall pass before you begin to find them insufficient.'

'I have travelled from beyond Princemont in them without trouble, but I shall not complain even if that which you say were to be so.'

'Very well.' Diana shouldered a canvas bag and strapped it to her back. 'I have already been to the village before you woke,' she said, 'and have purchased some food and supplies for our journey, which we will share. In addition, I have another bag here for you, into which I have divided our supplies between.'

Yvaine nodded, for she could see the wisdom of that arrangement, and copied the tall woman's manner of attaching the bag to her back, her own belongings now stuffed into the bottom of it.

'You must keep up with me,' Diana warned, as she added a quiver of arrows and a bow to her burdens, 'or I will leave you behind and you will be lost. If I tell you to do something, even if it seems strange, you must do it immediately. If you cannot agree to this, I cannot take you regardless of what we agreed on last night.'

'I will do as you say,' Yvaine said, though she chafed at being spoken to in this manner. She needed this woman's help, so she would not speak out of turn or in any way offend Diana during their journey. Her decision to be agreeable was starting to feel very hard to maintain.

Diana, her dogs and Yvaine left the cottage while mist was still clearing from the lowlands and the sun was not yet risen above the horizon. They broke their fast with hard cracker while they walked, but the thought of finally assuaging her guilt by finding Beau, at last, was all the salt Yvaine needed to make her meal flavoursome.

They walked in total silence, apart from the occasional sharp command to the dogs, in contrast to the chattering innkeeper's wife, but Yvaine preferred this. She was still not wholly comfortable in the company of other people.

'Wait,' Diana said, holding her hand up to indicate they must be still. Her dogs were alert and fixed on something ahead, and she drew her bow from behind her back and an arrow from her quiver. Yvaine looked closely and could see the young hare frozen still in the undergrowth. She felt her own muscles tensing, and a memory of muscles and sinews that she no longer possessed, as the arrow flew straight and true.

'We will eat well at noon,' Diana said, turning to address her. She looked at Yvaine with a look of puzzlement. 'Do you enjoy hunting?' she asked upon seeing the earnest expression, and the hunger, in the other woman's eyes.

'I do,' Yvaine managed to gasp as she forced her body to relax.

'Hm,' the tall woman sounded surprised. 'I would never have guessed.' She commanded the dogs to wait while she retrieved the hare herself and removed the arrow from its eye. 'What weapon did you use? Was it a bow, or a shotgun? Maybe a small hawk? You seem the sort of ladylike person who might have had a merlin upon your fist.'

'None of those,' Yvaine said, feeling in control of herself again. 'Although lately I have begun to instruct myself in the use of a rifle.'

Diana crossed her arms, the hare dangling still from one hand, and frowned. 'I feel almost as though you must be taunting me. Are you keeping some secret? I will not have secrecy on this journey; we must each trust one another enough to feel as though each is safeguarding the other's very life in this forest.'

Yvaine felt colour draining from her face. 'It is a secret which I fear to tell anyone at all, not yourself in particular.'

'You need not fear me, girl,' the huntress said. 'I do not judge others so easily as others have often judged me.'

'I cannot be certain of that, but if you must know I will tell you. And if you wish to leave me here to go on alone I will not blame you.'

'Go on, then,' Diana said with narrowed eyes.

'I have been until recently under an enchantment,' Yvaine said, watching the other woman carefully, but Diana made no change to her expression. 'For the last decade or thereabouts I was not a girl at all, but an inhuman beast in the form of a griffin.'

'A griffin?'

'Yes.'

'Head of an eagle, and body of a lion?'

'Just so.'

Diana began to laugh, full-bodied and vigorous, and Yvaine felt all her colour flooding back. 'I do not share this to be mocked!' she cried, and turned fully prepared to retrace her steps back towards the village.

She could find herself another guide, she decided, and one far more polite than this one.

'Wait, girl!' the huntress called after her. 'I do not laugh with mockery, please do not mistake me. I laughed in honest delight.'

'My name is Yvaine, not *girl*,' Yvaine spat. 'And I am glad that you are delighted by the condition which has given me only pain and torment.' She quickened her steps.

'Wait, Yvaine, wait! I did not mean to upset you, truthfully. Please forgive my unthinking offense, it was not meant as such, but then I have been told before that I speak quickly and well before I consider the impact of my words.'

Yvaine slowed her pace.

'And truth be told,' Diana said, 'I am actually rather jealous. I have often dreamed of being the fiercest predator in the forest, but have always woken to the sad truth of my actual limitations.'

Yvaine turned back. 'I do miss my old form at times,' she said. And then, quieter, 'More times than I would be happy to confess.'

'Would you mind, perhaps, telling me what it was like?' The huntress asked her with naked interest as they resumed their pace through the forest. And so they passed the first day of their travelling through the forest in companionable conversation as the trees grew thicker and the light grew dimmer with every step they took, and Yvaine told the huntress how it was to be hunting from aloft on silent wings.

Chapter 12

It was now fully night, though the darkness had been growing for some hours.

'We will build a fire,' Diana said when they could no longer see the ground and its obstacles. 'It may give us away to the unnatural dwellers of the forest, but it will keep away those natural predators which are more likely to find us and do us harm at this peripheral edge of the woods.'

As they sat before the comforting glow of the fire, Yvaine said, 'Now that you know all there is to know about me, might I know likewise?'

The other woman considered this. 'It is only fair enough, I suppose. I, too, keep my past a secret, but it would be poor form to have demanded such honesty from you only to repay you with falseness.'

'Indeed it would be,' Yvaine said, 'and I would be very cross if that were so.'

'Very well,' Diana said. 'Then it must be said. I am in truth a king's daughter, from a country far from here.'

'I was not expecting that!' Yvaine could not help but laugh in surprise. 'A princess, here dressed in leather and furs, leading me into the dread forest!'

'Then we are now even, for I no more expected my companion to have once been dressed in feathers.'

'Far more common to be dressed in feathers than silk and gold,' Yvaine said. 'Why are you now a huntress, and here in a land not your own?'

'Because my father, the king, was a foolish man who liked to wager. He enjoyed setting challenges to any man who approached him, and was so confident in his own supremacy that he wagered my hand in marriage to whomever could best him. When a man then won the wager I refused to be his wife and handed off so casually. It was not the fact that he was a common man which irked me most, it was the fact that my own father so poorly valued my person as to make me a prize. I left and will never return,' Diana said, and she frowned into the fire.

'I, too, refused to marry the person my parents had chosen for me,' Yvaine said. 'I could not see then, nor do I see now, the benefit to a woman to be married. A man might gain lands and heirs, but a woman does not gain either. Why, then, must we be subject to it, and accept the dominion of our husbands? I will never marry,' she avowed.

Diana watched her as she spoke, and now asked, 'And what if you find a man you love, and wish to remain with for the rest of your life?'

Yvaine said, 'I will chain no man to my side forever, but if he wished to stay I would not stop him.'

'There are times when a spoken vow is more than mere shackles. It tells the world that this person is yours, and you are theirs. There is pride in that, and comfort. Marriage can be a joyful state.'

'Then why did you not marry,' Yvaine asked, unmoved, 'if it were such a desirable situation?'

'I did,' the huntress said, but suddenly growls of warning came from her canine companions, and the earth began to tremor and shake beneath them. Diana swore.

'What is it?' Yvaine asked with widened eyes.

'It is a giant approaching,' the huntress replied. 'I was wrong about our safety here. Follow my lead, and do not run.'

Yvaine nodded, but the blood in her veins turned to ice and her teeth set to chattering in fear. She had never seen a giant but had heard tales of their ruination, turning whole towns to rubble when provoked into a foul temper.

'What dost thou want here, thou tiny flies?' came a voice like thunder above them. Legs thicker than the thickest tree trunks spanned higher than the fire's glow could illuminate.

'We are but warming ourselves before continuing on our way,' Diana replied. 'We will be gone from here before you can blink.'

'Before I can blink!' the giant staggered a step back, cracking several old pines in two. 'What wizardry is this?'

Diana whispered an aside to Yvaine, too quiet for the giant's ears to catch, 'Giants are strangely literal, and they fear that which they do not understand, very much like men in that regard. Do as I do, and speak as I speak, if it should address you directly.'

The giant seemed to gather itself sufficiently, and spoke again, making the loose rock around the two women shiver and disperse itself across the ground from the rumbling above. 'If thou wishest to stay here, little insects, first I must ask a toll of thee; go and fetch me a jug of water before I should blink and lose thou from my sight.'

'Had I not better bring the whole stream itself at once, and streambed, too?' Diana asked.

'What!' the giant cried. 'The whole stream, and the streambed, too? This taller of the small ones must be powerful indeed, be on thy guard, old giant. Best to discover if the smaller of the small ones is likewise.' It addressed Yvaine directly now, 'I would needest meat with my water, would thou shoot two or three wild boars for my supper with those arrows beside thee?'

Yvaine swallowed. *I have been a creature out of a nightmare who would have been able to give this giant a beating in a fight, so speak boldly and do not be afraid*, she thought in the space of an instant. 'Why not have a thousand at one shot, and all of them brought here before you?' she asked.

'What!' cried the giant again in great terror. 'A thousand in a shot? Let well alone tonight, old giant,' it said. 'Blink, and pray that thou tiny wizards indeed leave thy sight!'

'Be ready,' Diana warned, gripping Yvaine by the hand. They each looped their arms through the straps of their bags and belongings, so that as soon as they heard the sound of the giant's enormous eyelids shutting, like that of the sails of a windmill passing over, they sprang from the ground and into the cover of the forest, with the cowering wolfhounds running beside them in step.

Chapter 13

Yvaine, Diana and the dogs passed the night huddled together in the shelter beneath a stony outcropping, and awoke at dull daybreak with caution.

'You did well,' the huntress spoke as they broke their fast with dry bread. 'Let that be the first lesson of the forest. We must never let our guard down, and must always keep our wits.'

'How did you learn the weakness of giants?' asked Yvaine over a mouthful.

'You learn quickly, or die quicker, in the forest.'

Yvaine considered this. 'Do you suppose that Beau – my brother, that is – would have come afoul of such a creature?'

Diana shook her head, 'If any young men enter the forest they are picked out by the witch near as soon as they step one foot within. She then follows them like a hungry wolf, waiting for the right moment of weakness in which to make her move. If a witch has marked a man, no other creatures in the forest would dare interfere.'

Yvaine watched the huntress and was suddenly certain of a dreadful notion. 'Your husband,' she stated baldly. 'Is this what befell him?'

Diana chewed her bread slowly. She swallowed, and spoke, 'I came to B— because I sought a place of utter solitude, and it seemed the most insignificant kind of backwater village where simple folk lived simply and without intrigue. It was a perfect place to disappear. I did not seek out love, if anything I deliberately repudiated it, but that is often when it finds you.'

'What happened?' Yvaine prompted the other woman, when she had been silent for too long to bear.

'He was taken.'

'Did you not go after him?'

'I could not,' Diana said, 'not quickly enough, at least. I was no huntress then, it was he who was the huntsman. I beseeched the other men to help me, or at least teach me what I needed to know, but they laughed and would not lend their aid. I went into the forest nonetheless, but I got lost and could not find my way. Weeks later I found myself back on the edge of the village, having gone in circles and near death from starvation. By the time I recovered to try again it was too late. Another man had been taken, and it was known that the witch only ever took one captive at a time. My beloved was lost.'

'I am so sorry,' Yvaine said. 'I do not know what to say.'

'Nothing needs to be said,' the huntress smiled sadly. 'It was a long time ago now. I hope we can have a happier outcome for you.'

'I feel such impatience to find him quickly,' Yvaine said, feeling suddenly grim and ill at ease.

'It will not be very quickly, I am afraid to say,' Diana said. 'The witch lives some distance into the deepest, darkest part of the forest.'

'Deeper and darker than this?'

'It is so,' said Diana. 'You would not know if it were day or night, and never see stars from one night to the next.'

'Then I suppose we must not waste any more of this paltry day-light,' Yvaine said, standing. They gathered their belongings and were soon on their way.

As they walked, Diana spoke, 'Who is this Beau? I think we can both leave off pretending that he is your brother, as there is certainly no need to affect some idea of propriety here in my company.'

Yvaine was caught out mid-step, and stumbled in her distraction. 'He is a young man I know,' she said.

'Clearly,' Diana said. 'That much I figured out for myself. What is he to you?'

'He was at first my captive,' she spoke again with difficulty. 'When I was a beast he was my servant.'

'And now you go through all of these trials to save your servant? He must have been a remarkable one, indeed.'

Yvaine turned to see the huntress' smile, but it was not mocking. 'He became more than a servant, by the end. He was my friend, and my beloved.'

'I thought as much, indeed,' Diana said. 'But how does a beast befriend a man? How does it love him?'

'By first deciding not to eat him,' Yvaine said, 'and after that, the rest was simple. With the right man, love is not a difficulty, it is as simple as choosing to remain where he remains, to be each other's companion and friend. His goodness of character, and my enjoyment of his company, did the rest. His kindness, his sincerity, and his compassion towards the inhuman beast I once was – it was remarkable.'

'Then why is this remarkable, kind, sincere, compassionate man not with you, then?'

'You do ask a lot of questions, king's daughter!' Yvaine wrapped her arms across her chest, warming her fingers against her body. 'But, if you must know, I sent him away when I became human.'

'Why did you send him away? If your love was simple, why choose to be where he is not?'

'How can love exist between two people who no longer know each other? I changed into this person you see before you, and I did not even know who that is. I still find myself looking for paths into the sky, or living flesh to nourish myself with, and I long to spread wings I no longer have.' As she spoke those words she felt that longing, and her throat constricted with grief for what was no longer possible. 'I sent him back to his duty so that I could discover who I truly was, or am now.'

Still the huntress asked her questions she did not want to answer, 'Had Beau changed his mind about you, in your human form?'

It took a few moments for the passage of her throat to clear, but when it did Yvaine said, 'He claimed it was no difference to him.'

Relentlessly, 'And you think he lied, then?'

'I do not think he lied, or intended to lie, as he is as honest a man as ever there was, but he must have been fooled by his goodness into believing it was so,' Yvaine told Diana, and told herself. 'He may have found, in time, that he was now beholden to love a stranger.'

Mercilessly, 'How can you know that?'

'How can you not?' Yvaine cried. 'You ask too much, king's daughter or no. I cannot suffer this anymore! Leave me alone!'

'I will leave off,' Diana said. 'Only do consider that, from what you told me, your form changed but not the person who was inside, when you first became a beast. Why would it be differently when you changed back?'

Yvaine would not speak again, as this was the very question that plagued her waking hours since that day, and they walked in silence for some time. They spent their days in walking and their nights in a state of exhausted wariness, taking their sleep in turn.

One day, near the fullest height of the sun, as close as they could guess without seeing that orb itself through the tree branches, and they came to a small pond among the trees where a duck was swimming. Diana drew her bow but, before she could shoot, the duck saw her and cried out, 'Please spare me!'

'Oh,' she said. 'Of course, forgive me for almost making a meal out of you, little duck.'

'It was an honest mistake,' the duck said. 'I will not forget your mercy.'

'Much obliged,' Diana said, and the duck flew away. When it had gone out of their sight, she spoke to Yvaine, 'Rule number two of the deep forest: never kill anything that can speak.'

Yvaine nodded. Just when she had thought she was feeling unsurprised by this place, she found herself again mistaken. 'I will remember that,' she said.

Another day, when the walking began to blur together, the dogs began to dig beside an old, hollow tree. From within the hollow a resounding hum was heard, and it was clear that a great hive of bees was within.

'Leave it!' the huntress called off her dogs, who immediately turned and left the hive in peace. 'Rule three of the deep forest,' she said to Yvaine, 'Do not anger that which may do you harm.'

They spent that night huddled in a small cave, empty of erstwhile inhabitants. It was secure enough that both Yvaine and Diana allowed themselves to sleep and the dogs proved themselves adequate guards against the natural predators of the forest. They growled only once at a passing creature, but the night passed unremarkably otherwise.

They broke their fast solemnly and silently with handfuls of nuts and dry cracker. Diana felled two rabbits, after first calling a halloo to them and getting no reply. She gave one each to the dogs as a reward for their good service, who ate better than the women that morning.

Yvaine noticed a line of little black ants upon the rocks of the cave and as she felt little appetite, especially for such dry and unappetising fare, she crumbled most of her cracker and gave it to the insects on a whim.

Diana saw her act, and nodded, 'Rule number four of the deep forest, if you can do a kindness to another living creature, however small, then do. And ants are useful friends indeed. But on the same token, re-member rule number five: never accept food from someone you do not trust. Enchantments can lie within, and can trap you as neatly as an iron cage.'

And so they went on, and it was seeming to be another day like the one before, and the one before, and all those prior, with endless green and shadows. Then the dogs growled, Diana stopped still, and Yvaine looked up from her frowning contemplation of the unending forest floor.

A small man stood in their path, no taller than a child, with his long grey beard touching the pointed tips of his shoes.

'What dost thou here?' he asked with a grumble. 'These woods are not for the likes of thee.'

Chapter 14

'Forgive us, little gnome,' Diana said. 'We were just passing through.'

'Perhaps thou were once passing, but not any longer. None who go by this way may continue, until they satisfy me.'

'What trials do you ask of us, then?' Diana asked with impatience. 'I know your kind too well.'

'Harrumph!' he grumbled again. 'Such insolence! For that there will be not one but three tasks I ask of thee.'

'Oh, go on then,' Diana said, crossing her arms.

'First thou must retrieve this key,' and he flourished a small, bright brass key from beneath his beard, 'from out of yonder well.' They saw that they were beside the gnome's little thatched hut, and that indeed a small well stood not far from where they stood, into which the gnome threw the key. After a moment, they could all hear a small splash when the key entered the water, a good distance down.

Diana and Yvaine stepped towards the well, but the huntress drew the other woman close and whispered to her. 'Do not lean over the well,' she said, 'or that little man will throw you in,' so they both stood beside the well, but did not lean over.

'I have little patience!' the gnome said, crossing his little arms and tapping the foot of one stumpy leg.

'Give us but one hour,' Diana said, and the gnome stamped his feet, but agreed to leave them for the hour, and disappeared inside his little hut.

'Surely there is a winch?' Yvaine asked, looking closely at the well. 'Or even a rope?' But there was neither winch nor rope to assist them. The dogs lay down in the sun and took a nap, unconcerned about the trials of their human companions.

'Lazy hounds,' Diana said with affectionate exasperation. She unstrapped her bag from her back and looked within, and said, 'I do indeed have some rope, but I fear it may not be long enough.' They uncoiled the length of it, but it was indeed too short to reach the water of the well.

'If one of us goes in,' Yvaine said, 'we will not be able to come out.' And so they returned to their contemplations.

Then a noise overhead made them look up. They saw a duck flying low towards them, and it was that very duck Diana had spared some days earlier at the pond.

'I heard the whole of it,' the duck said, 'and, as I do not like to leave a favour unclaimed, I will fetch you that key in an instant!'

And having said so, it made no hesitation to do exactly that and dropped down into the well. Having gained the key, it was able to fly directly out again and drop the key on the ground between Yvaine and Diana.

'Thank you!' said the women to the duck, and they waved it goodbye as it flew back into the forest again.

When the gnome reappeared before them they placed the little key in his little palm.

'Harrumph!' he grumbled, but could not argue that the task had been completed. 'Now for the second task I put before thee. If thou wishest to pass, then gather every single grain of rice from the leaves and stones, and but only the rice alone, and place them back within this bowl!' From beneath his beard, the gnome produced a wooden bowl of rice, which he scattered across the leaf-strewn, stony, and twig-scattered earth at his feet.

'We will need an hour again, at least,' Diana said.

'I will not be so lenient again,' the gnome replied. 'Thou must complete this task in half the time of the last!' And so they had only a half hour to gather the rice.

When the gnome had gone back inside his little hut, Diana once more opened her bag and looked within.

'Perhaps I have a sieve,' she said. 'Or some fine mesh.'

While the huntress sorted through their supplies, Yvaine knelt on the ground and began to pick out each grain of rice she could see amongst the leaf litter.

276 | Arielle K Harris

'This could take all day,' she sighed. 'Certainly longer than a half hour. I do not know if we can complete this task. Maybe we will be the gnome's servants after all.'

Then, out of the corner of her eye, she saw a troop of ants marching towards her, and they were the same little black ants from the cave. They swarmed through the leaf litter and picked up every grain of rice therein, and placed them back inside the wooden bowl with precision.

'Very useful friends indeed,' Yvaine said.

'What?' Diana looked up from her bags and saw the neat lines of tiny insects gathering the rice. 'Oh! Well that is very helpful indeed!'

So when the gnome came out of his little hut they handed him back his wooden bowl of rice.

'Harrumph!' he grumbled, and stamped his feet, but he could not argue that the task was not done. 'Now, for the final task thou needest to complete, I will set you the most difficult of all! If thou wishest to pass then finally copy in wax the whole of my house, with everything that pertains to it, moveable or immovable, within and without. If thou should not complete this final task, then I shall imprison thee for ever to a life of dismal drudgery!'

With those words he took them inside his home and let them have a look within to observe his dwelling.

'Mark it well,' he said. 'For either it will be your masterpiece, or your prison. I have long wished for a domestic, but had not counted on a chance at two, to sweep, sew and cook for me!' His cackling laughter filled the room, from its frayed carpets to its dusty shelves.

Diana and Yvaine both shuddered at the thought, and looked around themselves apprehensively.

'We will certainly need an hour for this, if not longer,' said Diana.

'I shall not be so lenient again,' the gnome replied. 'Thou must complete the task in half the time of the last!' And so they had a quarter of an hour to make a model of the gnome's little hut.

When he had shooed the women from his home, remained inside and left them without, they began to survey the outside of the little hut and contemplate the impossible task in front of them.

'I think I would have rather stayed with the giant,' Yvaine said. 'At least it did not mention anything about cleaning. It could have just trod on us and that would have been a kinder end.'

'It is not over yet,' Diana said, and she pointed into the trees where a great buzzing sound grew nearer and nearer. It was the hive of bees, which she had saved from the dogs' destruction, flying between the branches towards them.

The bees descended into the gnome's little hut, to the sounds of indignation and alarm from within, and then quickly returned, having performed their observations. While the women watched, the bees set to work and soon the thatched hut was recreated in every detail, inside and out, with every object within exactly as it was.

When the gnome returned, rubbing his neck free of lingering beestings, he was smug with confidence that the women would not have done as he had asked. When he beheld the perfect replica of his hut in wax he stamped his little feet, threw himself to the floor and howled in outrage. The women had completed his final task and that he now had no power over them, so he would have to sweep his own floors after all.

Diana and Yvaine linked hands and fled, with the two well-rested dogs at their heels.

Chapter 15

When they could no longer hear the tirades of the gnome, and were a good distance from his dwelling place, Yvaine said to Diana, 'What other bizarre creatures might we find ourselves confronted with in this forest? I feel I am unpleasantly unprepared for these chance meetings, and need a more thorough education on the dangers around us.'

'You used to fly on wings, and you call these creatures bizarre?' Diana laughed. 'The greatest danger of the forest is that you simply cannot predict what you might find here. There are some known dangers, from the wolves to the giants to the gnomes, but then there are others we will not know until we see them. The forest is too large, and these creatures hide well.'

They continued for a time until Yvaine spoke again, 'Can you at least tell me with certainty how long it will take to reach this witch who has Beau? It seems as though we have been walking for weeks by now.'

'Indeed, it has been near enough a fortnight,' Diana said. 'And it will be several more days, at least, before we are there. Our path has not been the most direct, out of necessity. From here, we need only to follow the stream against its current, and the witch's hovel will become apparent when we draw near.'

Yvaine sighed, but did not mention the state of her feet, well-blistered and chilblained within their fur slippers.

Another cold day dawned reluctantly between the narrow gaps of the tree branches above them. They woke with frost in their hair, glittering their eyelashes and making their very breath come with difficulty through nostrils frozen and numb. Diana hazarded a fire for cooking beside the banks of the slow-moving stream, fearing that otherwise they might have been unable to continue.

'Is it safe to have a fire today?' Yvaine asked through chattering lips, but her mouth watered at the thought of the grain and water porridge which was now being placed in a pot above the flames on a tripod of sturdy branches. She could not remember her last warm meal, or the last time she was warm at all.

'It is necessary, I think,' Diana said. 'We will be drawing attention to ourselves, perhaps, but we are safer in this proximity to the witch than we would have been further away. It is known that she reigns over this part of the forest, and few are bold enough to trespass.'

No sooner than they were about to ladle the porridge into bowls then a cracking twig alerted them to their company. The dogs stood with their hackles raised and growled low and menacingly.

'May I join you?' asked a male voice.

Yvaine's heart nearly stopped when she saw the tall, cloaked figure of a man standing near them, for his stance and proportions were achingly familiar. Then he stepped nearer and drew back his hood and revealed his face and, while he was a good-looking man otherwise, he had a most peculiar blue beard that marked him as out of the ordinary sort.

'Who are you?' asked Diana, standing with her hand on her knife hilt.

'I am called Fitcher,' the man said, smiling at his ease, 'and I am remarkably hungry. May I be so bold as to beg the kindness of strangers?' He was carrying a large basket on his back, like that of poor beggars gathering alms, which did invoke some small sympathy on the part of the women.

Yvaine and Diana looked at one another, their hesitation clear on each of their faces.

'Rule four?' Yvaine asked the other woman, who seemed to come to the same conclusion herself.

'If you can do a kindness,' Diana said, 'then do.' The stranger still smiled, and set his basket beside him.

Their porridge stretched to three portions, though somewhat unwillingly, and they all sat before the embers of the fire and warmed themselves likewise at once within and without.

'I do not often meet travellers through the woods,' Fitcher said, and he spoke in such a sweet voice and with such fine manners that the women began to relax.

'We are looking for my brother,' Yvaine said. 'He is being held by a witch nearby.'

'I am sorry to hear of it,' Fitcher said with much genuine sorrow. 'That is a great burden for a sister to bear, especially one so young and so beautiful.'

Yvaine squirmed a bit, uncomfortable with the attention being lavished upon her.

'Do you have siblings as well?' he now asked Diana.

'I have several,' she said in reply.

'But not held in these woods, I should hope,' he smiled warmly.

'Indeed not,' she said. 'They are far from here in my father's country.'

Fitcher's eyes lit up with interest. 'Are you, then, a king's daughter? I can see it now in your noble disposition and great splendour.'

Diana swore internally, having not intended to reveal herself to a stranger. Being in the company of Yvaine for so long had left her usual cagey habits and withdrawn nature long behind. They had finished eating some time ago, and had rinsed their bowls and the cookpot in the frigid water of the stream, so she said, 'We should really be going on our way,' and began gathering their bags together.

'No, you must not go so soon!' Fitcher protested. 'Or if you must, do let me accompany you. The daughter of a king should have an escort!'

'I am well escorted already,' Diana said, pointing to the panting dogs whose mouths revealed long, pointed canines. Yvaine knelt beside her and helped pack away their belongings.

'I am feeling very uncomfortable,' Yvaine whispered as softly as she could manage in Diana's ear.

'Myself as well,' Diana said in a similar fashion. 'I had forgotten rule five of the deep forest: that which seems too good to be true likely is.' Then, loudly, for the benefit of all present, 'We really must be going now, but it was nice to have met you.'

Fitcher's face fell dramatically, the very picture of regret, but he spoke with reluctance, 'Very well, it was indeed delightful to have met you. May I just be so bold as to kiss your hand, king's daughter?'

Diana was taken aback, but before she could reply her hand was swiftly claimed by the blue-bearded man who gave her a gallant kiss. As soon as his skin touched hers, she felt the strangest sensation come over her, and she found herself drawn into the large basket on Fitcher's back.

'Diana!' Yvaine cried out. The stranger moved with unworldly speed, and soon disappeared through the trees with the huntress as his captive. The dogs ran in pursuit of their mistress, leaving Yvaine completely alone in the deep, dark forest.

Chapter 16

When Diana was finally in control of herself again, she saw that she was in the foyer of a magnificent house. All around her were room after room filled with beautiful furnishings and glittering gold chandeliers.

'You will be happy here,' Fitcher told her as he drew her out of his basket. 'There is nothing but the very best of everything here, and you are now to be mistress of it all.' He took off his beggar's cloak and revealed his own magnificent garments beneath.

'Release me,' Diana said. 'I will not be your captive, even in a gilded cage.'

'I think, perhaps, that you may come to like it here,' Fitcher said with his customary smile. 'For you are now my new bride, and I do not like brides who are not obedient.'

'Then I fear that you will not like me at all!' Diana laughed in his face, but as she laughed she felt a powerful blow to her stomach. She gasped and clutched herself, and looked up at Fitcher but he was smiling just as warmly as before.

'I have great hopes for you, king's daughter,' he said. 'Your nobility should predispose you to be a genial, yielding sort of character.'

Diana laughed again, this time bracing herself for the blow, and said, 'Perhaps that is why I was such a poor princess! You will be very disappointed, indeed!' This time he struck her square on the jaw, and she fell to the floor. Blood welled up inside her mouth, which she spat onto the floor.

'You do not want me to be disappointed,' he said, and his fixed smile, which once seemed so warm, now set chills up Diana's spine. 'I am being very gentle with you now. You do not wish to push me.'

His eyes, behind the smile, were eyes Diana knew well for she saw them whenever she looked in the mirror. These were the eyes of some-one who was at ease with killing.

Fitcher led her up to an upstairs chamber where she was shown an enormous dressing room filled with beautiful gowns in every colour, style and size.

'Choose one that becomes you most,' he said, 'and meet me downstairs for dinner in one hour.'

Diana sat among all the silk and chiffon, dressed in her own un-washed furs and leather and homespun, and found herself giggling hyster-ically. It was not just the strangeness of the situation, or the threat on her body and even her very life, no, it was how much she simply did not care.

She came to the realisation, during her hysterics, that she had two choices. The first, that she could continue to provoke this man until he eventually killed her, or the second, that she play along as the obedient bride until the right moment came for her escape. As much as she was drawn to provocation, and the power she felt to be defiant, she knew that the best choice was the second. She would be the obedient bride while it suited her to be so.

In an hour Diana was sweeping down the staircase in a dress that glittered like the stars. She had even remembered how to arrange her hair on top of her head in a pleasing fashion, probably a style which was a decade out of date by now but it looked well enough. The only thing which marred her was the spreading bruise across her jaw. There were cosmetic powders enough to conceal it but Diana allowed herself a tiny rebellion, and left it unhidden.

Fitcher was waiting for her, and his smile grew only wider to observe her deep curtsey as she drew level with him. He offered her his arm, and she accepted with a light hand delicately placed. It felt remarkably odd to turn her well-used muscles to this use, cast off from her previous life.

'I am glad to see you have reconsidered your behaviour,' he said when he had pushed her chair in for her and taken his place across the table. 'Wine?' he offered her a crystal goblet.

'Please,' she accepted graciously, but made no move to drink. 'How could I resist the charming accommodation of this place, and its charming inhabitant as well!' She fluttered her eyelashes, she simpered, and she even giggled; it was mortifying but necessary, she told herself.

'I am so very glad to hear it, indeed,' he said. 'And just at the right time, as well. I am afraid that I must go on a journey for some time, and will be forced to leave you in the morning.'

Diana pouted. 'How long for?' she asked with every indication of true disappointment.

'I do not know, my bride,' he said. 'But I will leave everything here into your keeping while I am gone.' From within his breast pocket, he drew out a large key-ring. 'I will give you these keys now, for I have to leave quite early and am sure that I will be gone before you wake.'

Suits me just fine, Diana thought, but she kept her face a picture of regret.

'These are the keys for all the rooms in the house,' he said as he flipped over each one in turn. 'From the pantries, to the stores of gold and silver plate, to the strongboxes of jewels. There is the master key to all the apartments, and this one to the kitchens, and this one to the wardrobes. But as for this little one here,' he held up a small golden key, 'goes to the closet at the bottom of the stairs on the ground floor. You may go into every room you wish, and count every precious thing inside, for they are to be yours very soon, but you are forbidden from entering that closet. If you do not obey me in this then you cannot obey me in anything and I will exact my final punishment upon you. But if you do obey then we will be married with all haste upon my return and you will be mistress of this house and everything within it.'

Diana gave him her best simpering grin, fluttered her eyelashes some more and giggled like an idiot, secretly wanting nothing more than to stab the man across from her with her fork. She only wished she had been given a steak knife.

Chapter 17

Diana slept poorly in the enormous feather bed despite its comforts, her stomach rumbling with hunger, as she had touched none of the food laid out before her, merely cut it into smaller pieces and made the pretence of moving morsels from fork to knife. As such, when the master of the house walked past her door she was wide-eyed and aware of his presence. His footsteps slowed as he approached, but he did not enter her chamber and soon carried on down the hall.

Her bare feet recoiled from the cold wood floor at first touch, but she slid out of the coverlet and crept to the window at the sound of the front door closing, a heavy lock bolting and a bar thudding into place. It was clear that she would not be leaving that way.

Her breath stirred the curtain, and she clapped her hand to her mouth as Fitcher came into view. He was wearing his beggar's cloak and basket again, and soon he was lost between the trees and out of her sight. Only then did she feel herself relax, and begin to breathe easily.

The first thing she did was to dress herself back into her old clothes, paying no mind to how badly they smelled. It made her feel stronger to be back in leather and fur again; chiffon was a poor armour.

The ring of keys lay on her nightstand, and Diana picked them up to inspect each. The tiny gold key winked in the dim light. In order for her to find an escape route she would need to look in all the rooms and apartments within the house, so she pocketed the keys and went into the hall.

All of the upstairs apartments were much like one another and it was not clear which, if any, was the resting place of her captor. They were all hung with glittering tapestries, and furnished luxuriously with high backed chairs, chaise-lounges, and dressing tables. The wardrobes were as full as the one in Diana's room with various beautiful garments within. The chimneys were all too narrow to admit her, and all of the windows were nailed shut. Even if the glass panes were broken it was a hazardous drop into thorny shrubs and jagged rocks on all sides. It was treacherous and possibly fatal to consider it as an escape route, so Diana left it as a reserve plan. Possible death would be better than certain lifelong imprisonment, after all.

There were no further rooms on this floor, and no further floors above, so Diana went downstairs to the main living quarters. She went from parlour to dining room to sitting room, and saw only decorative frivolity and excess in every one: damask cushions atop silken sofas, gilded portraits on every wall, and mirrors large enough to see oneself from head to toe. These rooms had windows that were nailed shut as well, only their panes were in a rather pretty lead latticework of small diamonds, so that breaking the glass would offer no possible escape through the tiny openings.

It was a beautiful cage, and Diana wondered if there had been others before her who had fallen under its enchantment. And if so, where were they now?

The next room she entered was a library and its shelves reached the full height of two grown men standing on top of each other. There were wheeled ladders spidering upwards, and high above came the source of the room's oddly-tinted light from an elaborate stained window as its ceiling. Everywhere she turned there were beautifully bound volumes with enticing titles and she ran a wondering finger down several of their gilt spines. The tomes were in many different languages, and they must have numbered in the thousands. It was simply magnificent.

She would have burned it all to the ground if it meant her freedom.

The next room Diana entered was the stronghold, and she opened each vault with her keys. One was filled with piles of gold and silver, and another filled with heaps of rubies and emeralds and sapphires. Diana found herself laughing, as she cupped the precious things in the palms of her hands, at the thoughts that came to her in that moment.

This house was designed perfectly to entice a person imprisoned in it into complacency. Offer her a king's ransom, and a scholar's learning, show her countless beautiful things and so surely something therein is bound to inspire her greed enough to overlook the fact that she is a prisoner. To overlook the fact that her captor is an abuser of women or, worse, to inspire false hope that she could change him, and make him treat her with kindness if only she would do his bidding and be an obedient bride. Riches enough could make someone willing to suffer plenty for the chance at material wealth.

She threw the jewels on the floor, and trod upon them as she left.

Next she found the kitchen and pantries, and they were as enticingly stocked as the rest of the house. Fresh bread cooled on the sideboard, cured meats hung from the rafters, wine and ale racked in casks against the far wall. There were baskets of apples, oranges and strawberries, and wheels of cheese sat invitingly beside them.

Then Diana saw the stairwell beyond and she descended to the ground floor. At the bottom of the stairs stood a simple door, with no embellishments apart from a gold-ringed keyhole which would fit a tiny golden key.

She had that key.

For a long moment Diana considered the door. *I will only take a look,* she thought, *after all, how would he know?*

The key fitted the keyhole exactly and with a smooth motion it turned the tumblers within the mechanism. The door swung slowly open, and the dim light made Diana squint as her eyes tried to adjust. She could not see from the stairs, it was too dim, so she stepped inside. All at once the room came into focus, and when it did it made her gasp. The key-ring fell from benumbed fingers, and she clapped both hands over her mouth to keep herself from screaming.

The room was full of dead women, dismembered into pieces. A great bloody basin stood in the centre of the room where the human remains were piled, and a block of wood lay beside it with an axe gleaming red. Smaller pools of blood lay in clots across the floor and arcs of red spray covered the walls.

Diana backed out slowly, and was about to leave, when she remembered the keys. With a shaking hand she knelt to retrieve them, only to find that they had fallen into a sticky pool of blood. She grabbed them, regardless, and locked the door again with trembling haste.

In the kitchen she scrubbed the keys in the sink again and again, but the blood would not be washed off.

'What is this magic?' she cried out. 'I will be betrayed by these damned bits of metal!' But nothing she tried would wash them clean. She wrapped the keys in a cloth and fled upstairs to her chamber to calm down.

'I must think,' she said. 'I must think clearly, and I will need a plan.' So Diana stayed in her room and planned and considered her predicament, and that was where she was to be found when Fitcher returned home that evening.

'I am returned!' he called as he entered the house, having unbarred the door and unlocked it. When he turned to lock the bolt again, Diana intercepted him with an embrace and prevented him from doing so.

'I am so glad!' she said. 'I was so lonely!'

Fitcher smiled down at her, 'I am sorry for your loneliness, my bride. You might never be alone again, now. Where are my keys?'

'Oh,' she said. 'I do not recall where I put them. I have been so enjoying your beautiful house that I do not believe I have picked them up at all.'

'Nevertheless, my bride, I will need them back to know if you have obeyed me while I have been gone.'

'I suppose they might still be in the library,' she giggled. 'I was spending so very long in there, reading so many fantastic books!' She indicated down the hall, and hoped he would lead the way.

'Let us go and look,' he said, but before he went down the hallway he turned and locked the front door. Diana suppressed a sigh. It would have to be the reserve plan, after all.

She made a big show of looking all around the library, lifting up books and checking under cushions and behind the curtains. 'Oh well,' she said. 'I suppose I did not leave them here, after all!'

Fitcher smiled, but she could see it was getting forced. 'Where, then, did you leave them, my bride?'

'They must still be on my nightstand,' she said brightly, attempting a vapid expression. Fitcher took her hand, somewhat harshly, and led her up the stairs to her chamber. She feigned a stumble or two, hoping to free herself, but his grip was strong as iron.

'There they must be!' she said, entering the room, and he released her to retrieve them. Instead of going to her nightstand, however, she made a sprint towards the window. The glass panes had already been smashed some hours earlier in preparation for this final confrontation.

Diana tasted the free air in her lungs at last, and gripped the wooden window frame to hoist herself through, hoping that her descent would not end too badly. But before she could clear the window she was intercepted, strong hands wrapped around her legs, which pulled her inside swiftly and made her hit the floor of the chamber with a shuddering force.

She must have been unconscious for a short spell because when she next opened her eyes she saw Fitcher before her, holding the bloody cloth with the keys.

'You have disobeyed me,' he said, and the words fell hard like physical blows. 'You have entered the forbidden closet against my will, and now you will enter it again against your own.'

He dragged her by her hair, and pulled her out of the room as she screamed and tried to wriggle free. She was thrown bodily down the stairs, and dragged again down the hallway below. Diana kicked her legs, twisted here and there, and raked her nails against his arms but could not free herself. Her hair tore from her scalp, but he caught yet more to hold her by. He then threw her down the last stairwell and she landed in a painful heap against the plain door with its golden keyhole. Her sides throbbed and jagged, and her every breath was an agony.

'I had higher hopes for you,' he said as he dragged her inside the bloody chamber. He pulled her head onto the wooden block, and hefted the axe over his shoulder. 'I thought you would be the one,' he said.

The last thing Diana saw was his blue-bearded smile before the axe fell.

Chapter 18

Yvaine swore as she stumbled again. It was difficult to manage both heavy packs at the same time, so she had ended up strapping one to her front as well as the one on her back. It meant that she could not see the ground directly in front of her, however, and she was constantly tripping over roots and stones.

She had survived the night on her own, unexpectedly. Without the company of Diana and her dogs Yvaine had not thought it would be the case, but she found her avian instinct to seek a high roost in times of danger proved a useful one. Using some ropes, she was able to pull the bags up into some branches and then hoist herself up among them after. It was an uncomfortable night, and she did not sleep, but she was safe from the natural and unnatural predators of the forest, at least.

In terms of unnatural predators, however, Yvaine was worried that she would never find the blue-bearded man who stole Diana away. She had fixed herself on the direction he had taken, but had no way of knowing if she was on his trail or not. Her own unfamiliarity in the forest kept her from being able to track him properly, and she was beginning to think it was a pointless exercise.

300 | Arielle K Harris

Crashing sounds through the trees startled Yvaine's heart into pounding hard in her chest. Thoughts about bears or wolves, or perhaps more giants, entered her mind as she stood there frozen to the spot, wearing her cumbersome bags fore and aft, barely able to walk sensibly, let alone run.

'This was a very poor decision,' she said to herself.

The crashing grew louder and nearer, and the undergrowth began to shake as whatever it was drew near. The leaves parted, and revealed a grey, shaggy two-headed beast that made her shriek with anxiety.

Then she laughed, because it was only Diana's two wolfhounds, searching for the trail that they, too, must have lost. They barely gave her a glance as they pressed their noses to the ground and sniffed here and there, but it lifted Yvaine's spirits immeasurably to see them.

It seemed like the dogs picked up the scent again, as they moved with renewed purpose through the forest, and Yvaine stumbled and tripped to keep up with them. She was soon perspiring from the haste and her uncomfortable burdens, but after several hours the trees thinned slightly to reveal a clearing, within which sat a grand house. It was a strange scene, as the house would not have been out of place in any cosmopolitan neighbourhood. To see it in the middle of a wild, untamed woodlands was a very odd picture to behold.

Yvaine remembered a command Diana had used, and bid the dogs to wait while she set down the bags. She turned the huntress' large bow in her hand, but put it aside soon after. It would have been next to useless to her and too awkward to carry to its owner, if this was indeed where she was being kept. Instead, she found two knives among the bags, and fixed both to her belt.

The first thing she did was to circle the mansion from the shelter of the trees and try to come to an understanding of what she was dealing with. It was as impregnable as a fortress, with no easy way to scale the outside even if she had that talent. The house itself was set in an immaculate border of lawn, forcing anyone approaching to expose themselves fully to the scrutiny of anyone within, though a thorny hedge sat among jutting stones at the very base of the structure.

The windows all appeared shut, and the front door firmly closed. There was one broken pane of glass from an upper window, however, which gave Yvaine a chill. Diana had either already acted out her escape or something else had happened to cause the window to break.

Movement at the front door made Yvaine duck behind a tree. When she peeked out from the trunk she saw the figure of Fitcher in his beggar's cloak and basket. She crept nearer as he busied himself with the door, and saw him rub at his face, after which he looked down at his hand and frowned. It had come away red.

Yvaine felt a flash of fury then, and her body moved of its own accord. She moved into the clearing, and cried out, 'Where is she?'

Fitcher looked up in surprise, but then smiled. 'Ah, yes, the dutiful sister looking for her brother. Are you now seeking your companion

302 | Arielle K Harris

as well? My word, you seem to have a habit of losing loved ones. One alone is a pity, but two is sheer carelessness.'

'There is blood on your face,' she said.

'I must have cut myself when shaving,' he replied smoothly.

She raised an eyebrow at his full, untouched blue beard. It was a bold lie delivered without hesitation, and she knew from experience that only a well-practised liar could accomplish that so easily. 'I know you have her, where is she?' she asked again.

'There is no one else in my home, but feel free to inspect it yourself.' He stood back from the door and extended his arm graciously in invitation. Yvaine stepped forward and mounted the stairs.

It was obviously a trap, but she was going in regardless.

Chapter 19

It was an astonishing house, Yvaine had to admit. The entrance hall alone was dazzling with gold, expensive fabrics and rich colour.

'Where first?' he asked, at ease.

'There was a broken window upstairs,' she said. 'Show me to that room.'

'You are my guest,' he bowed and indicated up the stairs. 'Lead the way.'

Yvaine narrowed her eyes. 'No, I think I will let you go first.' And so she watched his back as he mounted the steps in front of her. They went down a warmly decorated hallway, and then Fitcher indicated a door.

'Open it,' she said.

'As you say,' he said, and did.

The room within was a shambles, the wind from the broken window stirring the curtains. Bedding was strewn across the floor and a chair was pulled over on its side.

'What happened here?' Yvaine asked, looking at all four corners of the room, hoping to discover the huntress hiding within.

'I am a poor sleeper,' he said with a smile. 'Sometimes I have frightful dreams, and throw things without intending to. I must have broken the window in the night, and all the rest.'

Yvaine did not believe a word of it. 'Show me the rest of the house, then.'

'As you say,' he said, and did. They looked into every apartment along the hallway, but found no further trace of a struggle, or any other signs that Diana had been there.

'Downstairs, then,' she said when they had seen each one.

The floor below was as untouched, though marvellous in its grandeur. They went from parlour to library, from stronghold to kitchen, and no sign of the huntress.

'Have you seen enough?' Fitcher asked with a smile.

'What about down that stairwell?' she asked, pointing. 'We have not seen that yet.'

'It is a mere storeroom below,' Fitcher said, but his smile was looking tense. 'It is nothing.'

'Show me.'

'I do not believe that I will,' he said. 'You have tried my patience enough already.'

Yvaine pulled out both knives from her belt and swiftly crossed them beneath his blue-bearded neck. 'You will show me,' she said, and was pleased to see the whites of his eyes.

She kept one knife poised at his kidneys while they descended the final stairwell, and came to a plain door, which was locked.

'Unlock it,' she said, adding pressure to the knife.

'As you say,' Fitcher said, and did.

The door opened, and they entered.

Yvaine had found Diana, at last, but she was not going to be saved.

Yvaine's mouth formed a grim line, and she felt hot rage course through her veins. Without hesitation, she sank her knife into Fitcher's back to the hilt.

He was not expecting that, and staggered against the door. He lunged at her, but Yvaine was ready and she ducked with the instincts of her past life. With her other knife, as its pair was still in the back of the blue-bearded monster, she sliced deeply across his stomach. It was a good hunting knife, and sharp as broken glass. Fitcher clutched at himself to keep his viscera inside, and then fled from the bloody room.

Yvaine took up the axe from the wood block, and followed. Blood showed her his trail, and she found him hurrying along the hallway and hastening to the door. He reached for the bolts and bar, trying to lock her within, but she would not have that. She lifted the axe over her shoulder, and let it swing.

When he fell onto the perfectly green lawn, spilling his life onto it but not gone yet, the dogs were there waiting, and they had not eaten for some time. They waited for the release command, and she gave it.

Male screams filled her ears, but she did not listen as she went back inside the house. She had a friend's body to bury. His, on the other hand, was just meat for the dogs.

Yvaine returned to the bloody chamber with a white damask table cloth decorated with pearls and crystal beads. It was quickly stained red and black with congealed blood as she gathered together the huntress's body from the great basin in the middle of the room. Once she had found all of her limbs, her torso and head, Yvaine bundled the whole of Diana's body together in the cloth and dragged her up the stairs.

The dogs were gnawing on a thigh bone apiece, but their great heads lifted as Yvaine come out of the door with her grisly burden, and followed her into the trees.

Yvaine had never dug a grave before, and had not anticipated how difficult it was, particularly in the frost-hardened ground. Not only did the grave need to be long enough for the huntress' long body, as she would not pile the woman into the ground as just so many parts, but also be as deep as required. It took her the whole day to finish it, and even then she could hardly call it a job well done, as the hole had uneven lines and was deeper one end than the other.

When it was done, Yvaine began gathering Diana's limbs into the grave and put her parts in order, head, body, arms and legs in their place. When there was nothing further wanting, she placed Diana's bow in her lifeless fingers, and her sheath of arrows by her side. When she was done, Yvaine looked down upon the huntress and felt her limbs lose their power at once. It took all her effort not to fall into the grave beside her friend.

There was a new further guilt inside her to add to that which already existed within, which clawed at the confines of her mind and consumed her waking thoughts. Diana had come to such a cruel, horrible end because she had helped Yvaine in her search for Beau. Diana would not have been here, and would not have been killed, if Yvaine had not asked her to show her through the woods. And Yvaine would not have had to go through the woods at all if she had not sent Beau away, and Beau himself would not have needed saving.

It was all her fault, Diana's murder and Beau's capture, as her parents' death was likewise.

Yvaine spoke aloud through her misery and tears, 'I think I should not be around other people at all! I just cannot do good things for anyone, and everyone suffers poorly from my interference in their lives.'

The dogs lay beside the grave of their mistress as Yvaine filled it in with the dark, rich earth, her nose running and eyes weeping so that she could barely see what she did. She knelt there in the deep loam, like an animal, grunting and crying out as she pushed the mound of earth back inside its hollow bed.

Night had fallen while she was working, but she refused to take shelter in the mansion which was the scene of so much horror. She piled together a stone cairn for a headstone in the gloom, and then, when she was finally too exhausted to keep her eyes open, the dogs piled beside her on the ground and they huddled together in a miserable heap through the long night.

In the tepid light of dawn, frost clinging to her clothes and hair, Yvaine stood shivering before the mansion door. It was an unfeeling kind of practicality which made her enter the house again, and ransack the kitchen for as much as her bags could carry. But it was something else, something deeply emotional, that made her go back into the bloody chamber. She looked at the body parts of all the girls inside and knew that she could not leave them as they were, discarded like so many picked-over bones. It was some strange function of the room, its coldness perhaps, that kept the flesh from spoiling, and allowed Yvaine to identify which parts belong to whom as she lay each out in their entirety. She did not have enough time to dig graves for all of them, as there were six in total, but she had a plan.

She started in the upstairs chamber with the broken window, and piled the torn, skewed bedding into the centre of the room. She opened the wardrobes, and pulled out the delicate frocks with violence, making seams pop and beads skitter across the floor. Then she poured lamp oil over the lot of it.

Each room upstairs got the same treatment, and when those rooms were done, Yvaine went downstairs. The furniture in the receiving rooms she pushed over into a pile, and then took the bloody axe and began to hack them into pieces before pouring over the oil. In the library, she pulled books off of their shelves and kicked them into a heap, breaking spines without caution. They would not need much oil to light, but she doused them all the same.

Yvaine saved some of the books, but not for any altruistic purpose. No, these ones she desecrated even further, and began to rip their pages out of their covers, and gathered the loose paper in several large coverlets from the beds in the upstairs apartments. She then carried them down the stairs and into the bloody chamber, to add kindling where there was none. With care, Yvaine poured the lamp oil over the leaves of paper which surrounded the bodies of the unknown women like a blanket of snow. This was where she started the blaze, but she lobbed flaming sheaves of print into the rest of the rooms on the main floor but trusting the inferno to reach the upper level on its own.

She left, and did not turn back, with the dogs as silent shadows by her side.

Chapter 20

Yvaine made it for an hour before being sick, clinging to the rough bark of a tree.

What is wrong with me? She asked herself, *I have seen far worse, and done far worse, when I was a beast. I have ripped my prey in pieces with my bare talons, I have torn their beating hearts out from their chests, and yet am affected by what I have seen today?*

Nothing about being a human made any sense to her.

Instead of dwelling on these thoughts, Yvaine busied herself with the task of retracing her steps. She needed to regain the stream again, so she could continue on her search, alone. She was so utterly exhausted, physically and mentally, that she desperately wanted to find a quiet spot to sit, cry and sleep, but she could not. Beau was still in the hands of the witch. Yvaine had caused Diana to come to a foul end, but she still had it in her power to find Beau and hopefully extract him from whatever danger he was in.

If he still lived, that was. Yvaine was fully aware that this journey had been a long one, and that Beau had already been missing for some time before she set off to find him. She might be too late, and this might have all been in vain.

And she was not truly alone, either. The dogs were great company, sometimes haring off after creatures in the undergrowth, but returning when the chase was done. Yvaine did not have the control over them that Diana had had, but they seemed to accept her as a companion enough to stay nearby, and she was grateful for that.

Soon she heard the sound of water flowing over rock, and she quickened her pace. It would not be long now, she thought. This forest had been brutal, dreadful and bizarre, but she would not be defeated by it. Her feet hurt, her stomach ached with a hollow kind of emptiness, and her fingers and toes were itching with swollen chilblains, but she was nearly there now.

Every crunching step was a new victory, and each misting breath was a silent cheer. Yvaine no longer felt the straps of the bags on her front and back digging into her shoulders, and no longer even felt the cold. She could only think of how she would approach the witch's hovel, and how she would use her axe, which she had kept as a grisly reminder, to hack at the door, and strike the witch down. Beau would be freed, and would be at her side again. She would restore him to his parents' home, and then...

She did not know what then.

It felt never-ending, this green and black space, punctuated by white snow and dull grey skies. She spent another restless night in the hollow of a fallen tree, worn away by time and pests. The dogs lay with her like a breathing grey rug, and they passed the night together in shared warmth.

The next day was much of the same, and one foot followed another. Time seemed to have no meaning here, and the darkness just seemed to grow darker.

Then, there it was. A small cottage beside the embankment, smoke rising from its chimney. Candlelight flickered through its small, uneven window panes. Yvaine braced her axe in her hand, and prepared herself from a hidden place in the trees.

Then the door opened.

A woman stepped out, and she could see that this must be the witch. A part of Yvaine's heart sank when she saw her face. Until this moment she had not really known her own thoughts on the matter, but she had rather hoped that this witch would be the very same who had enchanted her into the beast she had been these last long years. It would have been a pleasant catharsis to vanquish that instigator of all her life's woes. Yvaine would never forget the face of the witch who had made her life a living damnation and this was not her. As Yvaine watched, nursing this disappointment, she saw the witch turn, called back by someone inside. A man stepped towards her, framed by the doorway. It was Beau.

Yvaine opened her mouth to call to him, her heart rising into her throat to see him hale and healthy, but what she saw next made her at loss for words.

Beau reached down to cup the witch's face in gentle fingers, smiling down on her with fire in his eyes. He drew her face close, and gave a lingering kiss.

Chapter 21

Branches lashed at her face as Yvaine fled through the trees. The dogs bounced by her side, convinced it was some kind of game, gambolling wildly and snapping at one another's faces in canine playfulness. One of them frisked into Yvaine, making her tumble into a heap among her heavy packs straight into sharp tangle of bramble thorns.

'Just go away!' she was scratched bloody, sore and angry, so she shouted at the irrepressible wolfhounds, who put their ears back but were otherwise unaffected by her words. She hid her face in the folded safety of her arms and let hot tears spill across her cheeks. *I cannot believe it,* she thought, *and after I have come all this way. And after Diana, for nothing…*

Cold wet noses shoved themselves under her hands, which were then licked vigorously. Yvaine lifted her head and could not help but laugh at the worried expressions on the dogs' faces as they tried to lick their apology through to her.

'Stupid creatures,' she said as she pushed herself up into a straight-backed sitting position, no longer letting herself be in a pitiful sprawled heap. 'And I as stupid as they. What foolishness this has been!' The dogs took this as an invitation, and each tried to occupy her lap unmind-ful of the fact that they each outweighed her again by half and were fully

316 | Arielle K Harris

the size of small ponies. What ensued was hilarious, with a small amount of real hysteria on Yvaine's part. She could barely breathe, but she laughed out loud despite herself.

'What a state of affairs,' she said to herself, and the dogs listened with open mouths and panting tongues, fully pleased with themselves. 'I come so far, travel for so long, and already he has found a new love.'

Do you know him to be so easily swayed, came a pernicious voice inside herself, *or as false as that?*

'No, but the evidence of my eyes tells me all I need to know.'

What evidence? That a witch has held Beau captive, and has done what witches do — enchant?

'Oh,' she pushed the dogs off her with sudden energy. 'Could it be?' They made their way back to that hidden spot where she had seen them before, and she waited.

She did not see Beau outside of the cottage again, but when the night was falling she saw the witch return. Beau opened the door to her, and welcomed her inside where firelight and candles illuminated through the nearest window.

Yvaine bade the dogs wait, and crept closer until she was able to peer inside. It looked like any normal domestic scene, the two of them sitting at a generous table which was spilling over with succulent roast meats and vegetables, dotted with ripe fruits and glistening jellies, hot breads steaming even in the warmth of the fire-lit room.

Careful not to let her breath steam up the glass, Yvaine looked at Beau. Now that she was close enough to see his features, she was struck by the familiarity and unfamiliarity of his features. He was the same person he always had been, only she was now different and her perceptions followed likewise. The lines of his face held the same perfect symmetry, his skin still smooth and his eyes still brilliant; he was still a beautiful man, but now she had the eyes to see it.

With that vision also came the memory of his kindness, his patience and the joy she had of his companionship. Why on earth and heaven had she not simply travelled with him back to Maison Desjardins? Her need for solitude, which had been so overwhelming at the time, now seemed so foolish. She had been alone for decades before his arrival, had it done her any good? What benefit would it have had to return to that state?

Yvaine watched Beau then, saw his easy manner with the witch, saw his smiles to her. He looked like a man in love.

But he loved me.

Could the man she knew, the honest, good soul, have been so fickle as to be proclaiming his love to her with such fervour, then change his heart and give it to another so quickly after?

Before she could be noticed through the glass pane Yvaine moved away again and regained her hidden spot beside her canine companions who seemed pleased to see her.

'I will need to think,' she told them, to wagging tails, 'and I will need to plan. It is not easy to trick a witch in her own home.'

Then she will not be expecting it.

Chapter 22

How does one overcome something seemingly insurmountable? How does the ex-enchanted overcome a master of enchantments?

Witches are known to have a cagey sorority, like she-cats sharing the same abode, or sisters who spend too much time together. They can be sweet to each other in one moment, but their softness belies their claws.

They mark each other by the scent of magic which lingers on them. Yvaine hoped that the remnants of her own enchantment would prove enough of a marker. They speak in riddle and metaphor, and have no fear. Yvaine thought she could fake what she needed.

The dogs were left in the hidden place, and Yvaine went to the door boldly and alone. She knocked with loud nonchalance, and arranged her expression into something at once impatient and frustrated as the door opened.

The witch stood before her, the being whose hated interference had captured Beau and changed him into a plaything.

'The moon told me how to find you, sister,' Yvaine said, trying to get the intonation as she had rehearsed, calm and smoothly spoken without haste nor hesitation. 'But I shall not trouble your hospitality long.'

320 | Arielle K Harris

'What the moon divulges, who am I to deny?' the witch said, looking at Yvaine with searching eyes. 'We have not met before, sister, or else I would have known you by the shining eye of the crow upon you. You make a light I have never seen before.'

Yvaine swallowed, wondering if she had been seen through.

Then the witch smiled, 'So I will introduce myself in peace, sister. I am the sickness and I am the mania, that which poisons the body and sickens the spirit. My heart has two souls, but my soul has no heart.'

Yvaine felt that the silence after this speech was awaiting her own likewise reply, so she opened her mouth and let the words spill. 'I am the flight and the soaring violence, the anger and the heated blood. My mind has two bodies, but my body has one mind.'

'Well met, sister,' the witch said, nodding.

'Well met, sister,' Yvaine replied.

And so Yvaine was welcomed into the house of the witch as a sister. She felt it was crucial to befriend this power which had ensnared Beau, to know it and learn as much as she could about it, in the hopes that she could use that knowledge against it. She knew she could not overcome the unknown, so she must therefore make it known to her. Make it a friend, a sister, so that she could draw it close and then, when it was relaxed, neck bared beside her, she could strike the fatal blow.

'Come and join us,' the witch was saying, and there was now a third chair beside Beau who looked at her blank and benign. Yvaine sat carefully upon it, looking deep into Beau's eyes as she did. He looked at her without recognition or interest. She felt a chill deep inside herself, and an aching in her chest.

'Who is this?' she asked carefully.

'My latest beloved one,' the witch said, reaching out her arm and drawing a long fingernail across the perfect recesses of Beau's collarbone. 'He is a rare beauty, and I am much pleased with him.' Beau caught her hand and kissed it with love and desire lighting his eyes.

'I can see why,' Yvaine said, keeping her face neutral.

The witch withdrew her hand and poured a cup of sanguine wine for Yvaine. 'Please,' she said, 'do help yourself to my table. And, oh my manners are shocking, please do remove your cloak, sister.'

'Thank you,' Yvaine said, but her heart was beating quickly and loudly in her chest as she uncovered the axe strapped to her back.

'Oh my,' the witch said. 'The wind did not tell me of this, nor the fall of evening mist. What dark suffering has this instrument inspired, sister? What toll of death has it wreaked?'

'Seven innocents,' she said. 'Seven girls who did not deserve what came to them, and one monster who did.'

'That is a greatly powerful object, my sister,' the witch said solemnly. 'She who wields it will be much feared. The rushing stream and the singing grass cannot hide the words I would speak of my desire for it. I wish not to bring discord to a table of sisters, but I must have it.'

Yvaine was surprised. She had thought that the witch would see the weapon as a challenge, and then Yvaine had prepared to find out if she could physically overpower her. It was by no means certain if she could, so the plan had been somewhat rash and desperate. Now it seemed there may be another way.

'If you must have it, sister,' Yvaine said, 'then perhaps some bargain might be struck.'

'A bargain?' the witch asked, her eyes alight. Nothing pleases a witch more than a bargain made, unless it be one she may win by trickery or deceit. 'Go on, sister, and divulge the bones and flesh of such a bargain.'

Yvaine was thinking quickly, more quickly than she had ever had to think before. 'Your beloved is such an extraordinary creature,' she said, 'worth, surely, the dark power I possess?'

The witch looked at the man in question. 'I could not give up my beloved, no. Not even for that which you carry. I could not give him up.'

'I love you,' Beau said with unsmiling fervour.

'I love you, too,' the witch returned the look.

'If not given,' Yvaine tried, 'how about shared? Would you allow me to sleep a night in his chamber?'

The witch chewed her bottom lip, caught between two desires. 'I could agree to that,' she spoke slowly, working through machinations in her mind.

After their repast, the witch first took Beau into his chamber, protesting that her dear sister must rest by the fire a moment longer and she must bid her beloved a good night. Within, she gave Beau a sleeping draught that would make certain that her prized beloved would be soundly asleep until morning. He drank, with the trust of love, and it was so.

When Yvaine was shown in next, the door was closed and locked behind her before she could protest. In the bed, Beau was curled in slumber and unaware.

Yvaine sat heavily on the bed beside him and let tears fall into her hands for several moments. She had come all this way, and she had found him, but she did not know what to do now. After drying her face with a sleeve of dubious cleanliness, she began to speak. She knew that he would not hear her, but she told him everything.

She told him of her determination to find him, of her trials and grief along the way. The people she had met, the things she had done, both in pride and in self-loathing.

Everything she told the sleeping man beside her, but he did not have the power to listen. And, heartbroken, Yvaine lay down beside him and eventually slept, broken and limp.

Meanwhile, a small mouse was listening from a crack in the wall.

Chapter 23

Breaking their fast the next morning was difficult for Yvaine, who was still overcome by the emotions of the night before. The witch was being eaten up by jealousy for having shared her beloved's very presence for a night, but she felt victorious in a bargain well designed.

Yvaine was going to take that victory away, and change that design.

'My dearest sister,' she said, 'you cannot have been aware of it,' although they both knew that she was, 'but this man was too insensible as to give me any satisfaction last night. A night spent with a sleeping man is not worth that which I carry, and which you desire to have.'

The witch withdrew her hands from around Beau's neck and pursed her lips, unwilling to admit to her intentions, which they both knew. 'What do you propose, sister?'

'I propose that you let me spend the day in his company, as you did the night, and if I am pleased then I will honour the bargain.'

The witch caught Beau's face in her hands and kissed him deeply, while his arms wrapped around her waist, the muscles beneath his shirt moving with strength and purpose. Yvaine could not watch.

'Very well,' the witch finally said, but she bade her sister finish her breakfast while she led Beau back into his chamber, and therein gave him the sleeping draught again.

Again, Yvaine was shut into the room, and again felt her heart break to see the man she loved brought to a state of insensibility. Without the vigour of life, and the way he used to look at her lighting his eyes, she felt she was with a stranger. Her task suddenly felt hopeless, and she wondered if it were even possible to reclaim the man she knew and loved. And if she could forgive him for the actions and feelings which he was making and feeling, despite being moved by the power of a spell. These were still his actions, and these were still his feelings. They existed, spell or no.

Nonetheless, he began her tale again, and spoke to the still body of her beloved. He would not hear her, but she felt moved to speak regardless.

This time she spoke more slowly, and the emotions no longer choked her. She felt removed from the story, a spectator, and at a distance from it. The sun's wan light moved across the room through the telling of it, until eventually, hoarse, she was done and it was dusk.

A mouse moved across the floor contemplatively.

It was a similar picture over their evening meal, the witch grown dark and sullen, resenting the time with her captive that she had given up to the other woman. Yvaine was listless and despondent. Beau was the only one unmarked by these events, still as certain for his love of the witch as ever, relishing her closeness and attention.

'Now may we conclude our bargain, my sister?' the witch asked, running her fingers through his hair. 'Are you not pleased?'

'I am not pleased,' Yvaine said. 'As you well know, dear sister. It will not do.'

'Fine,' the witch said. 'You may have this night as well. But that is all I will give you, and afterwards we are finished, bargain or no.'

'Yes,' Yvaine said. 'After tonight, it will be finished.'

This time the witch was so distracted by her jealousy and desire that she handed Beau the sleeping draught but did not watch him drink it. He was left in the room, holding it, while she invited Yvaine inside.

Beau stood like a carving of an angel, though wingless, holding the cup, and never felt nor saw the small mouse which climbed up his leg, torso and arm. With sharp teeth, the mouse bit Beau's finger, making his hand jerk and the draught spilled onto the floor. When the witch returned, all she saw was an empty cup, and so left, satisfied that the situation was under her control.

Yvaine saw, however, that this time, unlike the day and night before, Beau was not sleeping. He was still a vacant shell of himself, out of the sphere of his beloved witch, but he was awake. Yvaine took his hands and drew him to sit beside her, and looking deep into his beautiful eyes, the fire in them banked and dark, and began to tell her story for a third time.

First Yvaine began with the roses, though that was not the beginning at all. She told him that they had wilted and gave her a sign of his danger. She told him that she had sought out help from Eugénie, and then finding that her son had been the very person Beau had spoken to. Then, hearing his ill-advised route, how she had then followed it exactly.

Then she told him about the village of B--, on the edge of the forest, and the people she had met there. The innkeeper and his wife, did he remember them? Diana, the huntress, and her dogs, and the deal she had made for the other woman's guidance through the forest to find him. Her subterfuge in naming him as her brother, and the huntress seeing right through it. Their clashing stubbornness, their friendship.

Then she told him about the perils they had encountered in the deep dark wood. The giant, with his literal gullibility, and the gnome with his impossible tasks. Then she told him about Fitcher, and how Diana had been taken. And how Yvaine had finally found her, but too late. She cried again while she told him about Diana's burial, and then grit her teeth, white-faced, telling him about her vengeance. The axe, turned against its master. The gilded cage, burnt to the ground.

Then, she told him about finding him, at last, but seeing him with the witch and how that had made her feel. Lost, betrayed, alone.

Finally, she told him the true beginning of the story. How conflicted she had felt about him leaving. How much she missed him with her whole being. How dark her days were now that he was not lighting them with his companionship and love. That she loved him with her whole heart and soul, and did not want to be alone any longer if he would be by her side.

All of this she spoke of earnestly while searching his eyes for any spark ignited, any recognition at all of her presence beside him. But there was nothing.

'I love you,' she whispered, heart aching.

But there was nothing.

'Goodbye.'

But there was nothing.

Chapter 24

The morning dawned without light, and Yvaine felt that darkness echo in her soul. She had not slept, but her exhaustion lay deeper than merely the lack of sleep. She felt weary in her very bones and sinews, lost and hopeless.

The lock on the door clicked its release, and the handle moved with the movement of the witch's hand. Yvaine watched without interest.

There is a numbness which spreads when despair takes over, removing all feeling and sensation. Yvaine had been insensible like this before, too many times, so this was a familiar state to her. When her parents had died she remained like this for years after, removing her very sense of time or place or even her humanity. Her powerlessness then was a burden she had been unable to bear.

There had been too much loss, too much horror, for her to simply endure as she had done before. She had to reclaim her power, and banish the dread in her broken heart through action. Yvaine would no longer watch as the people in her life moved beyond her reach, not when she had breath in her body.

'Well, my sister,' the witch said, entering, hand upon the door. 'Will you make good on your bargain at last? Will you give the axe to me?

I spoke to the bracken and the heath and they said it would be in my hand this morning, and I rejoiced.'

'Yes,' Yvaine spoke to the silence which hid in the corners of the room. 'It will be so.'

She took up the axe, and did exactly that.

The witch screamed, and blood dashed itself across the walls and floor. She clutched the stump of her once-delicate hand to her chest and her eyes grew heavy with pain and magic. Yvaine watched death approach her, but she did not care. Nothing touched her any longer.

'Why, sister? Why?' the witch asked in gasps as her magic gathered.

'I am not your sister,' the woman who was a beast spoke quietly and with terrible gravity. 'Beau is my love, and I have come to claim him.'

'That is not-!'

But the witch spoke no more, for her head was parted from her body.

Chapter 25

There was blood everywhere, across the floor, the walls, even in Yvaine's hair. A spray of red, like some delicate stem of flowers, was cast across Beau's cheek while he continued to lay without movement or awareness. Only the regular rise and fall of his chest betrayed the life which still animated his body.

The witch was in pieces on the floor, and Yvaine could not tear her eyes away from the unsettling sight. This was the second person she had killed, but it was becoming no easier. The axe dropped from her numb fingers with a loud clatter.

There was a movement by the witch's disembodied hand. Yvaine's heart skipped a beat, but her eyes soon resolved that there was a small mouse which was making fluid motions towards her. The creature picked its way with near-human delicacy around the pools of blood until it stopped at Yvaine's feet. It sat up on its hind legs, whiskers twitching, and its bright black eyes met hers.

'Hello,' she said, feeling like she was being weighed and measured.

The mouse seemed satisfied by what it saw and it moved on past her and up the leg of the bed. It climbed over Beau's prone body and along one arm towards where his hands were loosely curled in sleep. Its nose sniffed one long, delicate finger of those hands, hands which girls had been known to swoon over, and then savagely bit the tip.

'Ah!' Beau cried, sitting up suddenly. The mouse flew from the bed and scampered away with the unnatural speed vermin possess when their lives are in sudden peril.

'Beau!' Yvaine sank beside him, clutching his hands in hers, heedless of the smudge of red beading up from the small wound on his finger. 'We must go, can you stand?'

His eyes were not yet seeing, but Yvaine helped Beau to his feet and dragged him into the waking forest, blanketed with white frost. The dogs ran out to greet Yvaine, clustering around her legs in quiet canine concern and eyeing up the newcomer with wariness. Breath puffed from their agape mouths as they panted nervously.

Yvaine wanted to get as far away from the place as possible, but without her guide, her friend, she was no longer sure what direction to go in. For all she knew they could be close to the other edge of the forest, and near Beau's home. Her eyes cast around the trees, but they all looked the same. All was dark and cold and lost.

'Yvaine?'

She froze at the sound of his voice behind her.

'I heard you speaking to me. I heard everything.'

Yvaine turned, and looked at Beau, and he looked back at her. The scales had fallen from his eyes, and he could truly see her now. The spell was broken.

'You did?' she asked quietly. 'I was not sure you had.'

'I heard it all,' he said. His jaw tightened and loosened, and he was stood at stiff attention.

Yvaine did not know what to say. 'I am glad,' was all she could manage.

Beau swallowed with some effort. 'I do not know what to tell you,' he said.

'Tell me about what?'

His eyes looked straight into hers but he was silent for a long moment, while that gaze sent chills of premonition down Yvaine's back.

'I love her,' he said and, as ever, the words he spoke were the honest truth, unencumbered and unenchanted.

Chapter 26

'Oh.' It seemed as though suddenly the earth was falling, and she with it, though she did not move.

'I did not intend for it to happen,' he said, 'but I have never felt this way before.'

'You have certainly never been under a spell before,' she said wryly, but her words only served to hide the hurt she felt deep inside. He looked at her with tormented eyes, but said nothing. 'So I should have never come to your aid?'

'I was not in need of aid. Pyometra found me when I was near death, frozen and starving, and fed me, clothed me, and showed me such love as I have never known. Kindness and charity which I have never before been the recipient of.'

Each word stabbed true into the very centre of her heart, prickling her conscience and stirring her ire. 'Kindness and charity?' she repeated. 'You are as ignorant as the fish calling the hooked worm a gift! What do you think the villagers tried, in vain, to warn you of? You were not the first young man to be entrapped so, though perhaps never so easily nor completely!'

338 | Arielle K Harris

The silence that followed told her to remain quiet and let Beau find the space to speak within it, within himself, so she waited, anger and frustration and despair roiling within her breast, and listened to the sound of his hesitation.

'I am so confused,' he finally spoke, hushed and passionate. 'I feel the way I feel, but here you are telling me that I am misled. That I am under a spell, that what I feel is wrong.'

'I believe that you feel how you feel,' she said with careful, deliberate tone, considering each word before she spoke it, aware that she was losing him but hoping that the right words, said in the right order, might bring him back to her. 'But I think how you feel could have been caused by forces outside yourself, inspired by something that is not real.'

'And if that is true,' Beau said, 'then how can I trust any of my senses? Any of my thoughts? If what you say is true, then it will destroy me. All that I am is the love that I feel and without it I cease to exist.'

'How is this love?' Yvaine asked. 'Love is not destruction, or obliteration of the self. Love makes you seek to be better than you are, not question all that makes up your being. It exists in simple acts, and in kind words. It shows light into the dark places, and taught a beast that she was a person worth loving.' Her voice cracked on the last word but she would not turn her face away, even as hot tears obscured him from her sight.

Beau did not speak, he ran his hands through his hair and looked cornered.

'I do not suppose,' she spoke with deceptive calmness, marvelling to herself that she was capable of this while inside her head she felt like screaming, 'that you recall the words of our parting?'

He did not speak.

'Do you not remember your promise?'

He did not speak.

'That you would never let me be lonely again?'

He spoke, quietly as a conscience, 'You said you would not hold me to promises made in ignorance.'

'You told me that you loved me. Do you deny even that?'

Beau crossed his arms, 'I did say those words; I do not deny it.'

His deliberate wording did not escape Yvaine's notice. 'Do you deny the meaning behind them?'

'I do not know what to say!' he said. 'I spoke the words, and at the time they had meaning, but since then I have known sensations, thoughts, feelings which I have never known before. Certainties which I have never had. With you I knew friendship, companionship and the sense of pride over sharing those accomplishments we worked on together. I have deep feeling for you, I do not deny that.'

Yvaine knew there was more, 'And yet?'

'Pyometra,' he breathed the word. He spoke with the gravity of an overawed youth, and suddenly Yvaine could see what was different about him. He was acting with all the dramatics of a young boy, in the body of a man who should have known better. 'I love her so much,' he was saying. 'She is the other half of my heart.'

Yvaine started laughing, and found that she could not stop. It was part hysteria, she acknowledged that, but the other part was true mockery. 'You are being ridiculous and dramatic,' she said. 'I will do as I set out to do, and take you to your parents. They will know how to deal with you, surely.'

'I cannot leave.' Beau would not look at her.

'Your parents must be frantic with worry for you,' she said. 'You know in your heart that you must at least see them to explain your absence. To simply never return would be cruel.'

His back was hunched and his arms gripped tightly by white-knuckled hands. 'I cannot leave here. I cannot leave her. Perhaps I am cruel, but for once I must do what I want for myself. All of my life I have done the supposed "right" thing and pushed my own needs aside for others. I have never done anything I actually wanted to do. Here, and now, I will start listening to my own needs.'

'You are refusing to live up to your responsibilities? To do what you know is right?'

'I cannot be parted from her, I would be leaving myself behind. I will not.'

Yvaine looked at him, this man for whom she had risked everything, lost a friend and seen such horrors. 'You are not the man I thought you were. You are not the friend I thought I had, the person who showed me how to be human again, to put my own needs aside for another. You are being as disgusting a creature as ever I was before enchantment showed me the true state of my being. You know what I have been through, and what I have seen and done to save you, and the feelings which we have shared, the promises you made. But you speak of them, and me, as if I were nothing.'

'I did not need saving,' was all he said.

She smiled, but it was a smile born from the predator inside of her.

'Then I wish you the luck of your chosen bride, Beau,' Yvaine told him, and her voice echoed within her ears as if it came from a source far distant from herself. She heard herself laugh again, a terrible sound, hollow and without humour, 'You may find her somewhat less than you knew, and in several more pieces than you might expect.'

At first he stared at her in incomprehension, and then disbelief, but something in her eyes must have told him all he needed to know. He paled, stumbled back from her and, tripping over himself in haste, fled through the trees.

Yvaine watched him go, taking all her dreams of happiness with him.

Something inside her had surely broken, she could feel its sharp, imagined edges making wounds inside her mind, her heart and her spirit. The solace she had found in the love of a man was now taken from her, and she was cast adrift.

I am not so weak as that, reminded the beast inside the girl, who would not let her forget herself again. *I am the thundering wingbeat and the mercy of death. A man such as that is not worthy of me.*

Yvaine smiled, and walked through the shadowing wood, even as tears fell upon the frost-laden loam and bracken.

Epilogue

She did not see how her tears melted the ice. She did not see the young, green shoots which emerged with the speed of enchantment upwards toward the weak, pale light of the bough-veiled sun. She did not see the small blooms which carpeted the frozen ground behind her footsteps.

Days came and went, and Yvaine wept, and walked. The dogs guarded her side as grey shadows, but no beings came forth from the forest to offer challenge.

It did not take long for her to reach the far side of the forest, but she looked upon the great expanse of exposed fields and the distant signal smoke of chimneys and was not impressed.

She turned back into the forest. It was then that Yvaine saw the flowers tracing her steps, and she stooped to pick one. It smelled so sweet that a strange impulse made her open her mouth and place it on her tongue.

The petals melted when she closed her mouth. They tasted like the salt of her grief and the bitterness of her sorrow, but there was another flavour, the sweetness of their perfume. This was the flavour of her strength; her heart had broken, but she had kept walking.

Yvaine smiled.

There was a gust of wind.

Feathers danced through the air.

A Note on Conventions

This story has been written using British English spelling and grammar conventions though I am myself an American and this book has been published and printed in the USA using American conventions in my front and back matter, which may understandably confuse some readers. So, let me explain: I wrote *Bestial* while living in the UK and adopted the writing conventions used there. Yes, I could have changed my novel's use of British-isms prior to publication, or continued in my use of British conventions throughout in the front and back matter, but by making the stylistic choice to use both I am deliberately being inconsistent and highlighting my own struggle to re-adapt to American life and culture after spending the better part of the last 12 years abroad in the UK. I will always be torn between two countries, two cultures and two literary traditions separated by a common language.

Acknowledgements

I would like to take this opportunity to thank my parents for all their support and help, allowing me the time to realise this dream. I promise to get a day job soon, honestly. I want to thank my mother in particular for being a sounding board and a proof-reader, a cheerleader and a toddler-sitter. A big thanks my sister, the dearest Noodle of my heart, and Melli — both of you have listened to me ramble about this book for years and you never told me to shut up. I'm putting you up for sainthood. Many thanks to Amelia Royce Leonards for your beautiful artwork, your helpful critiques and many discussions concerning wombats. Thank you to David Meyer for advising me on the route to self-publishing, your experience has helped guide my path. I also want to take the time to say a special thank you to all my friends and family, from both sides of the Atlantic, who have been such a support to me during an exceedingly difficult period of my life from which this novel was born.

Arielle K Harris spent her formative years in Scotland, which has irreversibly confused her accent and spelling conventions. Lately she has returned to her hometown in Massachusetts where she finished her first novel, *Bestial*, and is raising her young son. Arielle writes stories which focus on the human experience through the lens of fantasy, positing questions about reality to be examined through encounters with unreality.

www.ariellekharris.com

Printed in Great Britain
by Amazon